I0646555

SHADOW OVER MALVERN

JACQUELINE BEARD

VINCI
BOOKS

By Jacqueline Beard

Lawrence Harpham

The Fressingfield Witch

The Ripper Deception

The Scole Confession

The Felsham Affair

The Moving Stone

The Maleficent Maid

The Disappearing Doctor

The Camden Killer

Shadow Over Malvern

Vinci Books

vinci-books.com

Published by Vinci Books Ltd in 2026

1

A CIP catalogue record for this book is available from the British Library.
Paperback ISBN: 9781036709105

Chapter One

HUNTING AURORA

June 1, 1910

LAWRENCE HARPHAM GAZED up at an imposing stone facade, its shadow looming as if to swallow him whole. The sun fought through dense cloud cover, casting the building in a grim half-light. Lawrence raised a hand to the sky, half-expecting rain.

"Weather is the least of our problems," Violet said pragmatically. "We won't care once they shut us inside."

They glanced towards the gloomy, forbidding walled entrance enclosing the heavy wooden door to the Semer Poor Law Institution.

"You don't have to do this," said Lawrence.

"I must. You won't get within twenty yards of the women's ward. I'm our best chance of finding Luna and Aurora."

"There are other ways," said Lawrence. "I hate the thought of subjecting you to the workhouse again."

Violet replied with steely determination. "If there's the

slightest chance that Aurora's inside, I'll do my bit. Michael would never forgive us if we ignored this lead."

"Even so." Lawrence sighed as he regarded his wife and soulmate dressed from head to toe in the sorry cast-off clothes he had recovered from a rag-and-bone man's cart. The worn threads barely hung together and emitted a stale smell with a hint of decay. Lawrence had fared better with his outfit, chosen from various disguises he had collected over the years, all moderately well laundered and ready for use. He had donned a fraying suit, applied a fake moustache, and blackened his face, looking like a tramp by the time he finished.

The prospect of entering the workhouse was no more than an inconvenience to Lawrence. But he hated the thought of Violet enduring the indignities she had faced growing up after her family hit hard times. He reached for her hand and squeezed it.

"I hope this is worth it," he said.

Violet adjusted her bonnet, its oversized brim casting her face into shadow. It was too big for her head, but if Aurora was inside, they might need to return wearing different disguises to secure her release. Violet must keep her face well-hidden for now.

"We'll learn something, whatever happens," she said. "If we don't see Aurora, we can cross this workhouse off our list. But if she's there... wouldn't that be a relief?"

"We can but hope," said Lawrence, trying to sound more optimistic than he felt.

They had searched long and hard for Aurora, chasing their tails to find a clue to her dramatic disappearance. Then, finally, they heard a whisper so nebulous that it was almost wishful thinking. It had come from Vera Ponsonby, who remembered a conversation with Aurora from the previous year. Already fearful of Francis Farrow's sinister presence, Aurora had discussed the prospect of disappearing into an institution like a prison and living in plain sight. Aurora had no criminal record, no reason to hide from the law, and was too decent and moral to commit a crime in the name of self-protection. But entering a workhouse was a different matter. It might act as a fortress against an outside world that had failed her. Their supposition was hardly sound logic, but it was all they had.

Vera Ponsonby had acted quickly, contacting various workhouse masters to enquire about January admissions. She had found four potential sightings of a woman seeking entry with a child the right age: two in East Anglia, one in Dorset and another in Staffordshire. Through the process of deduction and applying Aurora's concept of disappearing undisguised in a nearby location, Semer seemed the most likely. But they would only know by finding Aurora. And that required covert detective work and plenty of patience. Aurora, traumatised and on high alert after Felix Crossley's past attacks, was likely to bolt if she saw them. Lawrence knew workhouse inmates could leave whenever they chose, and the slightest mistake could foil their plans.

"Ready?" asked Lawrence, reaching for Violet's hand.

"Ready," she agreed. They strolled wordlessly towards the door, crunching across the stony pathway. Violet grimaced as her thin soles ground into sharp gravel, but she said nothing and proceeded stoically to the entrance. They knocked, and a small hatch opened, revealing a sullen, whiskered face.

"Name?" the man barked.

Lawrence wiped a fine spray of spittle from his face. "George and Jane Rayner."

"For admission?"

"Sadly, yes. A terrible shame it has come to this."

Violet tugged a warning on Lawrence's sleeve. "Too much talk," she muttered.

Lawrence checked himself. "We're down on our luck, guv," he replied, lowering his eyes.

With a dismissive grunt, the man opened the door.

"Get inside," he sneered. "And none of that holding hands nonsense. "Men's ward to the left, women's to the right. You'll wait in the receiving hall until the master is ready to see you."

The man pointed towards a hard wooden bench in a cold, unlit corner of the entrance hall. "And no talking," he continued before passing through a set of double doors. They heard a distant mumble, and he returned, clutching a bundle of clothes.

"Take these," he said, thrusting them at Lawrence. "Now come with me."

"What about my wife?"

"Someone will fetch her in a minute."

"But..."

"Are you coming or not? This isn't the bleeding Ritz."

Lawrence glanced at Violet. She smiled courageously, though he knew she would find their separation daunting. But he followed the man down a long corridor and into a ten-bedded ward that felt several degrees colder than outside. Lawrence perched on a bed while the man turned tail and left without further comment. Moments later, the far door opened, and another two men arrived, one carrying a notebook, the other with a black bag.

The taller, more assertive man barked a series of basic questions, which Lawrence answered convincingly. Seemingly satisfied, he lingered in the background while the other man removed a wooden splint from his black bag and advanced towards Lawrence. After an undignified health check, the medical man ushered Lawrence into the bathroom, where he changed into the rough workhouse garb.

Lawrence's resolve briefly faltered as he watched his clothes bundled into a ball, ready for fumigation. Now unrecognisable and feeling the effects of his lowly status, Lawrence considered Violet's quiet dignity and followed suit, walking meekly behind as the warders admitted him to the able-bodied men's ward. With no time to gather his thoughts, a burly warder immediately set him to work. Lawrence grasped two buckets thrust towards him, one empty and the other containing a weighty rope of dubious quality. He spent the next three hours teasing Oakum from a nail, the tarry fibres scratching welts into his skin. Relieved to be in for the short haul, Lawrence watched the cold, dead eyes of weary inmates performing tasks they carried out repeatedly during the daily grind, marvelling at their powers of endurance. He felt sick with guilt, knowing he was there by choice, but his fellow workers were not. Lawrence worked silently until supper time when he joined the exhausted inmates in the dining hall.

Supper was a calculated, solemn affair; each man allotted a place in a vast, orderly dining hall. Lawrence preferred symmetry to chaos but found the rigid dining arrangements unsettling and the number of men crammed together distressing. God forbid there was a fire. They would never escape.

His potato pie supper lacked flavour, and he recoiled when drinking from an insipid cup of tea tasting like dishwater. Lawrence glanced across the sea of hunched shoulders, silently shovelling food while the guards looked on like circling crows. The vastness of the place unnerved him, its rigidity and unnatural silence designed to break the spirit.

By nightfall, Lawrence collapsed cross-legged by his bed, thoughts circling back to Violet, and he reflected on the next part of their plan.

Vera's research had uncovered a diagram that Violet carried with her. If the guards had not discovered it, she would know where to search within the labyrinthian walls for signs of Luna and Aurora. Lawrence had marked an alcove near the kitchen where they could meet to discuss her progress without prying eyes. But it was a mammoth task, and he wondered whether Violet would have time to check the women's wards before tomorrow. If not, they may need to stay another night.

Declining the offer of a card game, Lawrence settled for bed half an hour before the lights went out. Ignoring a minor scuffle between inmates, he fell into a deep sleep until the tolling bell rudely awakened him the following day.

———

LAWRENCE HAD BEEN DREAMING of his former home in Bury when the clanging bell put paid to visions of lustrous roses in his walled garden. He sat up with a start and remembered where he was. Still dressed, Lawrence rose and emptied his full bladder under the scrutiny of another inmate, intent on chatting through the most intimate of ablutions. The same man, introducing himself as Bryan, continued the one-sided conversation as they walked to the breakfast hall until the warder became so irritated by the chatter that he stationed himself immediately behind Lawrence's chair. After a depressing breakfast of tea and lumpy oatmeal, Lawrence was ready to put his plan in place, slipping from the column of men to head for the kitchen entrance.

"And where do you think you're going?" boomed the warder, his hands on his hips.

"To spend a penny," said Lawrence.

"Oh no, you don't. You know the rules. You can wait until later. It's time for work. Now get on with it."

Lawrence sighed, internally debating whether to risk the warder's wrath. If Violet had completed surveillance of the women's wards, they could leave and walk away. But it would be devilishly difficult to extricate himself with a warder offside if she had not. Sighing, he followed the guard to the workroom, hoping that Violet would know what to do when he did not arrive, inwardly cursing that they had not made a contingency plan for such an eventuality. But neither had foreseen any difficulty getting to the kitchens for their rendezvous.

The morning workday ran from seven to midday, each hour feeling like a week as Lawrence picked and prodded the filthy tar-ridden rope. But he did a good job, and the warders grunted their satisfaction when he presented several buckets of teased-out fibres. His original plan had been to meet Violet after breakfast. Failing that after lunch seemed the most logical prospect. After hours of menial labour, the dinner break was welcome, with the inmates inclined to surge towards the dining room, eager to rest and fill their stomachs. With men moving quickly and in vast numbers, it might be easier to slip away unnoticed before rather than after the meal. Lawrence's thoughts vacillated during his walk between the ward and the dining room, and he finally acted when a stumbling inmate attracted the warder's attention. Within seconds, Lawrence had turned tail and slipped away.

Lawrence slunk towards the kitchen, feeling vulnerable in the silent corridors. As he neared the doors, he could hear the hustle and bustle of busy cooks and kitchen staff beyond. But for all the careful planning, the exposed corridor was a terrible place to meet, with nowhere to hide and no believable excuse for being there. Lawrence waited nervously momentarily, prepared to flee if the doors opened to expose a guard. But suddenly, from nowhere, a draught shivered around him, and he heard a low hiss before turning to see Violet beckoning through a doorway.

"Thank goodness you are here," he said. "I'm sorry about this morning."

"Wait a moment," said Violet. "Quick. Through here."

Lawrence slid through a half-open wooden door and wrenched it shut behind him.

"Good God," he said, peering into the windowless room. "What is this place?"

"A store cupboard, I presume," said Violet.

"But what's that scratching noise?"

"Try not to think about it."

Lawrence shuddered and held Violet close. "I'm sorry I missed you earlier," he said.

"Didn't you make it either?"

"No. Didn't you?"

"Sorry, I couldn't," said Violet. "I was busy keeping Luna in sight. I couldn't risk moving away until I was sure."

"And are you. Have you found her?"

"Oh yes. I'd recognise Luna anywhere, bless her little heart."

"But you didn't see Aurora?"

"Not then. But I first noticed Luna holding hands with a woman. She had her back to me and was too far away to see properly, but in hindsight, it must have been Aurora. She'd have left the workhouse in a heartbeat if they couldn't stay together. Aurora must work, but perhaps they spend the day apart and get together at night."

"I still can't believe Aurora would choose to come to this hellhole rather than take a cottage somewhere."

"How would she do that, Lawrence? Aurora has no income or resources without Michael. However hard her life is here, she has secured food and a roof over their heads at no expense."

Lawrence scratched his nose. "I couldn't do it," he replied. "One night is enough."

"But we're fortunate. I remember what it's like to have nothing. We must help Aurora if she lets us."

"Do you want to risk making contact?" asked Lawrence.

Violet paused and considered. "I can't. If Aurora trusted me, she wouldn't have left."

"True," said Lawrence. "But perhaps time and uncomfortable circumstances have changed her views."

"I don't think we can take that chance."

"I agree. Have you seen enough? Can we leave now?"

"Yes. If Luna is here, Aurora won't be far. We've done enough."

"Good. Because three's a crowd, and we appear to have a visitor."

Lawrence glanced at the ground, where a pair of red eyes glowed from a whiskery face. He took a tentative step towards the door, and the rat sprang.

Violet darted outside without a word, Lawrence following close behind. Lawrence slammed the door just in time to trap the rodent before bolting to the nearest exit.

Chapter Two

UNDERCOVER

A QUICK BATH and change of clothing later, and Lawrence and Violet returned to Semer.

"I don't feel right about this," Lawrence said as they approached the entrance for the second time.

"But you look more convincing now," Violet replied. "That hat gives you an air of authority."

"That's not the problem. Arriving together for two days running is too risky. Especially if our whiskered friend is manning the door."

"I see what you mean. Should I go ahead of you?"

"Why don't I?"

"I'd rather do it."

"But, Violet, although it pains me to say it, they're bound to take a man more seriously."

Violet scowled. "It would be a sorry state of affairs if that were true."

"I know. But we must put our opinions aside and do the right thing by Michael."

"I think you mean by Luna and Aurora."

"All three of them. Look, why don't I go first, tell the guard I am expecting my secretary, and you can arrive a few moments later. That way, he won't associate our arrival with the poor, bedraggled couple he saw yesterday."

"Secretary," said Violet stonily.

"Or any other occupation you prefer. What would you like?"

"If that's your attitude, call me anything you choose."

"Don't be like that."

"How should I behave? You may be part of the so-called superior gender, but you are sadly lacking in general knowledge. Women have been eligible for election to the Workhouse Board of Governors for many years. I've as much right to masquerade as an official as you have."

"Oh. Then I'm sorry. Let's assume an equal footing, shall we?"

"Just go, Lawrence. We're wasting time."

"Alright, old girl. See you on the other side."

Ten minutes later, they had independently sailed through the workhouse past the same bearded guard who had admitted them the previous day. This time, he was courteous, escorting them into the master's office where they now sat drinking tea. Violet's mood had improved, while Lawrence still felt the sting of her earlier rebuke. Though hungry, Lawrence couldn't bring himself to accept the offer of a biscuit, having firsthand knowledge of the poverty on the other side of the wall. His stomach growled in protest as the master helped himself to a handful of digestives.

"So, you're on the board of guardians?" asked the master.

"I am. And my companion is also recently elected."

"What happened to old Carruthers?"

"Still grinding along," said Lawrence, hoping his vague lie would convince the master.

"Good. Do give him my regards. I last saw Carruthers a good six months ago. Leaving it so long is unforgivable, but time is always pressing."

"Isn't it just," murmured Lawrence.

"Quite, Mr Gibbs. You did say Gibbs?"

"I did. And this is Miss Sara Craven, who occupies a financial position on the board."

"I see. Now, let's get down to the nitty-gritty. What's the nature of your visit?"

Lawrence hesitated, temporarily stymied. He had planned down to the tiniest physical detail, swapping the previous day's rags for smart clothing. He had also learned about the master's background and habits. But beyond that, Lawrence had not given much thought to extricating Aurora. Fortunately, Violet had.

"The relieving officer is concerned about the provenance of one of your inmates," she said.

"In what way?"

"He thinks she should be in a different union workhouse with an alternative means of funding."

"I'm sure he is not alone in his views. But he is harking back to the bad old days. We are a modern organisation now. Poor Law is a thing of the past. We don't resettle inmates and can bear their costs flexibly."

"Indeed. But an unwise allocation of resources may affect your future access to funds."

"I don't see how." The master pursed his lips and eyed Violet angrily. But she confidently returned his gaze.

"An adjustment would not necessarily be to the detriment of the Union Workhouse. Rather, to its benefit."

"You mean extra income. But why?"

Lawrence and Violet exchanged looks, both now floundering.

Lawrence broke the silence first. "We cannot give specifics."

"Then you don't know?"

"I mean, my lips are sealed." Lawrence nodded and raised his finger to his mouth. Then, for good measure, he extended his hand and reached out. The master returned his grip, his eyes widening at the familiar, secret handshake. "Well, well. As you wish," he said, nodding towards Lawrence.

"Good. Your cooperation would be most helpful."

"And how would you like me to resolve this matter?"

"With care," said Lawrence. We want to remove and relocate an inmate from your institution. Miss Craven knows the woman by sight but not by name. She is likely here under an alias, you understand?"

"I see."

"And we will require her child too."

"When do you intend to remove them from our premises?"

"Today if possible. We have arranged transportation. Please bring them to this office, saying nothing about our plans until they are safely inside. The mother may be unwilling to cooperate, but if you allow us a few private moments to talk with her, we will make things right and be on our way."

"But dammit, Gibbs, there are processes to follow. We cannot allow this cattle trading."

"Correct me if I am wrong, but a workhouse inmate can discharge themselves at will."

"That's different."

"Is it, though?" Violet interjected. But the master, somewhat in thrall to Lawrence from his Masonic handshake, had no such allegiance to Violet. He purposely turned away from her, addressing Lawrence instead.

"I don't like this, Gibbs. Perhaps I should consult the board first."

"By all means, and I will do the same." Lawrence raised a confident eyebrow though he was blustering now, with no other plan. But a flicker of unease crossed the master's face as he wondered if Lawrence was a high-ranking Mason.

"Be a good fellow and do as I ask," said Lawrence, sensing the beginning of a thaw. "And I will put in a word with Worpleston."

The master fell silent at the mention of the only high-ranking Masonic officer Lawrence could remember from his short-lived foray into the brotherhood several decades earlier. It sealed the deal.

"Really? Would you? Well. Let's not delay this any further. Come with me, Miss Craven."

Violet stood and followed the master from the room, pausing only to turn at the door and raise her eyes heavenwards. Lawrence took it in the spirit she intended – a rebuke at Lawrence for using his well-despised Masonic credentials. And Violet was right to disapprove. He was a terrible fraud. Lawrence had no time for The Order, and his dislike of it had increased in line with Francis Farrow's upward trajectory through the ranks. And now that Farrow and Crossley had involved themselves in sinister satanic cults, his tolerance for any underground organisation was at an all-time low. Lawrence remained convinced that membership of one secretive society led to the desire to join another, rather like an innocent puff on a cigar might one day lead to an opiate addiction if the person was so inclined. And Violet evidently considered him a hypocrite, as well she might. But Lawrence had thought it worth the risk to get the master onside, and it seemed to have worked. He would make his peace with Violet later.

Alone in the room, Lawrence gave in to temptation and took two biscuits while he waited for the master to return. He duly appeared five minutes behind Violet, who arrived, pale-faced, her hair falling loose from its pins.

"I think she saw me," whispered Violet.

"It shouldn't matter at this late stage," said Lawrence.

"Unless she makes a run for it." Violet chewed her lip anxiously as Lawrence looked up at the opening door. The master entered first, followed by Aurora, Luna, and a plump wardress.

"Leave us, please," said Lawrence.

Aurora's panicked gaze flitted between Violet and the door. Lawrence, anticipating trouble, stood, and positioned himself next to it. "Do take a seat," he said.

"How could you?" hissed Aurora.

"We are only trying to help", said Violet.

"I was perfectly safe here."

"Are you my auntie Violet?" Luna reached towards Violet and tugged her skirt.

"I am, my darling," said Violet. "Do you remember me?"

"Yes. And Daisy. Where is she?"

"At home."

"Can I see her?"

"No," said Aurora, taking her daughter's hand.

Luna bowed her head disappointedly.

Violet reached into her purse. "Take this little box and sit over there," she said, pointing to a padded window seat at the end of the room.

Luna looked at her mother for reassurance and received a gentle nod.

"How did you find me?" asked Aurora resignedly.

"It was Vera's idea."

"I see. She's very clever. I miss her."

"And Michael too?" asked Lawrence.

Aurora blanched, fear and disappointment clouding her features. "How could I miss a man prepared to take a monster into our home?"

"And who has regretted it with every passing day."

"I don't care. Michael has ruined everything. I thought he loved me, but he put duty first."

Violet sighed. "I understand your feelings, but Michael is in a difficult position. Netherwood belongs to his brother, and although Francis appears contrite, he could take back the house tomorrow if he wished."

Aurora slumped in a high-backed chair, momentarily putting her head in her hands. Then she looked up at Violet through tear-filled eyes.

"I don't care about Netherwood. It's only a pile of bricks. Only Luna matters. Look at the conditions I am living in to protect her."

"There are better ways," said Lawrence.

"More dangerous ways," Aurora replied. "Don't presume to know how to keep my family safe."

Violet pulled up a chair and took Aurora's hands. "It's good to see your fighting spirit. The workhouse has brought out the mother tiger in you."

"Not the workhouse. Francis Farrow has. Crossley wants Luna, and Farrow means to give her to him. I will die before I let Felix Crossley take my daughter for his foul rituals."

"Michael honestly believes his brother has reformed."

"Then my husband is a fool."

Lawrence glanced at Violet, tacitly agreeing to change tack.

"What if there was another way?" asked Lawrence.

"Don't ask me to return to Netherwood."

"I won't."

"Or contact Michael."

Lawrence sighed. "I wish you would, but I won't try to force it."

"I wouldn't let you. But as much as I love Michael, I can't trust him while he's under Farrow's influence."

"Michael has already said he will ask his brother to leave, even at the risk of losing Netherwood."

"Good for him. But it makes no difference to me. If we return to Bury, Francis will know where we are. We will never have peace of mind, and Luna's safety will always be at risk."

"Would you consider living somewhere else?"

"Where?"

"I don't know yet."

"Not Suffolk or anywhere else they could find me. And only if you swore not to tell Michael."

"We wouldn't reveal your location. But we must let Michael know you are safe. He is desperate for news."

Aurora put her head in her hands again. "I don't know," she said, her voice quivering.

"This is no place for Luna."

"It was until you barged in."

Lawrence gently patted her shoulder. "I'm afraid it isn't now."

"That's your fault," said Aurora bitterly. "Children are resilient. Luna has accepted her life here, and I would have endured the discomfort for as long as it took to protect my daughter. But the master knows me now. You have spoiled everything."

"We only meant to help."

"You didn't." Aurora snatched her hand from Violet and wiped a tear from her cheek.

"Please come with us," said Violet.

"Can we, Mummy?" Luna skipped across the room and snuggled into her mother.

"I suppose so, sweetheart," said Aurora. "After all, what choice do we have?"

Chapter Three

MAKING PLANS

Cheltenham, July 1910

"WELL, Frank. I wish I could do more to show my appreciation. We haven't always seen eye to eye, but this has been uncommonly decent of you." Lawrence Harpham nodded as he listened intently to the voice on the other end of the telephone.

"Capital. I couldn't agree more. Yes, I'm sure we'll visit before long. When? Tenth of August, you say? I'll speak to Violet, and we'll have a meal together. Let us know when you arrive."

Lawrence covered the receiver and mouthed, "Frank is coming to Malvern."

"I know," replied Violet as she threaded a needle.

"Well, have a safe journey, and we'll meet soon. Good-bye. Sterling fellow," said Lawrence as he replaced the telephone handset.

"That's a change of tone. I can remember when you hated him."

"Be fair, Violet. I thought Frank was part of the group who tried to kill me."

"He wouldn't. The attack horrified Frank. He's not the kind of man to get involved in violence."

"Three men set upon me in the SPR Headquarters, and it's not as if they had that many members. I've often wondered who they were."

"They're nearly all dead now. You have nothing to worry about."

"But Frank Podmore was always your friend, rather than mine, wasn't he? You've kept in touch for years. It's only lately that he's given me the time of day."

"I rather think it was the other way around."

"Fair enough. I have only lately appreciated his finer points."

"You were getting on like a house on fire." Violet peered at the grey fabric on her lap and sighed. "Oh dear. I shouldn't have tried to darn Daisy's stockings in such poor light." She opened her workbox and removed a pair of tiny, ornamental scissors before snipping the woollen thread she had so carefully sewn.

Lawrence stared. "Why did you do that?"

"Because Daisy's tights look better on her than sewn to my dress," snapped Violet.

"Our darling daughter is no longer a child. Shouldn't she be mending her own clothes?"

"I was afraid she would ask you for a new pair."

"And I would refuse. Having plenty of money is no reason to encourage waste. Don't they teach needlework at the Girl's College?"

"They teach needlepoint and embroidery techniques. I'm not sure there's much call for making and mending."

"Fine. Buy Daisy all the hosiery she needs. But don't let's

spoil her. Now that she's passed through the practical joker phase, she's developing into a dear girl."

"Thank you," said Violet, rolling the stockings into a ball and throwing them into a nearby waste basket. "I'll take Daisy to Cavendish House on Saturday. Anyway, what were you plotting with Frank?"

"You said you knew."

"I know he's visiting Malvern. He didn't say why. Does it have something to do with Aurora?"

"No. That's just a happy coincidence. Frank takes a cottage at Lower Wyche every summer. He's done it for the last few years, and that's how he knew where to find suitable accommodation for Aurora."

"Of course."

"He rang her again, you know. He's stayed in touch."

"That's good of him."

"And part of the reason I have decided he's a jolly good type after all. Frank has taken a paternal interest and says he calls her twice weekly."

"Does Aurora mind?"

"No. She likes it. She's let her guard down since meeting Frank. He makes her feel safe. She's looking forward to his visit."

"That's good, but there's not much he can do from Broughton if anything happens."

"Why would it, though? Other than us, only Frank knows she's there. Though I'd feel much better if she was closer to Cheltenham or if we could persuade her to let us visit." Lawrence joined Violet on the sofa and crossed his legs.

Violet leaned in for a kiss. "Malvern is only half an hour away now you've bought a faster car."

"And it needs a good run out. I barely use it."

Violet laughed. "Perhaps you should have stuck to your principles and not let that eloquent salesman talk you into purchasing something you didn't need."

"Oh, come now. You enjoy a drive as much as I do."

"Rarely," said Violet. "But it doesn't matter. Aurora has settled happily, and that's more than we could have hoped for a few months ago."

"Yes. I'm so glad we trusted Frank with the problem. Michael has no connection with Malvern. Neither do we. Crossley will have a hard job if he still intends to pursue Aurora."

Lawrence pursed his lips. "Do you think he has given up?"

"No," said Violet sadly. "Crossley is determined to punish us for taking William and Millicent away. And he has never come to terms with losing his scarlet woman. I don't blame Aurora for hiding from him, but she should be safe living under an assumed name in a provincial town. She's still taking my telephone calls through the operator and doesn't seem to bear us a grudge."

"It's a shame we can't say the same about Michael. He's devastated that we won't tell him where she is and can't fathom our reasons."

"He does understand, Lawrence. Michael knows Aurora will bolt again if she feels threatened. This situation is awful for everyone. Aurora doesn't want to be alone any more than Michael does."

"But what if Crossley has given up? Surely there's some room for hope?"

Violet wound her darning wool and placed it in her workbox. She snapped the lid shut and pushed it out of sight by the side of the settee. "When I last spoke to Frank, he said Crossley had gone to ground."

"I wonder what he meant by that?"

"That he didn't know where to find him."

"Crossley often disappears abroad."

"But Frank's sources are usually well informed. It's rare for him to lose sight of Crossley altogether."

"Should we be worried?"

"Probably not. I'll call Frank in a day or two and see how the land lies."

"Good. Then everything is as it should be," said Lawrence.

Violet stared from the window, her eyes settling on Cambray Baptist Church as a cloud passed overhead. The skies darkened, and Violet involuntarily shivered. "I wish it was, Lawrence. But I can't help thinking this is just the start of things to come."

Chapter Four

PICNIC AT PITTVILLE PARK

Cheltenham, August 15, 1910

"VERA, it's been lovely to see you. I am so pleased you decided to come. What a pity you can't stay the night."

Violet Harpham leaned back on her elbows and wiggled her stockinged feet. The two women sat on a picnic blanket on a ground sheet near the bandstand in Pittville Park, listening to a wind quartet. Several yards away, Daisy Harpham, her back towards them, whispered to her school friend, Hilda, feigning embarrassment and pretending not to know who they were. Every now and then, Daisy cast a disapproving glare towards her mother, but Violet was in a good mood and enjoying the music too much to care. And Vera, often the stuffier of the Ponsonby and Cream duo, had cast caution to the wind and was mock conducting the orchestra while beating time with her foot. The sun shone brightly above, and Violet was as happy as she had felt in a long time.

"How's Cora?" asked Violet as the dulcet tune faded.

"Still betrothed to that frightful politician," said Vera.

"So, your opinion of him hasn't improved?"

"No. If anything, it has dropped further. Andrew Pennington is all show. He's got pots of money and comes from a notable family, but he's quite the chauvinist if you dig a bit deeper. Cora deserves so much better."

"Oh dear. She seemed quite smitten the last time I saw her."

Vera sniffed. "I daresay they'll marry, but I expect she'll live to regret it. She's no more than a bauble on his arm."

"It's been an age since I went to a wedding. We can enjoy the day, can't we?"

"They haven't set a date yet. And I'm not sure I'll make the cut."

"Don't be silly, Vera. You're Cora's dearest friend."

Vera gave a half smile as her eyes settled on the picnic blanket. "I'm sure you're right. Try one of these hog rolls. They're delicious."

"Seriously, Vera. We will both dance at Cora's wedding."

"I wonder who she'll choose for bridesmaids." Vera's eyes momentarily settled on Daisy.

"Oh, I doubt it."

"Why not? Cora doesn't know many children."

"Perhaps she'll appoint a maid of honour," said Violet mischievously.

Vera shuddered. "As long as she doesn't ask me. I can't think of anything worse."

"She'll make you wear a frock."

"Not on your Nellie. I do wish she could ask little Luna."

"Yes. It's a pity. I'm sure she'd love to if circumstances were different."

Vera sighed. "As long as they're happy."

"Happy is too strong a word," said Violet. "Aurora is

making the most of a difficult situation. She feels safe. I am sorry for keeping so much from you but needs must."

"I quite understand, and I wouldn't want you to compromise their safety. But bear me in mind if things become tricky again. Spending time with Aurora at Netherwood was an easy assignment. Or should I say, easy for me. The poor girl was an emotional wreck, fearful for herself and doubly so for Luna. I still don't understand what her husband hopes to achieve harbouring that wastrel brother of his."

"That's because you don't know Michael. Duty comes before all else."

"Then he will die a lonely man."

"Hard words, Vera."

Vera Ponsonby crossed her trousered legs. "I'm sorry. I know he's your friend. But I smell the whiff of a burning martyr."

"Michael isn't like that. He won't be feeling sorry for himself. Any weight he carries will be from trying to do the right thing."

"Oh, listen. This is such a jolly tune."

Vera tapped her feet again as Violet reached for a sandwich. Daisy watched her from afar, eventually giving in to hunger pangs.

"Can I have something to eat, Mummy?"

"Yes. Sit down and help yourself, girls."

"Only if you stop dancing. It's embarrassing."

"Why? I'm having fun."

"But you're too old."

"Daisy," exclaimed Hilda. "That's not very polite."

Daisy opened her mouth to comment, and her frown turned to a wide smile as she waved ahead.

"Look. It's Daddy."

"I thought he was lunching at the club," said Vera.

"So did I." Violet shoved her feet into her sandals and stood, peering into the distance as she spotted Lawrence's serious expression. "Wait here. I'll see what he wants," she said.

As Violet neared Lawrence, he checked his pace, allowing her time to reach him out of earshot of Vera and the girls. He leaned towards Violet and kissed her cheek.

"What is it, dear?" she asked.

"A phone call," said Lawrence.

"From whom?"

"Aurora. She's just called the house. It's Frank. He's gone missing."

Chapter Five

MALVERN LOWER WYCHE

VERA PONSONBY HAD BEEN in the right place at the right time. As Lawrence and Violet approached her, she immediately understood the imminent crisis and offered to mind Daisy without being asked. Violet had escorted Hilda home, taking Daisy with her, while Lawrence walked behind, earnestly talking to Vera. Though initially adamant he would not reveal Aurora's location, Lawrence wavered, finally deciding that if Vera were willing to remain in Cheltenham looking after their daughter, she should know why. He had confessed that Aurora was living in Malvern but kept her address to himself while revealing that Frank Podmore had booked Ivy Cottage at Lower Wyche, as usual. And though Lawrence hoped his stay in Malvern would only amount to a few hours, he would make himself known to the owners of Ivy Cottage so Vera could contact him there if she wished. Vera had been good about the vague information exchange, not asking awkward questions Lawrence couldn't answer or seeking details not freely offered. She had accompanied them back to Bath Street before settling into the spare room, promising to look after Daisy for as long as it took. After kissing their daughter goodbye, Violet slid into the passenger seat while Lawrence started the car.

They drove to Malvern through scenic countryside and would have enjoyed the view had their minds not been occupied with Frank's unexpected disappearance. Violet broke the silence a few miles into the journey.

"I'm surprised Aurora thought to call you," she said.

"She was lucky I was in. If I hadn't forgotten my wallet, I would be halfway through the cheese course at the club dinner."

"What did Aurora tell you?"

"That Frank had gone out in a storm last night and hadn't returned home."

"How did she know?"

"It's all over the town. They've organised a search party. That's where we're going now."

"Oh dear. This sounds serious. I had hoped it was a misunderstanding."

"I'm afraid not," said Lawrence. "And I don't like the sound of Frank's disappearance one little bit."

"Do you think he is hurt?"

"It's likely, Violet. Frank is a sensible man and would have sent word if he could. Aurora said he rented his regular room from Mr and Mrs Cross, who he knows from old. Frank likes to stroll across the golf links, and their cottage is nearby. The Crosses are fond of Frank and natu-rally asked where he was going late at night. They raised the alarm when he said he would return and did not."

"Poor Frank. This is awful."

"And the weather wouldn't have helped. Yesterday's storm was frightful."

"I know. We had to put waterproof sheets under our blankets at the park today. The ground was soggy even though the sun was blazing hot."

Lawrence changed gear and took a sharp left. Violet discreetly held onto the door, her heart fluttering. Lawrence had honed his driving skills in a small yellow Wolseley. Driving a car with a more powerful engine didn't come naturally. Now and then, the car would lurch, and Lawrence would curse beneath his breath. If Violet stayed calm, Lawrence would too. But if she overreacted, he would become flustered and bad tempered. Lawrence straightened the car and took an anxious look left. Violet smiled her encouragement. "What time did Frank go out?" she asked.

"Aurora didn't say."

"I suppose we'll find out more when we get there."

"Yes. Aurora will catch up with us on the links. But don't forget she will be using her middle name."

"I know, dear. And Luna will too – now Elizabeth and Constance, I believe."

"Lizzie and Connie, actually. Aurora said the long names were becoming a mouthful."

"I'm surprised she agreed to meet us after her initial resistance."

"Malvern has been good for Aurora. It's a small town with few people passing through unless they've come to stay. When I spoke to Frank on the phone, he said she'd lost that haunted look she wore when he first met her. I hope this doesn't prove a setback."

"We'll find out in a moment. There's a signpost for Lower Wyche over there."

Five minutes later, Lawrence stopped the car after seeing a group of scouts milling along the side of the road. To the rear was another group of adults, some with dogs.

"That'll be them," said Lawrence, opening the door for Violet. They squelched towards the group, both grateful for their outdoor attire.

Lawrence approached a uniformed officer at the rear of the crowd. "Is this the search party?"

"For Frank Podmore?"

"Is there more than one missing person?"

Violet saw the policeman's irritated glare and put a restraining hand on Lawrence's arm before he antagonised him further.

"Yes. Frank Podmore," she said.

"It is. Feel free to join us. The more the merrier."

"What do you know about Frank's disappearance?" asked Lawrence authoritatively.

The police officer shrugged. "He went out in a storm last night and didn't come home. That's about the size of it."

"I know," said Lawrence. "Was he with anyone?"

"Yes, a young companion who said Mr Podmore was taking a late-night stroll."

"Was that Mr Cross?"

"No. He owns Ivy Cottage. I'm sure Henry Cross would be pleased to hear you call him young, but I can assure you he is not. Mr Podmore's companion was a strip of a lad, perhaps in his twenties." The officer pursed his lips. "And then again, perhaps even younger."

"What exactly are you implying."

"Nothing. You're asking rather a lot of questions. If you want to help, put your best foot forward and get on with it."

"I'm sorry," said Violet, pushing ahead of Lawrence. "My husband didn't mean to be rude. We are old friends of Frank's and are naturally concerned about this news, especially as we were due to meet him this week. Do you know the name of his young companion?"

"No," said the officer.

"Please. It would help enormously."

"I'm not withholding information, madam. We know he did not leave Ivy Cottage alone, but his friend has yet to come forward. All I know is that the man was a casual acquaintance. If you want to know more, you should go to the police station where they are making active enquiries."

"We will, thank you."

Lawrence stepped forward, taking change again. "Who is your chief constable these days?" he asked.

"Colonel Walker," said the policeman.

"Ah. I've crossed paths with him," said Lawrence. "I think we might visit the station after we've helped out here."

"I wouldn't bother. The chief won't be there."

Lawrence raised an eyebrow and waited. The tactical silent pause did the trick, and the constable sighed, imparting information as if it were a heavy chore. "He's at Worcester Shire Hall for the next few days. Meetings and the like. You'll have to see him there."

"Whatever it takes," said Lawrence. "Now point us toward the best place to search."

Chapter Six

THE SEARCH PARTY

LAWRENCE AND VIOLET squelched through the dense undergrowth on the wet Malvern downs, searching in vain for signs of Frank Podmore. They had followed the scouts for a while, listening as the boys made a game of their mission. Neither minded the good-natured banter, which lifted their spirits as they tried not to think the worst. But after an hour, their enthusiasm dampened as the laborious walk failed to yield a single clue. Tired and demoralised but not ready to quit, they spied a familiar face through the mist; Aurora was with another group clad from head to toe in waterproofs and goloshes. She raised a hand to her mouth as she saw them, her expression momentarily one of alarm, but Lawrence strode forward with an outstretched arm.

"Hello, Lizzie," he said. "Fancy seeing you here."

Aurora's face relaxed instantly, relieved that Lawrence hadn't forgotten her alias and given the game away. Violet couldn't stop herself from hugging Aurora, who shrank back from the physical contact, making small talk until her companions moved ahead. Once she felt able to speak freely, Aurora's eyes filled with tears. "I have been so worried," she said. "Thank goodness you are here."

"Have you seen Frank?" asked Lawrence.

"Yes. Every day since he arrived in Malvern."

"Including yesterday?"

Aurora nodded. "I cooked for him. We ate breakfast together, and Frank played with Luna. She loves spending time with him."

"Did he seem normal?"

"Yes. I think so. Although he was getting frustrated with one of his London friends. He said he'd been waiting for some important information, which was slow to arrive. It turned up eventually, and Frank became irritated by the reply. But I wasn't listening properly. I'd been making Welsh cakes and left the heat too high. I was busy scraping charcoal from the bottom while Frank was reading his letter. But as far as I remember, he said nothing untoward."

"What do you think happened to him?" asked Violet.

"I don't know, but certainly not what the gossips are saying."

Lawrence cocked his head. "Which is?"

"Just silly speculation. I know you are both fond of Frank, and you should try to ignore it."

"Ignore what?"

"Some are saying that he killed himself," said Aurora. "But I know he wouldn't. We'd planned to go walking at the weekend."

"And we were meeting Frank for dinner," said Violet. "We were all looking forward to it."

"I know. Frank said so. It's a silly idea."

"Who suggested it?" asked Lawrence.

"One of the girls in the hairdresser's said she heard it this morning. Then another in the queue at the baker."

"Did you ask why?"

"No. I was reading a magazine while my hair dried and overheard a private conversation. It made me want to bolt from the premises and find Frank immediately, but I knew I'd draw attention to myself, so I kept quiet and waited until I'd paid. Then I went to see Mr and Mrs Cross as soon as I'd finished at the bakery."

"Were they aware of the speculation?" asked Violet.

"Yes. And it really upset Mrs Cross. She had already spent the night worrying. She said the gossip had added insult to injury, and she wished they would stop it."

"I wonder why anyone considered suicide?" mused Violet.

Lawrence caught her eye. "Frank has had a few troubles in recent years."

"If you mean living apart from his wife, he came to terms with the situation some time ago."

"I was thinking more about his sudden exit from the post office service."

Aurora wiped a sodden strand of hair from her eyes. "I don't know anything about that," she said.

"Now is not the time," said Violet, narrowing her eyes.

"Fair enough." Lawrence recognised her look of displeasure and swiftly moved on. "Did Mr and Mrs Cross say anything else?"

"Only that Frank had been out for a walk with a young companion."

"Hmmm. News travels fast. We've just heard the same."

"Although they don't know who he is," added Violet.

"I doubt it will help. Mrs Cross said the young man was

polite and friendly and had only recently met Frank. She doubts he can add much more information."

"But it's a loose end," said Lawrence. "And so far, the search has failed to deliver anything meaningful. If this chap was the last person to see Frank, we ought to find him. Unless, of course, Frank turns up in the meantime.

"I do hope so," said Violet. "It's getting awfully late, and the search party is thinning out. I fear people are losing interest."

"We won't," said Lawrence. "I'll find Frank if I have to spend the whole night on this blasted moor."

Chapter Seven

FRANK'S DIGS

THE AFTERNOON SLIPPED AWAY as they ploughed
through the undergrowth, damp earth clinging to their
boots with their eyes peeled for signs of Frank's where-
abouts. Eventually, Aurora reluctantly left to collect Luna
while Lawrence and Violet continued for miles, at first in a
group and then alone as, one by one, the searchers left to
resume their everyday lives. Lawrence's stomach was
cramping with hunger, but Violet wanted to push on while it
was still light enough to see. She had banked on a few more
hours of sunlight, but another sudden squall put paid to
that when black clouds darkened the sky. They turned back,
trudging to their car around seven thirty, having given little
thought to an evening meal, let alone accommodation.

Back in the car, they removed dirty wellingtons and
damp oilskin coats, stowing them in the car boot to keep the
upholstery dry.

"What now?" Lawrence asked, his fatigue almost
palpable.

"I wonder if we can find a hotel?" said Violet uncertainly.

Lawrence glanced at his watch. "If it's not too late. We'll drive into Greater Malvern and see what we can find."

"I'd rather stay here."

"We can't spend the night in the car," exclaimed Lawrence.

"No, silly. We should stay in Lower Wyche. We'll be close to Aurora and can get up early to resume our search for Frank.

"I don't know about you, but I'm tired to the bone. I didn't see any hotels on the way through, and it will soon be dark."

Violet sighed. "We shouldn't stray too far away, however uncomfortable. Do you think the Crosses will take us in?"

Lawrence mulled the idea. "They might," he said. "Frank's room should still be available, and they may let us use it. We might have to squeeze into a single bed, though."

"I'd sleep in a barn, if necessary," said Violet, stifling a yawn.

"Be careful what you wish for, old girl. That's on the cards if they turn us away."

But Lawrence was wrong. Once they announced themselves, Henry Cross greeted them like old friends.

"Come in," he said. "Make yourselves at home. It's the least we can do for Mr Podmore. Have you eaten?"

"No. We've been on the moor all day looking for him."

"Yes. I did a few hours searching myself at first light. I'd offer you a hot meal, but Fanny has gone to bed with a cold. Why don't I show you to Frank's room? Then I'll see what I can find in the pantry."

"That's very kind," said Lawrence.

"Frank's clothes are still in the wardrobe, so there's little available space. But I'm sure he'd want the room put to good use while he is out of action. Try not to move his things, though. We must keep his personal effects safe."

"Do you think he'll come back soon?" asked Violet. Her voice wobbled as she contemplated Frank spending another lonely night outdoors. Henry crossed his arms, and his face softened as he watched her anxious expression.

"I do," he said. "It's wild and wooded out on the hills, but Frank is familiar with the terrain. He has played golf every day since arriving and still walks several times a day for recreation. He is probably lying injured somewhere, or he would have returned by now. I'm confident they'll find him with a sprained ankle or a pulled muscle – something that has stopped him from returning under his own steam. Something with a reasonable explanation."

Lawrence squeezed Violet's hand reassuringly as he followed her upstairs. Although she had been brave and pragmatic for most of the day, Violet had a soft spot for Frank, more commonly seen between siblings. She was suffering, and Lawrence wished he could take her pain away.

Henry Cross stopped outside a crooked wooden door to the rear of the cottage and ushered Violet inside, standing back to allow Lawrence to join her. Lawrence set his bag down and looked around. Though not large, the bed beneath the window could comfortably accommodate them both.

"This is perfect," said Violet. "And it's kind of you to let us use the room while we look for Frank."

"It's the least I can do. Now settle yourselves in," said Henry. "Then join me downstairs."

Once alone, Violet perched on the edge of the bed

before collapsing backwards onto the counterpane. "I could roll over and sleep for a week," she said.

"And so you will, once we've eaten."

"It might be bread and cheese."

"I don't care. I'd sell my soul for a mouldy cabbage right now."

"We should have stopped for lunch."

"I would have if you'd let me. Strange. You're usually the one counting the hours until the next meal."

Violet sighed. "You do exaggerate."

"Not at all." Lawrence loosened his necktie and peered into a dusty mirror above a low bookcase. He was removing a spot of mud from his face when Violet interrupted.

"Look. There's Frank's compass," she said, pointing to the dresser. "That's worrying. Why didn't he take it with him?"

"He only went out for a stroll, Violet. I doubt he needed it."

"Even so." Violet roused herself and stood, casting an eye around the room before approaching the chest of drawers. A wash bag, cufflinks, and a bottle of cologne lay next to a pile of books. Violet removed the top one and flicked through it.

"Anything interesting?" asked Lawrence.

"Just an account of a fraudulent medium."

"They're all fraudulent in my experience."

"Don't judge everyone by Major Savage's standards," said Violet.

"And his dreadful wife. What was her name?"

"Jane."

"Ah, yes. What a reprehensible pair. Those poor children."

"They're safe now," said Violet, smiling at the memory

of William and Millicent, two little orphans stolen by the Savages to assist with their fakery.

"Yes. But that lowlife scoundrel would have given them to Felix Crossley had we not intervened. Savage by name and by nature. At least he's now safely ensconced at His Majesty's pleasure."

"I'm afraid not, Lawrence. I heard they released him last month."

Lawrence scowled. "What's the point of a judicial system if the likes of Savage only serve a few months inside?"

"Friends in high places, I suppose. But Jane Savage left London with her tail between her legs and no intention of returning to her husband. Karma will out in the end."

"Anything interesting in Frank's effects?"

Violet pulled open the upper right drawer, rummaged inside, and shook her head before systematically searching one drawer after the other until she had finished. "Only undergarments and shirts," she said. "Oh, and writing materials."

"That's a shame. But I didn't expect Frank to be knee-deep in mysteries. He would have told us."

"Oh. Look at this." Violet removed a brown leather-bound book from the pile and held it towards Lawrence.

"What have you found?"

"A journal," said Violet.

"You mean a diary?"

Violet licked her finger and turned a few pages. "No. Random jottings, really. Article prompts, a few brief scrib-blings on seances and other esoteric subjects. And a rather good pencil drawing of a curlew."

"I didn't know Frank was a bird spotter."

"Neither did I. Nor that he was such a splendid artist."

"You should recognise a masterpiece when you see one with your experience, my dear."

"Are you being sarcastic? I can never tell."

Lawrence put his arm around Violet's waist and drew her towards him. "No. I really mean it. Your paintings have improved beyond measure."

"Thanks to Walter."

Lawrence pursed his lips, fighting the impulse to remind Violet of his honest opinion of the pompous artist he had first met the previous year. But Violet still bore mental and physical scars from her encounter with Leonard Covington, and he decided not to dredge up memories best forgotten. Lawrence reached for the journal and removed it from her hand. "It's certainly a curlew," he said. "Look at the beak."

"I did. That's how I identified it. I wonder..."

But Violet, interrupted by a soft rap at the door, did not get any further.

"Come in," said Lawrence.

A young boy entered, his solemn face anxious at the sight of strangers. Violet flashed an encouraging smile.

"Excuse me. Papa asked me to fetch you both directly. He has set the dining room table and warmed up some soup."

"What's your name, young man?" asked Lawrence.

"William, sir."

"Thank you very much, William. Tell your father that we'll be down right away."

Lawrence snapped the journal shut, removed his hand-kerchief, and blew his nose. "That can wait for another day," he said, tossing the jotter carelessly onto the dresser. "Thank goodness our host has found something warm to eat. I fear I'm coming down with a cold."

Chapter Eight

SHIRE HALL

Worcester, August 16, 1910

LAWRENCE STOOD outside Shire Hall in Worcester, his head hunched as he blew into a soggy handkerchief. "I thought a warm bed and a bowl of hot soup would have killed this cold," he said.

Violet reached towards him and laid her palm across his forehead. "You're a little warm. I hope it's not flu."

"So do I. We don't have time for illness. Not with Frank still alone in the wilderness."

Violet sighed. "He's been away for two nights now. I'm desperately worried."

"Me too. But I feel a little lighter since speaking to Henry. He seems a decent chap and has Frank's interests very much at heart."

"Undoubtedly. But shouldn't we be searching the common with Henry and the others instead of chasing after this casual acquaintance of Frank's? It's hardly the best use of our time."

"I disagree. You know how I feel about loose ends."

"I'd understand if we were in the middle of a murder investigation. But these are only loose ends to you, Lawrence. The police will know all about Frank's companion by now."

"I'm glad you think so."

"Don't you? We should leave them to it and concentrate on more practical ways of helping Frank. Like searching Lower Wyche in daylight when we have a fighting chance of seeing something."

"We did that yesterday, and I would be out there now if I had more faith in the police. But how many crimes have we solved over the years by investigating clues they couldn't be bothered to deal with? Far too many for my liking."

"Frank's our friend. We have a vested interest in his safe return. We shouldn't rely on others."

"Agreed. But there's no such thing as too much knowledge. Let's find out more about his last outing. If we fail, we've lost nothing."

Violet hugged herself and sighed. "Very well. Let's go inside then."

Lawrence looked at his watch. "No. Give it another ten minutes until they finish. There's a bench over there where we can rest."

They sat, and Lawrence sneezed again, pulling out his handkerchief and blowing loudly.

"You can't keep using that; it must be sodden," said Violet. "Take mine."

"It's covered with lace."

"But it's also dry and not crawling with germs."

Lawrence grunted but did not argue. He blew his nose again and stared in silence at the Greek revival-style architecture of Shire Hall. The sun emerged from a clouded sky, and Lawrence leaned back, legs outstretched, as his eyes began to flutter closed. Violet prodded him in the side.

"Don't fall asleep. You'll feel worse."

"Chance would be a fine thing. My head's foggy, and I feel like I haven't slept in days."

"You were snoring fit to wake the dead last night."

"Well, it wasn't a very effective sleep. I'm dog tired this morning."

"And more than a little grumpy."

Lawrence raised an eyebrow but kept his counsel. "Ah, look. Someone's coming out." He pointed to the Shire Hall frontage, where a brace of officials were leaving. "Come on, Violet. Shake a leg."

They hastened to the steps and loitered as, one by one, the participants of the standing joint committee left the meeting.

"That's him," said Lawrence, pointing to a straight-backed man with a tanned, angular face.

"Who?"

"Colonel Walker, the chief constable for Worces-tershire."

"Do you think he will speak to us?"

Lawrence shrugged. "It depends if he remembers me. It's been a long time since we last met."

"And what's your plan if he doesn't?"

"I'll beg," said Lawrence.

They watched Colonel Walker meander slowly towards them, chatting earnestly with a uniformed man at his side.

"I wonder who he's with," said Lawrence.

The two men finally approached the bottom step, where Lawrence waited patiently. He strode forward and offered his hand to the colonel. "Hello, sir. You may not remember me, but my name is Lawrence Harpham. We first met on the Isle of Man. May I introduce my wife, Violet."

The colonel frowned. Seconds later, his face relaxed as an old memory surfaced. "Good Lord. I remember. A rather nasty murder, wasn't it? It's good that you mentioned your name, or I would have walked straight past you. How are things in the Suffolk constabulary?"

"I don't know, sir. I retired some time ago."

"You're a man of leisure? How very fortunate. Have you relocated to Worcester?"

"No. Cheltenham, actually."

The colonel turned to his companion. "You hear that, Anson? Danvers lives there too. On the edge of a hill, if memory serves."

"Cleeve Hill," said Anson, dourly, fidgeting with his button as if anxious to leave.

"That's right. Cleeve Hill. Do you know it, Harpham?"

"Vaguely," said Lawrence.

"Do you know Danvers?"

"Not at all."

Anson curled his lip. "I doubt he moves in those circles," he said beneath his breath.

Colonel Walker nodded. "Well, good to see you, Harpham."

He turned to leave, but Lawrence coughed. "Excuse me for keeping you, sir, but we're not here by accident. I hoped to speak with you about a particular matter."

The colonel glanced at his watch. "Time is pressing, Harpham. The quarter sessions will recommence within the hour."

"It will only take a few minutes. Five at the most."

"Very well. What can I help you with?"

"Violet and I are friends of Frank Podmore."

"Podmore, you say? Oh dear."

"I know that name," said Anson. "Where have I heard it?"

"He's a parapsychologist," Colonel Walker replied.

"Like Mrs Sidgwick?"

"Exactly. But Podmore is missing. Has been for a couple of days. I am sorry, Harpham. You must be very worried."

"We are," said Lawrence. "We spent hours yesterday searching for him on the common, to no avail."

"Yes, I know. We have feet on the ground too."

"Quite," said Lawrence. "We ran into your constable, and he suggested I might find you here."

"Did he now?" said the colonel sternly. "As much as I would like to help you, Harpham, I don't see how I can?"

Violet sighed, tired of waiting in the background. "We need some information," she said.

"What information?"

Violet opened her mouth, but Lawrence beat her to it. "Frank had supper with a casual acquaintance that night. I understand the young man is yet to make himself known."

"Well, I can allay your fears in that regard," said Colonel Walker. "We are taking every possible step to locate him. It's only a matter of time."

"That's a pity. I had hoped for some solid information. Here's my card. Can you let me know when you have found him? I would like to have a word."

Colonel Walker examined the offering. "I thought you'd retired. This card says private investigator?"

"I rarely take cases these days; when I do, it's mostly to keep my hand in. But this is different. Frank is a personal friend."

"Well, it can't do any harm under the circumstances."

"I disagree," said Anson firmly. "Don't get involved. The man's a civilian and will bring more trouble than it's worth."

"I take your point, old man. But I've worked with Harpham before. He was a good policeman and very reliable."

"Thank you, sir," said Lawrence.

Anson scowled. "I was under that misapprehension when I tried to help Conan Doyle with the Edalji case. You remember, don't you? That damned troublemaker from Great Wyrley who slaughtered livestock and wrote filthy, anonymous letters. And look how that turned out."

"Yes. I realise how much Conan Doyle's indiscretion harmed you. But this is different. Harpham was one of us."

"But he's not now. The man is a private detective and has lost the right to expect access to information before it appears in the press."

Colonel Walker turned to Lawrence and shrugged. "Anson has a point, you know."

"I daresay, but if you're referring to Arthur Conan Doyle, he's a writer, not an ex-policeman. I know how to keep my counsel and assure you of my absolute discretion."

"And," said Violet, interrupting her husband. "I doubt Mr Conan Doyle had a personal interest in your case. Frank Podmore is our friend. I have known him for a decade. He's missing, possibly injured and alone on the moor, and nobody has interrogated the last person who saw him. It's not good enough."

"Try not to get upset, Mrs Harpham."

"It's hard not to. We are only asking for a little informa-tion when you have it."

"Absolutely not," said Anson.

Colonel Walker grimaced. "It is my decision."

"I'm only trying to warn you," said Anson. "So you don't

fall into the same trap as me. The Edalji family have been laughing at the police force since their precious George left prison. He should be serving a long sentence. Instead, he's free to do as he chooses, and it's all down to that interfering amateur detective."

"Three years in jail is hardly getting away with it."

"But Edalji is back in society and working as a solicitor. So much for justice."

"You're letting that case colour your judgement," said Walker. He turned to Lawrence. "I will take your card and pass the information on as soon I can. No details, of course. Just the bare bones. Will that do?"

"Yes, sir. Thank you," said Lawrence.

"Well, good day to you both." The colonel touched his forelock as he turned to leave. But Anson's face was red with unconcealed rage. Lawrence and Violet could still hear him muttering under his breath as they walked away.

"I think you're making a big mistake," said Anson, strolling into the distance.

"Come on. Let's get back to the car," said Lawrence. "I feel like death warmed up."

"You don't look well at all. We'll take it slowly."

Lawrence started the motor, and they left Worcester, driving south towards Malvern.

"Who was that awful man?" asked Violet.

"Walker's friend?"

"Yes. He seems surprisingly irate. It can't be good for his health. I wonder what's really troubling him?"

"I don't know. Anson clearly holds a grudge about an old case. It's a terrible shame to have such a thing hanging over you. Move on, I say. Forget all about it and concentrate on the next investigation."

"That's fine coming from you, Lawrence. You're like a

dog with a bone until you've got to the bottom of a mystery."

"Yes. As I will be until we find Frank."

"This isn't an investigation, Lawrence. Frank is a missing person, nothing more."

Lawrence momentarily took his eyes off the road and gently caressed Violet's cheek. "I know you're worried. But we will find him."

"But what if we don't? What if we never find him?"

"We will, old girl. I promise."

Crossing fingers while driving was no mean feat, but Lawrence did it anyway, knowing he had just declared an oath beyond his powers to keep. And as the clouds slid back over the sun and a drizzle fell on the outskirts of Malvern, Lawrence wished he could take back the words. He had a terrible sense of foreboding.

Chapter Nine

TRAGEDY AT NEW POOL

Malvern, Friday, August 19, 1910

LAWRENCE OPENED the front door of Ivy Cottage and inhaled the delicious smell of a cooked breakfast. He headed contentedly for the dining room, where Violet sat opposite Henry Cross while his wife, Fanny, dished fried eggs directly from the pan onto their plates.

"Just in time," said Fanny as Lawrence shrugged off his jacket and sat at the table.

"Thank you. I'm ravenous."

"Did you get it?" asked Violet.

Lawrence nodded. "The telegram? Yes, I did. It might mean another trip to Worcester, but Walker came up trumps though Frank's friend knows nothing of his subsequent movements."

Violet smiled. "Good for Colonel Walker, especially after the warning from that awful man, Anson."

"I expect that's why he cooperated. Walker disliked taking orders from a fellow chief constable."

"Have you made any progress?" asked Henry Cross.

"A little," said Lawrence. "It's still not enough, though."

"I'm beginning to lose hope," sighed Violet, her eyes heavy with lack of sleep. "It's been five nights. Frank may be injured and alone, waiting for someone to rescue him."

Henry Cross cocked his head and smiled encouragingly. "Or he may not be outside at all. He could have approached the road and caught a lift from a passing vehicle. Keep your spirits up, Mrs Harpham. The longer this takes, the less I worry."

"I wish I had your optimistic nature," said Violet. "I won't be happy until Frank bursts through the door, telling us about his adventures."

Lawrence speared a forkful of food, but it hadn't reached his mouth when someone rapped loudly at the door.

Violet gripped his arm. "Frank," she whispered.

Lawrence lowered his fork and turned towards the entrance as Henry Cross approached the front door. They waited silently, food untouched, listening in vain to the murmur of voices coming from outside.

Moments later, Henry appeared, solemn faced. "I was wrong," he said, sitting at the table with his head in his hands.

Nobody spoke until he sighed and looked up. "I am sorry to have to tell you that they've found a body near the golf links."

"Oh no." Violet's voice trembled as she covered her mouth with her hand, tears welling in her eyes. Lawrence patted her shoulder, but she moved his hand away.

"It may not be Frank," said Lawrence.

"Of course it is." Violet pushed away her breakfast and

looked distantly over the Crosses small garden, too stunned to cry.

"The poor man," said Fanny. "How awful." She put her hand to her mouth and stifled a sob.

"Now, now," said Henry Cross. "Don't take on so."

"We must tell Lizzie before she hears it from somebody else," said Violet, springing into action.

"Shouldn't we wait first?" Lawrence stared longingly at his cooling breakfast, still hungry despite the awful news.

"No. She can't hear it from a stranger."

"Finish your food first," begged Lawrence. "Mrs Cross has gone to a lot of trouble."

"I'm sorry. I couldn't eat a thing." Violet stood and took a moment to compose herself, then strode towards the door with the air of a woman determined not to let her emotions get the better of her.

"Do eat, Mr Harpham," sniffed Fanny. "You're no good to anyone if you're hungry."

Lawrence shovelled his food down in minutes, replete though he had eaten with little enjoyment. Fanny was right. If Frank were dead, and he knew he must be, he would need to fuel his body for a long and depressing day.

"Did they give an exact location?" Lawrence asked.

Henry Cross nodded. "New Pool," he said. "He's in the water."

"Oh God. Poor Frank. I hope he didn't suffer."

"I expect it was quick and painless."

"Tell me the way, please," said Lawrence, his voice heavy with grim determination. "I've delayed long enough. It's time I examined the place before too many people trample any clues away."

"It's easier to show you."

"Thank you. By car or on foot?"

"Both. Give me a moment, and I'll join you outside."

Lawrence grabbed his coat and started the engine with a heavy heart, staring through the windscreen as Henry Cross appeared. Henry draped an arm over his wife's shoulders and kissed her gently on the cheek. A few moments later, the door opened, and he clambered into the car.

"Fanny's upset," he said. "But she's trying not to show it for Mrs Harpham's sake."

"She mustn't worry about Violet," said Lawrence. "Violet is terribly fond of Frank, but she is pragmatic and resilient. Bad news brings out the best in her. Don't worry. Violet won't rest until we get to the truth."

"I doubt there's much to discover. New Pool is deep, and the banks are steep in places. Poor Mr Podmore probably slipped and drowned. I doubt it took more than an instant."

"You're probably right," said Lawrence, "but I must be sure."

They drove for a few minutes before Henry Cross gestured for Lawrence to pull over. He parked the car and followed Henry down a narrow path to the water's edge. They scanned the pool, now peaceful and shimmering below a gentle August breeze.

"Over there," said Lawrence, seeing a small group of people, including several uniformed officers.

"Ah, it's young Culver. You might get some sense out of him."

"Who?" asked Lawrence as Henry Cross pointed to a young police constable.

"Is that Culver? Good. We met yesterday. It took a bit of coaxing from Violet for him to cooperate."

"Don't worry about asking for help. I know his father." Henry Cross winked encouragingly.

PC Culver detached himself from the other men as they

approached the group and headed towards them. "No farther, please, gentlemen," he said, firmly raising an arm to block their passage.

Lawrence produced his card and handed it to the young constable.

"I don't care who you are. You can't go any farther."

"Come on, Gerry. You'll let us in, won't you?" asked Henry.

"I can't," said PC Culver, unwavering in his duty.

Henry Cross chewed his lip, taken back by the refusal. "But your father…" he said.

"He has nothing to do with this." Culver pursed his lips and lowered his eyes, clearly embarrassed.

Lawrence recognised the young PC's discomfort and pounced.

"I spoke to Colonel Walker yesterday at your suggestion," he said casually. "And he sent me some important information earlier. Should I bother him again, or will you let us pass?"

"Did you really?" asked the constable, arching a sceptical eyebrow.

Lawrence produced the telegram and thrust it forward. The PC's eyes widened.

"I see. Well, that throws a different light on matters. You can pass, but don't touch anything."

"We won't," said Lawrence. "I'm only here for information."

"Right. Now stand aside for the medical examiner."

Lawrence watched as a suited man wearing goloshes examined a body at the water's edge. Lawrence leaned forward for a better view, then winced as he recognised Frank's overcoat. Seconds later, the examiner's assistant turned the body over, revealing Frank's greying face.

"Oh God," said Lawrence.

"Do you recognise the body?" asked PC Culver.

Lawrence nodded. "Yes. It's Frank Podmore."

"Good. We've sent someone to fetch his brother, George. He should be along shortly for a formal identification. But thank you for confirming in the meantime."

"Where did you find Frank?" asked Lawrence.

"We didn't. That young man spotted him in the lake this morning."

Lawrence followed the direction of PC Culver's finger.

"Who is it?" he asked.

"John Harvey, a pupil of Mr Edmonds, that chap over there." Culver nodded towards a man in a brown jacket squatting beside a young boy. "And no, you may not speak with either of them. The boy is very distressed, as I am sure you will understand."

"I wouldn't dream of it," said Lawrence. "What happened?"

"We don't know yet. But Mr Podmore likely slipped and fell. If you want to know more, the coroner is arranging an inquest for tonight."

"So soon?"

"Yes. Mr Podmore's family arrived in Malvern as soon as he went missing. They were expecting the worst and expressed a wish for a quick burial when we sent word of the discovery earlier this morning."

"I'm surprised the family didn't come to see me," said Henry Cross. "Frank's possessions are still in my house."

"Keep them safe. We'll send an officer over before the inquest, just in case," said Culver.

"In case of what?" asked Henry.

"Never you mind. Now, I must assist my colleagues. Oh dear. My inspector has arrived."

"Come," said Lawrence, hastily casting an eye towards the approaching officer. Securing the cooperation of a young and somewhat naïve constable was one thing, but Lawrence didn't like his chances with a more senior policeman around.

"Where are we going?" asked Henry.

"For a stroll around the lake."

"Why?"

"In case they've missed anything."

They walked silently for a few moments before the loud shriek of a whistle pierced the air. Lawrence looked over his shoulder to find the inspector and two other men running anticlockwise towards a third civilian waving by the waterway.

"On the other hand," said Lawrence, turning to retrace his steps.

The two men covered the ground quickly as Lawrence approached the medical examiner, now conducting his business with no audience save for a bearded man staring distractedly ahead.

"Ignore them and get on with the job," snapped the coroner, glaring at his assistant, now preoccupied with the antics of the officers. "Write this," he continued tersely. "No obvious external marks of violence."

The assistant repeated his words, his eyes now fixed on his notepad.

The examiner looked up as Lawrence's shadow loomed over them. "What do you want?" he snapped.

Lawrence straightened his back, trying to project an air of authority. "Are we looking at death by drowning?"

"It seems that way."

"And did I hear you say there were no external marks of violence?"

"You did."

"Did you find anything on the body?"

The examiner huffed a sigh and looked up. "Who are you?" he asked.

"Harpham's the name. I'm collecting information for the chief constable ahead of tonight's inquest."

"If it happens."

"I'm sure it will."

"The deceased carried four pounds and a gold watch to answer your question," said the examiner. "And the body was fully dressed when recovered."

"Anything else?"

"Yes. They found a walking stick a few yards away."

"Where?"

The medical examiner pointed west. "In front of the farthest bush, I believe. Now I must press on," he said.

"Of course. We'll leave you in peace."

"I wonder what all that's about," said Henry Cross, pointing to the police inspector, standing with his hands on his hips while two constables tentatively prodded at the reeds by the water's edge.

"I don't know. Let's hope it keeps them busy while we search the bank."

"What are you looking for?"

"Anything. Signs of a struggle. Something our police friends have missed."

"Right. I'll help."

Lawrence stopped. "Do you mind walking a few paces behind me?" he asked.

"Why?"

"I know what I'm looking for, and it's all too easy to trample over the evidence."

"Right you are." Henry Cross grimaced, and for a

moment, Lawrence thought he'd offended him. But Henry remained a discreet distance behind, whistling quietly to himself.

Lawrence tiptoed towards the bush, where the imprint of the stick was visible in the still-wet mud.

Henry peered over his shoulder. "They've taken it away then?"

"So it would appear."

"What now?"

"Try to provide some screening."

"What do you mean?"

"Stand in front of me; there's a good chap. Block their view."

Lawrence waited until Henry had positioned himself, then dropped to his knees, gently patting the surrounding ground. Then he pushed forward, blindly searching beneath the bushes, grunting as his hands closed over a small, mud-covered object.

"Ah," said Lawrence, sliding it discreetly into his pocket.

"Watch out," said Henry.

"What's wrong?"

"The police are on the move."

Lawrence resisted the urge to examine the tiny object, now safely inside a handkerchief, and turned towards the lake. He covered his eyes from the piercing early morning sun and squinted at them. "What are they doing?" he asked.

"Returning to the body, I think. Sorry, I meant returning to Frank."

"It doesn't take long," sighed Lawrence.

"Sorry, I didn't mean anything by it."

"I know. It's life. One day, a man; the next, a corpse. It's the way of things."

"The inspector keeps looking at you."

Lawrence brushed damp earth from his trousers. "We should avoid him, if possible. Or he'll start asking awkward questions. Let's go to the bank, and then we'll leave." Lawrence took a pace towards the water and examined the slope before him.

"No marks at all," he said.

"None," agreed Henry.

Lawrence moved closer before noticing the inspector powering towards them.

He waved a cheery hand before spinning around and walking swiftly away. "Time for a quick exit," he said.

Chapter Ten

THE FUNERAL

Saturday, August 20, 1910

"THIS IS DEPRESSING," said Lawrence, huddling with Violet by the entrance to Malvern Wells Cemetery.

Violet stared witheringly. "What do you expect with a funeral about to take place?"

"I meant the weather. It's seasonably inclement."

"As it has been all month, which is why I am wearing a raincoat."

"It was nice enough this morning."

"I'm surprised at you, Lawrence. You're usually better prepared. You'll catch another cold standing in this shower."

"It's only drizzle, and I wouldn't be in it if you joined me in the chapel."

"I can't. I promised Aurora, I mean Lizzie, I would meet her outside. But you can wait wherever you like."

"I'm not leaving you. Not on a day like this."

Lawrence pulled Violet closer and planted a kiss on her

forehead. She smiled for the first time that day and squeezed his hand.

"That's more like the Violet I know and love," said Lawrence.

"I'm sorry I've been so miserable. It's not your fault."

"Don't be sorry. You've known Frank a long time. He's only recently grown on me."

"There she is," said Violet, pointing farther up Green Lane. Aurora rushed towards them, holding her hat as she hurried up the road. She arrived breathless, her cheeks flushed.

"Sorry. Mrs Gibson was late."

"You should have come with us," said Lawrence.

"I was babysitting and could hardly abandon Marion while expecting Mrs Gibson to watch Luna for me later. It was kind of her to drive me at all, let alone with two little girls in the back."

"You called her Luna," whispered Violet.

Aurora clapped her hand over her mouth. "Oh dear. I expect so much from everyone else, but it's not the first time I've slipped. And Luna has too. She's old enough to wonder why I keep calling her Connie. But perhaps I have been too cautious. Things are quiet here, and even with Frank's awful accident, I doubt anyone would recognise me."

"You can never be too cautious," said Lawrence, chewing his lip.

Violet cocked her head, and he turned away before she could see his worried expression.

Lawrence subconsciously thrust his hand into his trouser pocket, feeling the object he had pulled from the bushes the previous day. His fingers brushed the ruby-covered cufflink, shaped into a unicursal hexagram, and he wrestled with his conscience as he had the previous night when deciding to keep his discovery secret until after the funeral. For a moment, he almost gave in. Violet's spirits were low, the day bathed in melancholy. In some ways, it was the perfect time to tell her that Crossley may have been present at Frank's death, and if not Crossley, then some other member of The Order of The Crescent Moon. But Violet had been so sad, and the news would plunge Aurora into a new panic. Lawrence was mindful of his duty to keep things peaceful until they'd safely buried Frank.

He checked his watch. "Come now. We'll be late."

"What about Mr and Mrs Cross?" asked Violet.

"They arrived ahead of us. We'll see them inside."

They approached the small chapel, where several ministers waited by the entrance. After greeting Frank's family, they squeezed into the rear pew behind a full congregation. The service was brief but solemn, punctuated by heart-rending sobs from an elderly lady in the front pew.

"That's Frank's mother," said Violet, her voice quivering while tears streamed down her face in empathy at the old lady's distress. Aurora stood, head bowed, gripping Violet's arm. George Podmore strode to the front of the church, stoically reading a eulogy, his tearful eyes downcast and focussed on his notes. Then silence descended. After a few moments, Violet looked up and stared narrow-eyed at the front of the chapel.

"She isn't there," said Violet.

"Who?" whispered Lawrence.

"Frank's wife."

"But they're separated."

"That's irrelevant. She could have paid her respects."

"But there's a history. It wasn't an amicable separation."

Violet glared. "Now is not the time."

They listened quietly to more readings and hymns

before leaving the chapel behind the pallbearers and congregation. Then, they walked silently to the graveside, standing away from the family as the minister blessed Frank's body. The rain had stopped while they were inside, but Lawrence's clothes were still damp, and he was eager to go home to change. He waited impatiently for a few minutes before broaching the subject with Violet.

"She shook her head unsympathetically. I should speak to the family first," she said.

"You and everyone else, by the look of things," said Lawrence, casting an eye towards the queue of people surrounding the Podmore family.

"Then we'll look at the wreaths while we're waiting."

Lawrence trailed behind as Violet and Aurora stood side by side, commenting on the beautiful flowers.

"Look. That one's from Henry and Fanny," said Violet, pointing to the Crosses' tribute.

"And a beautiful one from his mother," said Aurora. "Someone's put a lot of time and trouble into it."

Lawrence huffed and detached himself from the funeral party, waiting on the pavement where the sun had timidly crept from behind a cloud, casting gentle rays. Stretching his neck, he thrust his shoulders back and basked temporarily in the more temperate weather. Then, hands in pockets, he stood mesmerised by the gravestones and was deep in thought when someone loomed behind him.

"Friend or family?" asked the man in soft Scottish tones.

"Friend," said Lawrence.

"Did you know Frank well?"

"Decently. My wife knew him better. She met Frank ghost hunting, would you believe?"

The man stepped back, raising his eyebrows in surprise. He moved a hand to his bushy moustache, which bristled as he inhaled. "What a remarkable coincidence," he said. "The same thing happened to me."

"Really?" asked Lawrence sceptically.

"Truly. When I was in Dorset – I will never forget it. I knew Mr Podmore a little through the Society for Psychical Research."

"I did too, and I've had some dealings with the SPR. We haven't met, have we?"

The man thrust his hand forward. "I'm Arthur Conan Doyle, a writer of some renown. Pleased to meet you, I'm sure."

"Ah. I thought you looked familiar. I'm Lawrence Harpham and a private investigator for my sins."

"What a pity. You could have been useful to me a few years ago, but I've solved the case myself."

"I'm sorry. I thought you said you were a writer?"

"I am, but an unspeakable injustice made me step into a different role for a while. The police were utterly useless. I got no sense from the authorities and elected to investigate the Edalji incident myself. And a jolly good thing I did."

Lawrence, who could see Violet approaching, was only half listening.

"Are you ready, Lawrence?" asked Violet. "We really must pay our respects to the family."

"There you are, Violet. This is Mr Conan Doyle. He writes books. This is my wife and our friend Elizabeth."

"I know who you are," said Violet. "It's a pleasure to meet you. I have very much enjoyed your stories."

"How kind of you to say so." Conan Doyle puffed out his chest and beamed.

"And how do you know Frank?" asked Violet.

"Through the Society for Psychical Research, as I was

just telling your husband. We did a spot of ghost hunting together."

"Well, I never. You must tell me all about it."

"I thought we were leaving," said Lawrence, fingering his still-damp collar.

"There's no rush," said Violet. "Where did this happen, Mr Conan Doyle?"

"Please call me Arthur. And the spectral events occurred at a haunted house in Charmouth."

Lawrence smiled sympathetically at Aurora, who seemed as ready to leave as he was. But Aurora, with a more pressing reason to go, had no hesitation in excusing herself to collect Luna from the Gibson house.

Conan Doyle was in full flow when Lawrence's attention returned to the conversation.

"It was a slow investigation over several days. Your friend, Mr Podmore, was initially reluctant, having encountered some deception in previous cases. So, we took precautions, setting threads around the hallway and across the stairs. Nothing happened during the first night, but the next was a very different matter. On settling down after supper, we heard an almighty crash from downstairs. Not one sound but a succession of them, as if someone were thumping the floor with a heavy object. My heart leapt from my chest in fright."

"What was it?" asked Violet, clapping her hand to her mouth.

"I thought it must be a poltergeist," said Conan Doyle. "The sounds were unreal, otherworldly, as if Satan and his minions had invaded the home. But Frank was more circumspect. He thought the son of the house was up to no good. But there was no reason for his suspicions. The young man was sitting downstairs with us when the noise erupted."

"How fascinating," said Violet. "Frank and I investigated a haunting at Chelmondiston Rectory. We never got to the bottom of it, yet nobody ever accounted for the mysterious sounds and sightings."

"Spiritualism is a fascinating subject," said Conan Doyle. "I could talk about it all day."

"But sadly, we must leave you," said Lawrence.

Violet shot him a glare. "Not until we have said goodbye to the family," she said. "We can't interrupt them; they are still talking to the ministers. Tell me, Mr Conan Doyle, are you familiar with any more of Frank's work?"

"I have read several of his books and wish I had spent more time joining him in psychic research. Podmore was a remarkable man with unusual clarity and judgement. I learned much from him and applied it later during my own investigative work."

"Mr Conan Doyle is an amateur detective," said Lawrence sarcastically. "Unlike his creation."

Violet frowned, and Conan Doyle remained silent, trying to decide whether Lawrence was overtly hostile or poor at irony.

"And he dislikes policemen," Lawrence continued.

"Some policemen," said Conan Doyle. "Or to be more accurate, one particular member of the force."

"George Anson," said Lawrence.

Conan Doyle gasped. "How did you know that?"

"We had the pleasure of running into him a few days ago, didn't we, Violet?"

"Yes. We found him rather disagreeable."

"My thoughts entirely," said Conan Doyle, his sudden beetroot cheeks returning to their usual colour. Did you read about it in the newspapers?

"Your feud with Anson?" asked Lawrence.

"There was no feud. Just a distinct lack of cooperation on his part."

Lawrence shook his head. "I did not read about it. Anson spoke of you directly."

"In what context?" Conan Doyle reddened again; his cheeks flushed with inner rage.

"We asked Colonel Walker for help finding Frank," said Violet, trying to calm the situation.

"Walker is the chief constable for Worcestershire," said Lawrence. "They ran in pairs that day, and Anson was beside him. He couldn't resist interfering and stated the many reasons Walker should not cooperate with us, citing you as an example."

"Damn the man," said Conan Doyle. "His arrogance knows no bounds. And I won't have it. An innocent man languished in jail for three years thanks to his flawed attempts at policing. Thank God the poor victim thought to seek me out."

"And how did you resolve the case?" asked Violet.

Conan Doyle smiled. "I found another, more likely suspect."

"Did he confess?" asked Lawrence.

"No."

"Did you provide solid proof?"

"No. But I gave a raft of irrefutable evidence."

"So, the suspect is now incarcerated?"

"He is not, but only because of police incompetence."

"What reason did they give for denying justice?"

"That the evidence provided was entirely circumstantial."

"Ah," said Lawrence. "So, your case was no better than theirs?"

"Lawrence!" exclaimed Violet.

Conan Doyle narrowed his eyes. "It's a fair point," he said through gritted teeth. "But my deductive process was as watertight as it could reasonably be. And it saved George Edalji from a lifetime in prison. No detective in the country could better my conclusion. Not even you."

Violet crossed her arms. "Don't you dare," she warned, glaring at Lawrence through narrowed eyes.

Lawrence smiled. "Challenge accepted," he replied.

Chapter Eleven

HINTS OF DANGER

Sunday, August 20, 1910

"WHY MUST you be so rude, Lawrence?" asked Violet as they left Ivy Cottage the following day.

"And why must you repeat yourself? We had this out yesterday."

"Yet you still haven't answered satisfactorily. You humiliated poor Mr Conan Doyle. I don't know what you stand to gain from baiting him like that."

"As opposed to you fawning over him?"

"How dare you suggest that my justifiable admiration for an excellent writer makes me obsequious? There's a balance between adoration and loathing. It's called being pleasant."

"Obsequious? What do you mean by that?"

"To ingratiate oneself, like Uriah Heep, which you would know if you ever read anything worthwhile."

"Ah. Dickens is too dry for me. But let's not fight. I wasn't frank with you yesterday. There's something on my mind which we'll talk about in a moment. But I ought to tell you I have met Conan Doyle before."

"Really? He didn't seem to remember you?"

"He wouldn't. Conan Doyle runs an organisation called Crimes Club, which I had the misfortune to attend a few years ago, against my better judgement."

"Why didn't I come?"

"You were in Suffolk, and I was working a case alone in London."

"I've never heard of Crimes Club."

"You wouldn't. It only admits men, I'm afraid."

"Really. In this day and age?"

"Don't worry. You're not missing anything – just a group of middle-aged chaps discussing crime and detection. One or two have professional expertise which some writers use to increase the chances of lining their pockets. I'm not sure I agree with that level of collaboration."

"I have never heard anything quite so cynical. Why shouldn't authors improve their knowledge?"

"They'd do better consulting officials."

"I'm sure the police force has better things to do with its time."

"The Crimes Club members wouldn't listen, anyway."

"How do you know?"

"I spoke up about a case I was personally involved with. They refuted my expertise, preferring conjecture to cold, hard facts."

"That sounds like sour grapes."

"It isn't. I have little faith in their way of doing things. It's all theoretical."

"Why don't you write to Arthur and tell him you got carried away yesterday? We can't get involved in a contro-versial crime for the sake of a bet. And we must return to

Cheltenham soon. There's nothing more to do in Malvern with Frank gone."

"No. I'm not backing down. And I'm afraid we must stay here a little longer."

"Why?"

Lawrence sighed. "Frank may not have died naturally."

"According to whom?"

"Me."

"But the inquest said he drowned."

"I'm not disputing that."

"Then what?"

Lawrence reached into his pocket, withdrew his hand, and thrust his open palm towards Violet.

Her eyes widened as she saw a tiny cufflink with a faulty clasp. "Where did you get that?" she demanded.

"By New Pool. Henry and I found the imprint of Frank's walking stick a few inches away."

"God, no. How awful. There's no innocent reason for it to be there."

"Unless Frank was part of The Order."

"Never. He despises Crossley. You can be certain the cufflink doesn't belong to him."

"Frank could have found it."

Violet shook her head. "And was holding it when he fell? Why? That makes no sense."

"Then somebody else must have been there."

"Oh, Lawrence. It's looking that way. How long since you found the cufflink?"

Lawrence chewed his lip. "Henry and I picked it up on the day Frank died."

"Well, you should have said something sooner. Malvern isn't safe. What were you thinking?"

"That whatever happened, you'd want to attend the funeral. I was trying not to upset you."

"My feelings are irrelevant. What matters most is Aurora's safety."

"I know. But one wrong word and she could bolt again."

Lawrence and Violet rounded the lane, passing a cow chewing noisily by the fence.

"Oh, for an easy life," said Lawrence, enviously gazing at the cow. "Nothing to think about. No difficult decisions. I'd love the mundanity."

"Then resume your retirement. But you'd be bored to death without problems to solve."

"I wouldn't count on it. Anyway, what do you think we should do?"

"We must tell Aurora. She's responsible for Luna's safety. You've kept this from her for long enough."

"Now?"

"Right this minute."

"Fine. We'll head straight to the cottage."

———

AURORA WAS WHISTLING CONTENTEDLY in her kitchen when they arrived. She had thrown the windows open to make the most of the bright, sunny day and was busily scrubbing pans when they knocked on the door. She smiled and enthusiastically waved through the window before greeting them in the hallway, wiping soap suds on her apron before kissing Violet on the cheek.

"How are you both?" she asked.

"Very well," said Violet sombrely. "You seem in good spirits?"

"I'm still sad, of course," said Aurora. "But life goes on.

Luna had a lovely time with Marion yesterday. She seems settled and has stopped asking for her Daddy."

"That's sad," said Violet spontaneously.

Aurora's face fell. "I didn't mean it like that. We haven't forgotten Michael. We never will. I love my husband and miss him every day. But I must make the best of a bad situation."

Lawrence nervously chewed his lip, knowing he was about to ruin Aurora's peace of mind, but stalled with some well-chosen small talk. "Will you ever return to Netherwood?" he asked.

"Not while Francis Farrow is there."

"What if he leaves?"

"Unlikely, although I might consider it if he went aboard. But Luna will always be vulnerable at Netherwood. Crossley knows where we live. It hardly matters now whether Farrow is there or not. My home isn't safe."

"You don't know that. Michael would look after you and believes Farrow's repentance is real."

"Well, I don't. And Michael cannot guarantee Luna's safety. It's not in his power. Can we talk about something else? I was in a good mood, and thinking of Michael makes me sad. Come through to the kitchen. I've made scones."

Lawrence and Violet positioned themselves at the table. Violet prepared to deliver their dreadful news, but Lawrence gently nudged her on the shin. There was plenty of time to deliver the unpleasantness. They might as well enjoy their food first.

"Those scones look delicious," he said.

"Help yourselves." Aurora passed over a jar of strawberry jam and a butter knife. "Dig in. Luna doesn't care for scones, and I will be the size of an elephant if I eat them all myself."

Despite his hearty breakfast, Lawrence polished off two scones in a few bites. But Violet nibbled the offering with an air of apprehension. She nodded towards Lawrence, and he steeled himself.

"What would you do if you felt threatened?" he asked.

"Strike out, kicking and biting, if necessary," said Aurora firmly. "Is that the right answer?"

"I mean, would you run away again?"

"Yes. If I had no other choice."

"But what if you did? What if you assessed any potential danger and planned for it?"

I suppose that would give me other options. Why? Do you think I should?"

"Yes," said Lawrence. "Life is uncertain, and I think it's time to consider a plan."

"Why?" Aurora sat heavily on the third kitchen chair and peered anxiously at Lawrence.

Violet reached for her hand. "You'd better prepare yourself," she said.

Lawrence dropped the cufflink onto the table. It fell face down, and Aurora reached forward uncertainly, before turning it over. She flinched as if burned when she saw the unicursal hexagon.

"Where did you get this?" she demanded.

"I found it near Frank's body."

"Oh no. It's all over. I must pack at once."

"Wait," said Lawrence. "Let's not be hasty. Have you seen one of these before?"

"Not on a cufflink, but I'd recognise the unicursal hexagon anywhere. You know it's Crossley's sign."

"Or that of The Order?"

"Of course. But it amounts to the same thing."

"You can't leave here, Aurora. Where would you go?"

"Nowhere, anywhere. But one thing's certain. I wouldn't tell you."

"Please don't do anything rash."

"But Crossley could be nearby."

"He could be anywhere. The cufflink was near Frank's body. Not here at your house. Not close to you. If Crossley's business was with Frank, he may not have known you were in Malvern. If he did, he would have been here by now, don't you think?"

Aurora stroked her chin. "I suppose so," she said uncertainly.

Violet closed her eyes, relieved at Aurora's measured consideration. She turned to Lawrence. "You mean Crossley was looking for Frank, not Aurora? I didn't think of it like that," she said. "You're right, of course."

"Even so, staying here much longer is too risky," said Aurora. "I won't be able to let Luna out of my sight."

"What does Crossley want with you?" asked Lawrence.

"Revenge. You know that. And he wants a vicar's child to use as a human sacrifice."

"He'd never go through with it," said Lawrence. "The man's mad, but that would be cold-blooded murder."

"But for you, he would have killed me in Akenham churchyard," said Aurora.

Lawrence shook his head, unable to articulate the gulf between his concerns for Aurora's safety and cynicism about Felix Crossley's intentions. He knew the man was unhinged and unsafe, but still doubted he would risk murder to satisfy his ludicrous satanic beliefs.

"You ought to tell Crossley the truth about Luna," said Violet.

"What? Confess that Luna is his child. Never. She'd be in more danger. He would want her for his own."

"Crossley has other children."

"Not like Luna. She's special."

"Why?"

"Because she's mine."

Lawrence leaned forward. "I've never asked you about your time with Felix Crossley. But we must know why he's so possessive of you. I've spent hours researching Crossley and his cult. He's bestowed the scarlet woman title on other women, yet he cannot keep away from you. Is it because you were the first?"

Aurora lowered her head and stared at a knot on the table.

"Please answer honestly," said Violet, squeezing her hand.

"Alright." Aurora looked up, but her gaze did not meet their eyes. Lawrence smiled encouragingly, ignoring the shame in her eyes.

"I wasn't the first to fall for Crossley," said Aurora. "And I tried to leave him when I realised his words were all lies. But our relationship was innocent to start with. I first met Felix in a coffeehouse on the banks of the Thames. I had only recently arrived in London straight from the orphanage. I was lonely and he started a conversation and made me feel like I'd made a friend. Our paths crossed again and this time, he told me all about The Order. He made it sound thrilling but safe, like a fraternity — a group of like-minded individuals striving towards friendship and knowledge. But I soon learned about the dark side. Crossley's dark side, that is. And some of the other members of The Order were Satanists too."

"They misled you," said Violet. Aurora nodded.

"I know. But I was foolish. I wanted to believe in their benevolence. I had no friends or family to counsel me, so I closed my eyes to the early warning signs. Felix Crossley's research into astral travel fascinated me. I was happy to act as his guinea pig, his test subject. Night after night, we pushed ourselves harder, trying to reach the astral realm."

"Poppycock," said Lawrence under his breath, and winced as Violet kicked him hard.

"Did you succeed?" she asked.

Lawrence shot a look of disdain at Violet's question.

"I don't know," said Aurora.

"Why not?"

Aurora closed her eyes. "Felix gave me little white pills. I don't know what they were, but they made me feel hazy. He said they would help me reach the celestial heavens if I worked hard at my technique. And occasionally, I thought it had worked. I would lie on my bed, and if I concentrated hard enough, I felt as if I was rising. I could see my body beneath me, and Crossley's too. That's what he's after, you know. He is determined to master dream walking. Think of the possibilities if he succeeds – crossing time and distance through the power of thought. He wants me because we worked well together, and he thinks I can help him achieve his dream."

"And Luna?" asked Violet.

"She's my daughter and, in Crossley's eyes, might have powers of her own."

"The man's a fool," snapped Lawrence.

"But he believes his own rhetoric, which is why he's so dangerous," Violet said as she rose and paced the kitchen.

"Will Crossley come for me?" asked Aurora.

Lawrence shook his head. "I still don't think he knows you are here. But he might in time."

"Then what should I do?"

Violet glanced at the stricken woman. Aurora had

turned pale, all the fight knocked from her. "Why don't I telephone Vera?" she asked. "She's helped you before and can offer advice."

Lawrence nodded. "Good idea."

"Will you stay in Malvern if we stay with you?" asked Violet.

Aurora looked up with tear-filled eyes. "If you move in with me. Luna and I can share a room."

"Yes, dear. We'll do whatever it takes," said Violet. "I'll call Vera now."

Chapter Twelve

PROTECTING AURORA

Monday, August 21, 1910

"IT'S SETTLED, DEAR," said Violet, placing her carpetbag in Aurora's kitchen.

"Thank goodness," said Aurora. "It's kind of Vera to change her plans."

"She can't indefinitely." Violet passed over a folded telegram.

Aurora's face fell as she scanned the words. "Oh, that's a shame. She can only manage a few weeks. I will need to move on after all. I suppose it was bound to happen. What a shame. I like it here, and so does Luna."

"Why don't you wait and see how things work out," said Violet. "Lawrence telephoned London earlier to speak to Lonni Carpenter."

"Who?"

"His reporter friend. We may find Crossley's where-abouts if Lonni has the right contacts."

"Good. It's unsettling not knowing where he is. Frank

kept a close eye on Crossley, which was an enormous relief. I hate mysteries. For all I know, he could be living next door."

"Not a close enough watch," said Violet, tears suddenly pricking her eyes. "Frank's information source let him down when Crossley or his minions came close enough to leave the cufflink."

"Who was Frank's contact?"

"I don't know. He never told me. But it could have been someone from Crossley's inner circle, which would explain why Frank was so secretive."

"Who's been keeping secrets?" asked Lawrence, striding through the door, suitcase in hand. He parked it by the stairs and joined the women in the kitchen.

"Frank had. Did he ever tell you who updated him about Crossley's location?"

"No, Frank kept his source close to his chest. A pity, as they would have been a useful contact."

"Who should be accountable for their failure to protect him," muttered Violet.

Lawrence scratched his nose. "Being an informant isn't easy, especially one who works for both sides. I am sure they did their best under difficult circumstances. And don't fret; we can't be sure the cufflink was Crossley's."

"I suppose not. Did you reach Lonni?"

Lawrence smiled. "I did, and he was eager to help. News is slow, and Lonni is bored. He will try to use his resources to track down Crossley. I'll call him from the local press office in a few days to see what he's found."

"Let's hope he comes good. Lonni sometimes promises more than he delivers," said Violet pessimistically. She glanced at Aurora's worried face and checked herself. "It's good to know there are newspaper resources nearby."

"Come now, Violet. Lonni means well. And when I say press office, it's better described as a small set of rooms inherited by the Malvern News from their predecessor. The office is at the town end of Edith Walk. I hear it's a bit of a hoof."

"So, not walkable from here?"

"No. But it's an easy drive, as you'll soon discover."

Violet frowned. "I was about to have a cup of tea with Aurora. Isn't it too soon to expect anything from Lonni?"

"Of course. But I'd like to drop in for another reason."

Violet eyed him suspiciously. "What?"

"To look through their archives."

"Why?"

"For some background on Conan Doyle's case."

"Oh really, Lawrence. Must we? I hoped you'd forget all about it."

"We might as well read about the case, now we're here. It will keep me occupied."

"But what about Aurora?"

"Don't worry about me," said Aurora. She straightened a tiny picture hanging on the wall and stepped back to check the angle.

"Of course, we are worried. We've stayed in Malvern to protect you. And there's little point unless we keep close. Isn't that right, Lawrence?"

"Aurora won't want us hanging around all day. We'll drive her mad."

"He's right," said Aurora. "It's enough to know you are near if I need you. You won't be leaving Malvern, though, will you?"

"Definitely not." Violet reached for Aurora's hand. "Are you sure you don't mind if we pop out for a while?"

"It's fine. I've got things to do. Like hanging this picture."

Lawrence strode over and tilted the frame a fraction to the right. "There you go," he said.

"That's better. I'll see you later."

"I'm sorry, but it doesn't feel right. Why don't you go alone, Lawrence? You don't need me with you."

"But Aurora said…"

"I know. She's being polite. I'll keep you company here, my dear."

"Oh, for goodness' sake. Aurora, please tell my wife that she's free to leave for an hour."

Violet shot him a glare.

"On the other hand, if I've misread the situation, ask us to stay. You won't hurt my feelings. According to my wife, I don't have any."

"Lawrence," Violet hissed.

Aurora rejoined them at the table. "I'll be honest with you both. I am frightened," said Aurora. But I refuse to live my life as a prisoner of circumstance. If it weren't for Luna, I'd risk it all to confront Crossley. But my daughter comes first. That doesn't mean we need round-the-clock babysitting. You don't need to watch me all the time."

"There," said Lawrence, crossing his arms triumphantly.

Violet shook her head. "You have spectacularly missed the point."

"Oh," said Lawrence. "Now I understand. Violet is afraid you will run away again if we leave you alone. And she has a point. If we strike a balance by being here when you need us while giving you privacy, will you promise not to leave Malvern without telling us?"

Aurora chewed her lip. "Must I?"

"Yes," said Lawrence, firmly. "We will do anything to

help – our friendship is unconditional. But you can't take off alone again. Michael has barely spoken to us since we refused to tell him your whereabouts. And he will never forgive me if we lose you again after all our assurances."

"I understand," said Aurora. "I have put you in a terrible position."

"Don't worry about that," said Violet. "We still think you are safe in Malvern in the short term, but only you can decide your future. Just promise that you will talk it through with us first."

"I promise," said Aurora.

"And you mean it?"

"I do. I will need your help to move away. And you were right about one thing. We need an emergency plan, and I can't do it alone. Give me time to think, and we can work it out when you return."

"I haven't said I'm going yet," said Violet.

Lawrence flashed his most winning smile. "But you will. Come on, we'll only be an hour or two. And if I can wipe the smug grin off Conan Doyle's face, it will be time well spent."

Violet raised her eyes heavenwards. "Let's get it over with then."

Chapter Thirteen

THE MALVERN NEWS

"THIS IS IT," said Lawrence, pulling his vehicle onto a patch of rough ground by the side of the press office. "Number two, Edith Walk."

Violet left the vehicle and stood outside, hands on hips. "I have a strong feeling of déja vu."

"Why?"

"How often have we relied on the local press for information? Too much. And they're not always accurate."

"It's a risk we must take," said Lawrence. "Otherwise, our only recourse is the local police or, God forbid, the old gasbag, Conan Doyle himself."

"Why must you always take against other men?" asked Violet, frustratedly.

"That's hardly fair. What other men?"

"Arthur Myers, Walter Sickert and Frank when you first knew him."

"Goodness, Violet. I may have misjudged Frank, but Myers was a killer and Sickert a pervert."

"Walter was nothing of the kind."

"He painted nude figures, and I caught him in *flagrante delicto* with a woman of very dubious habits."

"You mean his lady friend? Honestly, Lawrence. You are so strait-laced."

"It's called having standards."

Violet sighed. "Let's go inside before we fall out."

"Right." Lawrence strode towards the door and let himself in without knocking. He flung open another door in a room and announced himself to the solid-looking gentleman sitting behind a desk, poring studiously over a newspaper. The man looked up and removed his spectacles as Lawrence approached.

"Who are you?"

"Lawrence Harpham. This is my wife."

"And your business here?"

"Research."

"I don't know anything about it."

"Lonni Carpenter spoke to your office this morning."

"Who or what is Lonni Carpenter?"

Lawrence frowned. "Can I have a word with your manager?" he snapped.

"No."

"Your editor then?"

"Again, no."

"Why?"

"Mr Welsh is in Worcester if you must know. Not that it's any of your business."

"Then I'll speak to whoever is in charge."

"That would be me. Jocelyn Wiseman. I'm the assistant editor and a very busy man."

Wiseman glared at Lawrence as if about to evict him from the room.

"We are so sorry to have disturbed you," said Violet,

stepping forward. "Mr Carpenter is a journalist. He spoke to one of your staff this morning. Who might that have been?"

"Whoever answered the phone," said Wiseman curtly.

"Where do you keep the telephone?"

"In the compositor's office."

"Which is where?"

"Last left along the corridor."

"Thank you. You have been very helpful." Violet sailed from the room, Lawrence following in her wake.

"You see," she hissed.

"The only thing I saw was a trumped-up pipsqueak."

"Oh, Lawrence. I was nice to him, and you were obnoxious. It's too bad. You should be better at dealing with people by now."

"I am when I want to be."

"And that's what's so sad. You are more than capable of behaving well. It's a pity you are unwilling. You should retire again and mean it."

"Perhaps I will after this," said Lawrence. "My patience decreases the older I get."

"You were born impatient," said Violet, but she gently kissed his cheek before opening the compositor's office door.

Two heads looked up, one dark-haired and one white.

"Ah, you must be Lawrence Harpham," said a smartly dressed woman, extending her hand. "Mrs Harpham, I presume?"

"I am," said Violet.

"This is Ferdi Schmidt. Your friend, Mr Carpenter, spoke with him this morning. My name is Mildred. Would you like a cup of tea before we start?"

"Thank you," said Lawrence, relieved at the friendly reception.

"Very well. I won't keep you a moment. Do take a seat. I'm sure Ferdi will tell you all about us."

"Park yourselves there," said Ferdi in a part Germanic, part Yorkshire accent. "Don't look so surprised. I was born here, a third-generation immigrant. Father wanted to anglicise our name, but Mother said no; we should be proud of our heritage."

"German?" asked Lawrence.

"Austrian. My family came from Seefeld. Sadly, I have never been there."

"What a shame," said Violet. "The name sounds familiar. I feel I should know it."

"Have you visited Innsbruck?"

"No. I've barely left these shores. Ah. I remember. Is it in the Tyrol?"

"That's right."

"That's why it sounds familiar. I read about the pilgrimage site."

Ferdi shrugged. "You know more than I do. Perhaps I will visit one day."

"So, you're a compositor, Ferdi?"

"No. But I'm working towards it."

"I thought this was the compositor's office."

"It is. But I am a lowly office clerk until Mrs Agg finishes training me. She's clever and will teach me well."

A slow smile crept over Violet's face. "Is Mildred's name Agg?"

Ferdi nodded.

"Did you hear that, Lawrence? A lady compositor."

Lawrence flashed a feeble grin. He had nothing against women in the workforce. And it was impressive to see a lady who must be well into her fifties, if not beyond, tackling a skilled profession. But he knew it would encourage Violet's increasingly militant suffragist views. He worried she might take things beyond peaceful protest and into the realms of criminal action in the future. Lawrence had narrowly stopped Violet from joining a march up the Embankment in June. She had agreed to hold back pending a November review of the Conciliation Bill to advance women's rights. But if that failed, then so would Lawrence. Violet was determined to do her bit for the movement. Recently, he had consigned the problem to the back of his mind but now sensed danger as Ferdi gushed reverently about Mrs Agg. Meeting another self-confident professional woman would doubtless spur Violet onwards.

"I'm parched," said Lawrence, wondering what Mildred Agg was doing with the tea.

Violet narrowed her eyes. "I hope you're not implying that tea-making is women's work."

"Why would you think that? I'm genuinely thirsty," said Lawrence, puzzled.

"Mrs Agg enjoys fussing around the kitchen. I offer to make my fair share of hot drinks, but she rarely lets me. She likes to look after us," said Ferdi. "I think she's been lonely since her husband died."

"How sad," said Violet.

"You wouldn't know it. Mrs Agg is a trooper. Ah, here she is now."

Mildred Agg entered the room bearing a loaded tray.

"Pop this into the reading room," she said, handing it to Ferdi. "Now, what are you good people looking for?"

Chapter Fourteen

THE EDALJI CASE

"WE'D LIKE everything you have on the Edalji case," said Lawrence. "Have you heard of it?"

Mildred Agg raised an eyebrow. "Hasn't everyone? They covered the story extensively in the national press. And Sir Arthur Conan Doyle wrote a long piece about it. His article would be a good starting point. Would you like me to locate it?"

"No, thank you," said Lawrence. "It's important that the prejudice of others doesn't tarnish our research."

"I understand, and it's interesting you use that word. Prejudice cost George Edalji three years behind bars."

"Go on. We don't know much about it."

Mildred Agg cocked her head, staring at Lawrence as if he were teasing. Violet intervened.

"My husband spent many years avoiding the press. He retired too soon from our private detective agency and lost interest in current affairs. We stopped taking a newspaper. I picked up a little of the day-to-day news when chatting with friends, but Lawrence pointedly ignored it. We are both a little behind on newsworthy items from the recent past."

"I see. That's a rare attitude, fortunately, or we'd go out of business."

"We knew we'd made a mistake when we realised how much we'd missed after taking a private case last year," said Violet. And now we take a national and a local paper."

Mildred nodded. "Good. Follow me, and I'll take you to the archives."

The well-furnished reading room was a short stroll down the corridor with old-fashioned desks that would not have looked out of place in a schoolroom.

"Let me consult my trusty cards," said Mildred, gesturing for them to sit while she stood in front of large oak filing cabinets with rows of tiny drawers.

"E for Edalji," she continued before withdrawing a solitary card containing a few lines of writing. "Not much here, I'm afraid," she muttered, handing the card to Lawrence. Then she flipped its neighbour to a ninety-degree angle, marking the space.

"Slim pickings," said Lawrence, disappointedly, as he read the sparse information in heavy bold print. "*Edalji, George – trial; Edalji, George – release, Edalji – Charlotte – thank you letter.* Well, it will have to do," he continued.

Violet coughed and stared pointedly towards him.

"I mean, we'd be grateful if you could locate the articles on the card. And thank you for helping," muttered Lawrence.

Mildred Agg fixed him with a penetrating stare. "Oh, I don't give up that easily," she said. "Bear with me." She carefully closed the drawer and ran her fingers down the furniture until she reached a metallic label holder bearing the letter W. "Ah. This is more like it." This time, she produced two cards, the first filled on both sides and labelled one of two. *Wyrley Great – Outrages, Wyrley Great – hate letters, "Wyrley, Great – Suspects,* each bearing lists of dates and filing codes. "Goodness. You'll be here all day," she continued.

"We have a few hours at most," said Violet.

"It will take me that long to locate all the articles," said Mrs Agg. "Why don't we start by summarising the circumstances leading up to Mr Edalji's arrest? One of our reporters covered this only last year, and it will give you a good starting point. I'll track down a full reading list in the meantime, and you can help yourself whenever you are free."

"Perfect," said Violet.

"I'm sure Aurora won't mind if we are an hour or two longer," said Lawrence.

Violet narrowed her eyes.

"On the other hand, perhaps not," he continued. "Yes. Please put them together, and we'll visit again tomorrow."

Mildred Agg bustled away, returning moments later with two copies of the Malvern News, passing one each to Lawrence and Violet.

She left without another word as they opened their newspapers, reading in silence for several minutes.

"This is not what I was expecting," said Violet on reaching the end of the article.

"I agree. Great Wyrley seems to have experienced the livestock version of Jack the Ripper."

Violet shuddered. "Don't use that filthy expression. No sane man could have committed such crimes. It's barbaric. But why on earth blame a respectable solicitor? And a man who is also the eldest son of the local vicar. This article suggests an intolerance for his skin colour."

"It does, though things are rarely that simple."

Violet shook her head. "You might not think so, Lawrence. But as a woman, it's easy to understand the attitude of the establishment towards those less powerful."

"Be careful. We must both be objective to fully understand this case. If the story is accurate, then Edalji experienced a great deal of unfairness, but we can't assume his innocence as Conan Doyle did if we are to examine the case with a critical eye."

"You are right," said Violet. "The article is sympathetic to Edalji. It's hard not to feel sorry for him."

"But we must be impartial," said Lawrence. "Let's take the meat and bones of the case. Would you like to rewrite it, or shall I?"

"I will," said Violet. "And then I'll read it to you. Give me ten minutes."

Lawrence sighed and fidgeted while Violet removed a pencil from her bag and wrote an unbiased precis of the article. She cleared her throat.

"I'll read aloud, and you can tell me what you think."

"Go ahead."

"Great Wyrley was the scene of several livestock killings during the winter of 1903. Gossip in the village ran rife, and before long, some accused George Edalji, the eldest son of Parsee Vicar Shapurji Edalji. The quiet, mild-mannered vicar's son suffered from poor eyesight, leaving him virtually blind."

"Long or short-sighted?" asked Lawrence.

Violet scanned her notes. "He could see close objects but nothing more than a few inches away without it appearing blurred. And his eyesight was dreadful during dusk or after dark."

"Hmmm. And we've previously heard that these outrages occurred mainly at night."

"Exactly. Shall I continue?"

"Please.

"Now suspected by the villagers of conducting the killings, George Edalji received several anonymous letters accusing him of the crime, which he passed on to the local police. Despite his full cooperation, the chief constable suspected Edalji of writing them himself."

"Our friend Anson, you mean?"

"You must put your dislike of the man aside, Lawrence."

"I know. But it isn't easy to disregard such a loathsome character."

"Moving on," said Violet. *"There were another two atrocities in August of 1903, and Inspector John Campbell interviewed Edalji at the vicarage, first to take a statement and again, three days later, to arrest him."*

"Remind me what evidence they found?"

"Wet boots, blood on a jacket sleeve, horse hairs on his trousers and a cutthroat razor stained with blood."

"Could be circumstantial," said Lawrence. "But it requires an explanation. It was a fair question to ask. How did Edalji reply?"

Violet traced her finger down the page. "He said he hadn't worn the suit on the day in question. He had no idea where the horse hairs came from, and the blood stains on his bathroom razor had been there for some time."

"What was he doing outside at night if his eyesight was so poor?"

"Delivering boots to a local cobbler. He left the vicarage at eight o'clock and returned home at nine fifteen."

"Well, it would be light in the summer months. His explanation could be reasonable or a flimsy excuse."

"Arthur was keen to discount anything that might be questionable."

"Then he promptly provided a case utterly reliant on circumstantial evidence of his own."

"We don't know much about that yet."

"I realise that," said Lawrence. "But I'm reluctant to read Conan Doyle's account in case it influences my investigation. I suppose I must eventually. Conan Doyle believed that a young troublemaker named Royden Sharp was behind the outrages and hate letters. But that's the extent of my knowledge. Conan Doyle's case seems weak, and he took offence when I said so."

"Which is why we are where we are," said Violet dryly. "Why you couldn't just let it go, I will never know. And now you must spend every waking moment in this office reading about it. I hope you get what you need before we must return to Cheltenham."

"I'm sure I will. But Great Wyrley isn't far. If push comes to shove, I'll drive over and have a nose about the place. It didn't happen that long ago. I'm sure I'll be able to find a few people who can give firsthand accounts."

"Absolutely not," said Violet. "There is too much in Malvern to worry about. Aurora comes first and well ahead of any silly investigation."

"Livestock killing is extremely serious."

"I don't doubt it, but you only care because Sir Arthur wounded your pride. You should focus on the poison pen letters. Just because someone connected them to the slayings doesn't mean they are."

"How can you possibly know that?"

"I don't for sure. But I've studied the human condition long enough to know they are two very different crimes. Slaughtering livestock requires great physical strength and a certain boldness. But hate letters are underhand, devious, and spiteful, generally written anonymously behind closed doors and often by women. It's hard to imagine two less similar crimes."

Lawrence stroked his chin. "A good point, Violet. But why would the letters start at the same time as the killings?"

"Are we sure that they did? I suggest…"

Violet's words trailed away as the door opened, and Mildred Agg appeared carrying a single sheet of newspaper.

"Here, take this," she said. "It's only a little light reading, but quick and easy to digest."

"What is it?"

"A precis on the occupants of the vicarage. I'll leave it with you. Speak to Ferdi if you need anything else. I must fly off to a meeting."

"Well, this is helpful," said Lawrence, scanning the page.

"Show it to me."

"Wait one moment. Let me finish. Oh, George's father Shapurji married an English woman."

"So?"

"It's unusual, isn't it? That might have added a further layer of prejudice."

"It shouldn't happen in a decent society, but I take your point. Some people are still narrow-minded." Violet raised an eyebrow at Lawrence as she spoke.

"Don't look at me so disapprovingly. I'm simply stating an uncomfortable truth. I don't feel that way."

"Good. This family has suffered enough."

"Oh, Violet. You will struggle to remain objective if you take up the mantle of a protector. It isn't like you at all."

"I'm worried about Daisy, Lawrence. She's not used to us being away from home for so long."

"Are you missing her?" asked Lawrence.

"Of course, I am."

"She'll enjoy spending time with Vera."

Violet snorted. "What teenage girl wants to waste her leisure time with her parent's friend? She'd prefer you or me to Vera, and that's saying something. Daisy seems permanently embarrassed to be seen with either of us. She wants to be with her friends, but we can't expect Vera to supervise that. Daisy must be miserable, virtually confined to quarters."

"It won't be for long."

"But where does that leave Aurora?"

"We'll work it out, Violet."

"Let's see this article." Violet reached over and removed the piece of paper, placed it on the desk, and read aloud.

"*George Edalji was the eldest son of Shapurji Edalji and his wife Charlotte Stoneham. Shapurji, an Anglican vicar, had received the parish living from Charlotte's uncle after marrying in 1874. George was born in 1876, followed by their second son, Horace, in 1879 and daughter, Maud, in 1882. George attended Rugeley Grammar School and worked as a solicitor.* So far, so relatively unremarkable."

"Yet he found himself in the dock for an appalling series of crimes."

"And was exonerated."

"Read on, Violet, and you'll see that George Edalji was pardoned but never compensated."

"Why?"

"Either due to the failings of the British justice system or because they doubted his innocence."

"Typical. Guilty until proven otherwise."

"Hello. What's this?"

Lawrence reached down and removed a small cutting from the floor.

"Damn," he exclaimed as a pinprick of blood welled

from a tiny wound on his finger. Lawrence removed his handkerchief and started dabbing.

"Don't. You'll ruin it," said Violet.

Sighing, Lawrence sucked his finger, grimacing at the metallic taste. "Watch the pin," he said as Violet pulled the clipping towards her.

"This is interesting," said Violet, comparing the two articles. "The holes line up identically. Someone must have pinned one to the back of the other."

"Any relevance?"

"Yes. It's a letter from Shapurji Edalji to the editor of the Morning Post. The title sounds intriguing – *A Warning to Tradesmen*. Shall I read it?"

"Carry on."

"Sir, Some evil-disposed persons have been sending me letters for the last six months threatening to do a great deal of annoying things unless I agreed to do as they wished. One threat was to send false advertisements of various kinds to the newspapers in my name. They have already done this within the last six weeks and have been successful in deceiving a number of newspaper managers all over the country.

Last night someone picked up a letter near the kitchen door of this house. It says, among other things, 'If your kid speaks or rides or walks with Fred Brookes, grocer's kid, we shall have revenge at once by sending lots of orders for Christmas cheer.' This, of course, means that they would again forge letters in my name and send them to tradesmen in the same manner as they had recently forged advertisements for the press. The writer adds, 'I shall do the same for the Brookes.'

Therefore, will you kindly allow me to caution all tradesmen against any imposition that this gang of scoundrels is about to practice upon them? It will save them much trouble, inconvenience, and a loss of money if they note my name and address. Yours, etc. S EDALJI, Vicar of Great Wyrley, Walsall.

Well, Lawrence. What do you think of that?"

Lawrence scratched his nose. "The threats are very juvenile and probably penned by children. When did they publish the article?"

"December 1892."

"That's years before the livestock killings."

"Exactly. I thought we'd get more context from the letters than the violence. It's a curious document, though."

"I expect the poor old vicar was at his wits' end."

"No doubt. But it implies other letters and previous acts of mischief."

"You're right. And who is Fred Brookes that he deserves such censure?"

"The grocer's son, apparently. But why should they single him out?"

"Boys will be boys, I suppose. This is clearly a school-child's prank."

Violet peered at the letter again. "On the face of it, yes. But let's take the vicar at his word. He said he'd received many letters over six months, some hand-delivered to the vicarage door. Now, children could easily slip in and out of the grounds with little inconvenience or cost. But he then mentions false advertisements in the plural. And that costs money. The culprit also threatened to do the same to the Brookes, so what does that imply?"

"A rather expensive pastime," said Lawrence.

"Exactly. Most children couldn't afford it, and if they had the money, they would find better ways to spend it."

"So, you think this is an adult purposely disguising his activities to look like a childish prank?"

"Perhaps. And it may be more than one person. The vicar mentions a gang of scoundrels."

"I wonder if he still lives at the vicarage."

"I should think so. There's no reason to suppose otherwise if he's still alive. Perhaps you could write to him?"

"He'd probably ignore a letter. After all, he has good reason to fear them."

"You could tell him you're a friend of Conan Doyle."

"What? Lie to a godly man? I'm surprised at you."

"Very well. Say you are an acquaintance then. Although that might not yield any results."

"I don't think a letter will do. And a thorough review of the case would mean contacting the grocer."

"Writing two letters is well within your grasp."

"It wouldn't work. Letters are easy to ignore and don't clarify physical facts."

"Such as?"

"The distance between the drive and the vicarage kitchen door. How much the householders might reasonably see? And above all, why did the vicar and the grocer receive dozens of threatening letters long before the crimes that convicted George Edalji occurred? It's a nice fresh puzzle, not one of your historical crimes. There should be plenty of people who still remember the details. I doubt it would take more than a few hours out of my day to find out."

"No, Lawrence, it's out of the question."

"I could drive to Great Wyrley first thing tomorrow and be back for supper. No need for you to join me."

"You really shouldn't. We're in Malvern for Aurora."

"You'll be with her. You can sit down and compose Aurora's emergency plan should the worst arise."

Violet shook her head and sighed. "It's a terrible idea."

"That's settled then. I'll take the car, and you can have a relaxing day. Make the most of it, Violet. You could always do some sketching."

Chapter Fifteen

GREAT WYRLEY

Tuesday, August 22, 1910

LAWRENCE PULLED up near St Mark's Church in Great Wyrley, opened the car door and stretched his legs. His anticipated one-and-a-half-hour drive had turned into two following a blockage caused by an upturned milk float, followed five miles later by a herd of dairy cows taking a leisurely stroll to the field. An impatient Lawrence had tutted and scowled his way through the rest of the journey, having found little to enjoy in the landscape and a lot that displeased him in architectural terms. On a different day, in a better mood, he would have enjoyed the pretty villages and swathes of open countryside, but Lawrence was a creature of habit. And if he expected an unrushed, unimpeded journey, anything else was trouble and bound to disappoint.

Heaving himself from the car, Lawrence shut the door and walked towards the stone-built church nestled beneath a tiled roof. The August sun and recent downpours had left the churchyard vegetation brown in places and overgrown in others, and a scattering of gravestones created a some-what haphazard effect. Lawrence cast a critical eye towards the church. Though the early English style pleased him, the random exterior and asymmetry did not. He entered the church, still feeling disgruntled.

Inside, Lawrence found the interior disappointingly free of life. He had hoped to see Mr Edalji Senior, fussing around the church doing whatever vicars do when not conducting services. It would have been a more straightfor-ward encounter at his place of occupation than for Lawrence to intrude into his personal domain at the vicarage. Now there was nothing for it but to locate Shapurji at home. Sighing, Lawrence reached into his pocket and flipped a coin into the locked wooden collection box, removing a one-page printed leaflet for future contem-plation.

Lawrence left the church and wandered back towards his car before hearing a sudden noise. In the distance, a caped constable, cap perched high on his head, accelerated towards him at a rate of knots.

The constable gestured towards him, bellowing at the top of his lungs. "Have you seen a boy in your travels? He's about ten years old and wearing grey flannel trousers and a green jumper. The little blighter has just stolen my truncheon."

"I'm afraid not," said Lawrence. "The church is empty. Your boy's not here."

"Damn it. I could have sworn he ran in this direction. I'll give him a good clip around the ear when I get hold of him."

"The youth of today," sighed Lawrence.

The policeman cocked his head and narrowed his eyes.

"Who are you, sir? You're not from around these parts, judging by your accent. Or lack of one, I should say."

"You're right. I've driven up from Malvern today."

"Ah. I went there once on a mystery coach tour. Can't say I was that impressed."

"Each to their own."

"A day trip, is it, sir?"

"No," said Lawrence. "I was hoping to see the vicar."

"Were you now? If the vicar's not here, he'll likely be at the vicarage."

"You don't say. But it's a pity to disturb a man at home." Lawrence glanced at his watch. "I hope I don't interrupt his lunch."

"It depends on what time he eats," said the policeman. Or if he lets you in at all. Mr Edalji keeps himself to himself these days. He still plays a role in vestry matters, but we don't see much of him about town, or socially, for that matter."

"Do vicars often socialise?"

"If they want to."

"Or if they're invited."

The policeman narrowed his eyes. "Why wouldn't they be?"

"If they suffer unwarranted prejudice."

"You remind me of that interloper Conan Doyle."

"I hope not. I don't aspire to his arrogance."

The policeman put his hands on his hips, stepped back and sized Lawrence up from top to bottom. Lawrence did likewise, staring back into a tanned face, still speckled with perspiration, beneath greying hair. Smartly dressed from his immaculately laundered cape to his well-polished shoes, the constable seemed a cut above the police force specimens

Lawrence was more familiar with. This was a man who cared about his profession.

"Who are you?" barked the policeman.

"Lawrence Harpham."

"And your reason for being here?"

"Must there be one?"

"Alright. Your profession then?"

"None. I no longer take paid work."

"Why does it feel as if you're withholding something?"

Lawrence sighed. He had hoped to slide into the village without fanfare or disclosing his intentions to the first person he encountered. He momentarily considered activating his alter ego, Alistair Blatworthy, and donning the mantle of a quantity surveyor. But it was too much trouble. Instead, he decided on a different approach. He would skirt close to the truth and try to make a friend of the police constable.

"Look," said Lawrence. "I'm an ex-policeman. I started my career in the Suffolk constabulary and finished it as a private detective. I do very little these days but take the occasional interesting case."

"You're too late," said the policeman, shaking his head. "Sir Arthur Conan Doyle beat you to it and solved our only high-profile crime, which happened to involve the vicar's son. Is that why you want to see the reverend?"

Lawrence ignored the question. "I know about Conan Doyle and his contribution to freeing George Edalji."

"Then what's the purpose of your visit? We've had enough interference from outsiders to last a lifetime. Can't you people let us forget all about it so we can live our lives quietly?"

"That's fine for you, but it might not be so easy for Conan Doyle's target, young Royden Sharp."

The police constable cocked his head. "You're remarkably well informed."

"I'll be honest with you," said Lawrence. "I barely know anything about this case, but I recently bumped into Sir Arthur, and in my opinion, he has swapped one case of circumstantial evidence for another."

"Meaning?"

"I understand Conan Doyle's reasoning and why he believes in George Edalji's innocence. And I've read a few newspaper articles. If accurate, the establishment failed Edalji in every way. He should not have seen the inside of a courtroom. But the law has no interest in anyone else despite Conan Doyle's theories. Why not?"

The policeman sighed. "Don't come here stirring up a hornets' nest."

"I don't intend to. But are you satisfied with the outcome? Is it fair that another young man must suffer the ignominy of an author's theoretical reasoning? I wouldn't be content knowing that."

"That's as maybe. But we are sick to death of the whole sorry matter. Edalji is a free man. He doesn't live here anymore, and we are free of the taint of his crimes. It's in our past."

"Recent past."

"Conan Doyle came here three years ago. We've mostly lived without scandal since then."

"I won't make things worse; I promise. I'm not here to open old wounds. And between you and me, I'd rather like to prove a point. And perhaps right a wrong."

"Clearing Sharp's name?"

"If it's justified."

"He won't care. And you'll have to work quickly. Royden Sharp has booked a berth on a ship sailing to Canada in a few months. He has better things to do than worry about village scandal."

"You seem to know him well."

"I should. I've lived here long enough."

"Since the outrages began?"

"No. I've spent some of my career in Birmingham. Not that it has anything to do with you."

"Look, I'm sorry. We started on a bad footing. As one policeman to another, I could use your help. What's your name?"

The policeman frowned, and Lawrence felt his potential cooperation slip away.

"With a little assistance, I could keep a low profile. I'm not here to cause any ill feeling. I intend to spend as little time in Great Wyrley as possible. Can I rely on your help and perhaps pick your brains?"

"I told you I wasn't always around."

"But you lived locally?"

"Not at the time. My mother did. We live together now."

"Then you must be better informed than I am."

"Most people are, by the sound of it."

Lawrence drifted into silence, unused to the rebuff. A shared background in policing had often brought mutual gain in previous cases. He had misjudged his ability to present a symbiotic scenario. He was about to turn away when the constable removed his cap and unexpectedly offered his hand."

"Martin Newlove," he said. "You're not alone in having concerns. After all, if George Edalji didn't commit the crimes, then somebody else did. I'm off duty at five o'clock. Meet me at The Royal Oak. It looks rough and ready from the outside, but they've worked hard on it over the last few years. It's a decent place to drink, and they serve a good ale."

"Thank you," said Lawrence.

"And a word of warning. This is a mining village. I've known these people for a long time. They are straight-talking, and listening to their concerns makes my job much easier. I don't want them to know I'm involved in your investigation. Do you understand? Policing is my life, and I won't risk the wrath of my friends or superiors by talking out of turn."

"Understood," said Lawrence.

Chapter Sixteen

THE VICARAGE

LAWRENCE'S WALK to the vicarage was short and uneventful. He left Constable Newlove by the side of the church, still casting an eye out for his missing truncheon, but not before he had given directions to the Edaljis home.

Lawrence approached the vicarage cautiously, arriving at the driveway and gazing towards the handsome, substantial brick building, making a quick mental assessment. It met most of his standards of architectural beauty, though lacked symmetry and needed minor repairs. But he'd seen far worse and would happily have spent a few days residing there given half a chance. But as things stood, he would need cooperation from a family that was often unkindly treated and with no reason to let him cross the threshold. To what extent they had suffered, Lawrence was yet to judge. But the sheer volume of hateful letters and nasty pranks would have laid anybody low. And then, to lose their eldest son to prison would have been an almost unrecoverable blow. Lawrence did not expect a warm reception, and his stomach clenched in anticipation of their response.

Lawrence wavered as he walked down the driveway, approaching a gothic-style arched doorway where he lingered momentarily before knocking apprehensively on the wooden door. He waited, heart thumping, knowing he would rather intrude on a criminal in his den before disturbing a mild-mannered vicar in his place of refuge. But when the door opened, his eyes widened at the sight of an elderly lady, white-haired and elegantly dressed in a high-necked dark blouse and ankle-length tartan skirt.

"Good day, madam," he said, doffing his hat.

Charlotte Edalji's eyes darted to his face, looking him up and down before she spoke.

"Yes?" she asked.

"My name is Lawrence Harpham." Lawrence offered his hand and prepared to speak.

"I see," she said, turning on her heel. "Shapurji, your visitor is here."

Lawrence waited, puzzled. Although he had said his name clearly, she seemed to have mistaken him for an expected guest.

A minute ticked by, and then another. Lawrence sat on the low wall in front of the house, glancing down the hallway from the open door. He was distractedly tying and untying his shoelace when he heard a shuffling noise across tiles. He looked up to see the vicar, clad in a customary dog collar and dark jacket, walking towards him.

Shapurji Edalji was a small man with a kindly face and a receding hairline. He shuffled down the corridor with an unusual gait, taking small, measured steps as if walking a tightrope. Lawrence jumped up and offered his hand. Edalji accepted with a warm, confident handshake.

"Come in, Mr Harpham," he said, directing Lawrence down the corridor.

"Take the door to your left," he continued. Lawrence entered uncertainly, finding Charlotte Edalji perched on a settee set by a large bay window overlooking the lawn, her face tense and pale.

"Take a seat," said the reverend, turning to his wife. "Are you sure you want to hear this?"

Charlotte nodded and removed a handkerchief from her sleeve before dabbing her nose.

Lawrence chose a high-backed chair by the fireplace while the reverend joined his wife opposite.

"We wondered when you would arrive," said the vicar.

"Or indeed, whether you would come at all." Charlotte peered at Lawrence, scrutinising his face as if trying to decide whether to trust him.

"I don't understand," said Lawrence.

Shapurji Edalji leaned forward. "Arthur telephoned," he said. "He told us about your conversation and warned us that you might call by."

"I see."

"And here you are," said Charlotte bitterly. "As if we haven't suffered enough."

"I have read newspaper reports. They have treated you dreadfully, that much is evident," said Lawrence. "But after everything you have endured, don't you want to see the real perpetrator brought to justice?"

"Not at the expense of our privacy," said Shapurji. "Or my poor son's peace of mind."

"I hear that George moved away."

"It's hardly surprising," snapped Charlotte.

"No. Of course not. His position would have been intolerable."

"We have lost our son to all intents and purposes. He

will never live here again." Charlotte's mouth set into a firm line as she gazed into the distance.

"Doesn't George visit?"

"Occasionally. But it's not the same. And now Maud speaks of joining her brother one day."

"Maud?"

"Our daughter," said Shapurji, his face breaking into a gentle smile.

"Is she here?"

"She's resting upstairs," said Charlotte. "And we won't be asking her to join us. Maud misses her brother and resents his poor treatment. She has repeatedly written to the Home Office demanding compensation for him, but they will not listen. They have no interest in fairness."

"I'm sorry to hear that," said Lawrence, "truly I am. I'm not here to make matters worse."

"Then leave," said Charlotte.

Lawrence leaned back and crossed his legs, torn between seeking information and a genuine concern about further disruption to their lives. For a moment, he contemplated returning to Malvern.

"The truth must out," said Shapurji, unexpectedly. He patted his wife's hand. "My dear, this won't be the last of it. Mr Harpham will go, and another man will take his place in the fullness of time. And so it will go on until someone finally identifies the guilty party. A mystery will always attract armchair detectives. We've discussed this already. It is easier to cooperate, don't you think?"

"You know my feelings on the matter,"

"And they are not dissimilar to mine, but I can't see an end to this without a resolution."

"Dear Arthur gave us one."

"For which I will always be grateful. He saved our son,

but for all his efforts, the culprit remains at large. We don't know who killed the livestock and tormented us with those terrible letters. It could start again at any moment. How will we ever be free?"

Charlotte Edalji looked up, glanced at her husband, and then at Lawrence.

"Shapurji is right, of course," she said bitterly. "We will never escape this persecution."

"I will do my utmost to help."

"Arthur said you would say as much. But I warn you now, he does not have any faith in your methods and has advised us not to indulge you." Shapurji Edalji wagged his finger in Lawrence's direction.

"I expected nothing less," said Lawrence.

The Edaljis exchanged glances. Charlotte finally spoke.

"I'm a good judge of character," she said. "I think you sincerely wish to help for all the good it will do. What would you like to know?"

Chapter Seventeen

A COMPLICATED FAMILY

"I FIND it helps to start at the beginning," said Lawrence. "Which, according to the newspapers, was the incident in 1903. My instincts say it may have occurred earlier."

Charlotte sighed. "It feels like a lifetime." She raised a hand to her head in concentration. "Oh, my dear, we've suffered for over two decades."

Shapurji gave his wife a reassuring smile. "But it's stopped now, thank the Lord."

"Although more interference might provoke the letter writer again," Charlotte said, raising a trembling hand to her face.

"I will be discreet," said Lawrence.

"You must. I cannot put my family through any more than they have already endured." Shapurji peered earnestly through deep-set dark eyes which did not meet Lawrence's gaze.

"If you mean what I think you mean, then the fault lies with the community. No man should suffer prejudice because of his skin colour."

A burn of anger welled in Lawrence's chest as he regarded the ageing vicar, brow-beaten and shadowed by guilt, not from any wrongdoing on his part, but the burden he inadvertently brought on his family.

"Most people have treated us kindly," said Shapurji. "Though I cannot always agree with them in vestry-related matters, let alone local politics. This is a mining area. And with that comes disputes between the working men and landowners. I am responsible to my flock and often deal with opposing views. I will not hesitate to upset the great and good if the situation warrants it."

"I'm sure any reasonable man would understand that."

"They don't all take that view, and in any event, I take my duties seriously and will not appease anyone if action is required. What is right is right, no matter what people think of me."

Lawrence smiled. Far from being downtrodden, Shapurji Edalji was a man with clear opinions who would not be easily silenced. A man whose no-nonsense manner might make him enemies. Lawrence felt an urge to remove his notebook and start jotting down ideas, but it would only add to the palpable tension in the vicarage drawing room. He hoped his memory would stand up to recording the salient points of the conversation.

A sharp knock at the door preceded the arrival of a young woman.

"Did you want me, ma'am?"

"Yes, Dora. Tea and water, please."

The maid left, and Lawrence wondered how she had known that Charlotte required her. He had seen no interaction and heard no bells or alarms; not that it mattered. A cup of tea would be very welcome and more than he expected under the circumstances.

"So, how did your troubles begin?" he asked.

Shapurji and Charlotte exchanged glances. "Tell him if you must. It's too painful for me."

"Why don't you leave us?" asked Shapurji, turning to his wife.

"No. I have never hidden from trouble. But I won't participate."

"Very well." Shapurji Edalji gave a half smile. "I will bypass the unhappy events of 1903 for now and tell you about our servants. You've just met Dora. She's a good girl, obedient and hard working. But we have not always been as fortunate with our domestic staff. Now the first anonymous letter arrived in the summer of 1888. I will never forget the silly, childlike wording."

"What did it say?"

"That I must order a particular Birmingham newspaper or suffer the consequences."

"How peculiar," said Lawrence. "What difference would your reading habits make to anyone?"

"You are missing the point. It was a means of control, of someone attempting to influence my life. Naturally, I ignored it."

"You mentioned consequences. What were they?"

"That the writer would smash the vicarage windows if I did not comply."

"Not so innocent then. That's a nasty threat."

"Well, I didn't think so at the time. I put it down to juvenile antics from the local children. You know how boys are. I ignored it and several other letters that followed. They were irritating, but no more than that. Then, in December, things changed for the worse."

"What happened?" asked Lawrence.

"I received another letter, this time threatening to shoot

me if I did not follow their instructions."

"Shocking," said Lawrence.

"That letter certainly gave me pause for thought, but once again, I decided to put it from my mind. But within days of receiving the letter, I came downstairs to find glass over the floor where someone had smashed the windows. Well, I had a duty to my family. I couldn't ignore a threat that someone had carried out, nor did I relish the idea of a hidden enemy taking potshots at me as I went about my parish duties. So, I telephoned the police, but not before my servant girl revealed that she had also received threatening letters of a most unpleasant variety."

"Can you tell me more about them?" asked Lawrence.

"I would rather not."

Charlotte Edalji grimaced. "My husband is reluctant to give details because the filthy letters also contained threats to shoot Elizabeth when her black master was out. They were full of unkind references to my family's skin colour and cast us in a malevolent light."

"I am sorry to hear that. And equally sorry to bring up this painful subject."

"And all for a gentleman's bet," said Charlotte perceptively.

Lawrence blushed. "It might have started that way and believe me when I tell you that I am ashamed of myself. But let me try to do some good now I am here. Get this thing out in the open and find the real culprit."

"You do realise that the letters are only part of the problem," said Shapurji.

Lawrence leaned forward. "If you are referring to the livestock slayings, I have read about them and will naturally seek more information. But as my good lady wife says, there is a world of difference between bloodied killings and anonymous hate letters."

Shapurji nodded. "Your wife is a wise woman. We have always felt the same way."

"George could never hurt a living creature," said Charlotte. "He is simply not made that way."

"Did the police react to your complaint about the letters?" asked Lawrence.

"Oh, yes. Sergeant Upton came from the Cannock police station. He listened to us, and we showed him every document. Then, our servant, Elizabeth, showed him her letters. Upton seemed concerned and took the matter seriously, placing a watch over the vicarage for several nights. We slept peacefully in our beds for the first time in months. No further letters arrived, and Sergeant Upton removed his constables from duty. We hoped that was enough to frighten the culprits away. But the moment the police left our home, the letters began again, turning up in the oddest of places. We found one in the yard and others in the house. But then I picked up a letter that sent a chill through my bones. The fox was in the hen house."

"What do you mean?" asked Lawrence.

"Someone had used flyleaves taken from my children's books to write their wicked letters."

"Are you sure?"

"Yes. The coverless books were still in the nursery. It could mean only one thing. Elizabeth Foster must have been the author."

"Your maid?"

"Yes. She did it."

"Who else lived here at the time?"

"Other than me, my wife and our three children?"

"Three? You've mentioned George and Maud. And the third?"

"Horace is our middle son," said Shapurji.

"Is he home?"

"No," snapped Charlotte. "And we do not expect to see him."

"Where is he, if you don't mind me asking?"

"In his lodgings, I expect."

"Where?" Lawrence, sensing an obvious reluctance, pressed Charlotte gently for details. She was not forthcoming.

"I can't remember."

"How old were your children?"

"George was twelve in 1888, Horace and Maud, nine and six or thereabouts," said Shapurji. "All far too young to understand such things. Anyway, I told Sergeant Upton what happened, and he searched for evidence of Elizabeth's handwriting and found some examples in her trunk. On close comparison, they were similar to the letters."

"Similar?"

"Close enough."

"Did you dismiss Elizabeth?"

"No. She ran away to her aunt in the village. She couldn't face the consequences. I was disappointed in her."

"And that was the end of it?"

"No. Elizabeth had greatly wronged us, and I felt obliged to set an example. I instructed Sergeant Upton to charge her with criminal mischief before she ran away. But then I relented, and asked Upton to offer her the chance to redeem herself. If she confessed, I would drop the charge against her. It was a very generous offer. But Elizabeth continued to deny writing the letters and, as I said, she left for her aunt's house at the first opportunity. It was a sign of guilt if ever I saw one."

"Did you follow through with the prosecution?"

"Naturally. It was only right and proper."

"And we had done a lot for the girl," said Charlotte. "It's why I find this so hard to talk about. Elizabeth professed to be frightened when she opened the first letter. I was worried about her and allowed her to sleep in my room, so she was not alone at night. This continued for several weeks. I spent hours consoling the girl and mopping up her tears. And all the time, she was the one tormenting my family with her wicked deeds. I should have realised when she brought in the letter on New Year's Day."

"Why?"

"The gum on the envelope was still wet," said Shapurji. "I noticed at the time but didn't think much of it until I took it to Sergeant Upton. He said it must be an inside job."

"What happened to Elizabeth?" asked Lawrence.

"The case went to court," said Shapurji. "And we attended as prosecution witnesses."

"Both of you?" asked Lawrence.

"And my son George."

"Wasn't he a little young?"

"Yes," said Charlotte. "And I'd have preferred to leave him at home. But George saw a shadow through the door when one of the letters arrived. Moments later, Elizabeth came sailing through. Sergeant Upton thought it would be useful for George to speak up. We were all convinced of Elizabeth's guilt, but the police could not offer a hand-writing expert and had limited evidence. George attended court to be on the safe side."

"With the greatest respect, I'm surprised they success-fully prosecuted the girl," said Lawrence.

"I dropped the charge to a lesser one," said Shapurji. "The defence thought it would ruin her parents if the girl went to trial at the assizes. And I wanted the matter over with."

"You could have dropped the case altogether."

"Absolutely not. My family had suffered for months on end. I had a position to uphold and a family to protect. So, I agreed to a lesser charge of using threats, providing that the girl confessed and agreed to be bound over to keep the peace."

"And did she?"

"Only for the sake of the court. She said what they wanted to hear, and as soon as she left the courtroom, Elizabeth denied all charges and threatened revenge. We'd harboured a serpent in our midst."

"Yes, my dear. She was what you might call a wrong 'un," said Charlotte.

"And yet you were still receiving letters in 1903?" asked Lawrence.

"Yes. The letters stopped temporarily after the court case," said Shapurji. "We had three relatively peaceful years, and then it all started again. Not so much for us to begin with. William Brookes, the grocer, took the brunt of it. But it was another painful chapter in our lives."

Charlotte Edalji clasped her hands to her chest. "I've had enough for today. You may come back another time if you wish. But I really can't take any more questioning."

"I'm very sorry," said Lawrence. "I can see how difficult this has been. Of course, I will leave."

"Good day, Mr Harpham," said Charlotte, staring into the distance as Lawrence stood.

Shapurji Edalji accompanied Lawrence to the front door. "My wife tires easily," he said, offering his hand.

"I understand," said Lawrence. "And I appreciate her offer to let me to return. Please thank her on my behalf. I am grateful for your time."

"You could try asking in the village if you want to know more, providing you do it discreetly."

"Of course. I want to speak to the Brookes family, if possible."

Shapurji frowned. "I'd prefer it if you did not."

"But the anonymous letter writer targeted them too."

"Brookes is troublesome and no friend to my family."

"I would have expected him to be a kindred spirit."

"Quite the opposite. Please do not discuss my private business with that man."

Lawrence sighed. "Arthur must have met the Brookes to make his case."

"Not with my approval. But he succeeded in freeing my son, so his methods were sound. This is a different matter. I have as much to lose from your belated investigation as any possible gain."

"I understand your position, and God knows, I sympathise."

Shapurji Edalji winced.

"Sorry, Reverend. That was clumsy. I apologise for the blasphemy, but no unresolved criminal matter is ever over."

Shapurji closed his eyes as if shutting out the world. Silence briefly reigned as he considered Lawrence's words. "Do as you must," he said, "but don't expect my blessing."

"But..." Lawrence's words trailed away as the beleaguered vicar quietly closed the door. Lawrence walked away from the troubled family, his thoughts a tangled knot of guilt. But selfish matters soon overtook his concern for others. Something was missing, and only when he licked his parched lips did Lawrence realise the Edaljis had still failed to achieve an orderly household. Though he'd been there for the best part of an hour, Dora had not delivered the tea.

Chapter Eighteen

THE BROOKES BOYS

LAWRENCE STRODE DETERMINEDLY towards the village centre, knowing he must meet the Brookes family one way or another. The Edaljis had spoken of them, and the plaintive letter from the vicar to local tradesmen also mentioned Frederick Brookes. If he were to make any progress, he must question them and try to uncover a reason for the unpleasant spate of letters.

Lawrence zigzagged through Great Wyrley, eventually ending up on the Walsall Road near a depressing row of terraced properties perched like sullen vultures along the side of the road. Lawrence glanced suspiciously towards the steeply pitched roofs and multi-paned windows, trying to decide what architectural feature made them seem so predatory. He concluded that, from a distance, the roof dormers looked like raised eyebrows scowling beneath a darkening sky. As if on cue, Lawrence felt the patter of rain on his jacket, immediately regretting his earlier decision to leave his raincoat in the car. Pacing quickly beyond the offending properties, Lawrence soon spotted the welcoming signage of

The Royal Oak a little way up Norton Lane. He could ask the barman for directions while browsing his choice of ale for consumption with Martin Newlove later that day.

After a quick conversation with a preoccupied barmaid, Lawrence soon possessed directions to the grocery and sub-post office owned by Mr William Brookes farther up Walsall Road. Under other circumstances, he would have waited for the rain shower to stop and lingered in the bar for a quick refreshment, but he doubted the barmaid would rustle up the enthusiasm to serve him quickly. She had barely managed to respond to his polite request for help. Pulling up his jacket collar, Lawrence strode up the street until he finally arrived outside a building where a row of crates displayed their fruit and vegetable contents near the frontage by the door. Lawrence selected an apple and walked inside.

The doorbell jangled, and an elderly man glared at Lawrence through heavy-lidded eyes. Lawrence paused, wondering if he had accidentally wandered into someone's residence, but a cursory check of the room revealed a counter, a cash till and well-stocked floor-to-ceiling shelves. The shop contents were all as he expected, except for a man whose faraway stare and haggard frame suggested he was either unwell or one step away from meeting his maker.

Lawrence held out the apple uncertainly. "Just this, please."

The man grunted and prodded a key on the till, which dinged before the drawer sprang open with a satisfying rumble.

"Thruppence," said the man, gruffly.

"For one apple?"

"That's right."

"No. It can't be."

"That's the price. Take it or leave it."

"I think I'll leave it." Lawrence plucked a solitary plum from a small pile on a knitted mat. "I'll have one of these instead unless that's even more expensive."

The old man fixed Lawrence with a steely glare. "That will be a shilling."

Lawrence shook his head in exasperation. He badly needed to find common ground with this man if he were to extract information about the Brookes family. But that did not include paying unreasonable prices for half-rotten food items. He replaced the plum and tried again with mounting frustration.

"I want to speak to Mr Brookes," said Lawrence.

"What for?" The elderly man took a step backwards and slumped onto a chair behind the counter.

"It's a personal matter," said Lawrence.

"Then go to a doctor."

Lawrence frowned and briefly wondered if the man was suffering from the beginnings of senile dementia, but his last snippy retort, in a sing-song Black Country accent, made him seem fully aware.

The man stared balefully, and Lawrence met his eyes, locked in a battle of wills. Then, an inner door opened, and two younger men arrived, one in his late twenties and the other a little older.

"What are you doing here, Father?" asked the younger man, surprised.

"Your sister popped out. The young 'un's acting up. She asked me to sit for a while."

The taller man sighed. "I'll be having words with Eliza. She should know better. Edgar, take the old boy home. He looks worn out."

"Can I help you, sir?"

He turned his attention to Lawrence, now quietly standing and contemplating the confusion.

"Some fruit, please," said Lawrence.

"The nosy sod wanted more than fruit," said the old man.

"Quiet, Father. Away with you now."

Lawrence retrieved the apple. "How much?" he asked nervously.

"A halfpenny."

"Don't give it away," snapped the old man.

"That's a better price than three pence," said Lawrence.

The man raised an eyebrow.

"Your father asked for more. But good for him trying to make a decent profit." Lawrence smiled and winked, trying to break the ice, but the old man took immediate offence.

"Shopkeeper marks up goods. Well, I never. Put the pig on the wall, why don't you?"

The taller man raised his eyes heavenward. "Edgar, go on, lad. Take Dad away. See you later, Father."

Edgar gently shoved the old man from the store while his brother inserted himself behind the counter and placed his hands on the wooden top.

"Sorry about that," he said. "I don't know what's got into my sister. She took advantage. Dad's a well-respected businessman, but he's been ill lately, and it's affected his spirits, if you know what I mean?"

"I think so," said Lawrence uncertainly.

"Dad ran the stores for years. He's well known in the town, but he's been rather melancholic since his last illness. It's altered his personality. Dad was always a gruff straight talker, but lately, he's been uncooperative and belligerent. Not just with you but with everyone. I hope it isn't a sign of worse to come."

"He probably needs a good rest."

"I keep saying that, but Dad potters around doing odd jobs come fair wind or foul. He's long retired from the grocers and can't remember what to do behind the post office counter. It's too bad of Eliza to impose on him. I'm surprised my mother allowed it."

Lawrence nodded. "You must be one of the Brookes boys?"

"I am. We've owned the grocers for decades. You're not a local then?"

"Can't you tell from my accent?"

The man laughed. "Too right. Don't take offence, but you sound like a proper toff."

Lawrence smiled. "No offence taken, but I had hoped to speak to Mr Brookes."

"So, Dad was right when he said you were a nosey sod?"

"Arguably nosey, but less of the sod, if you don't mind."

"I'm Fred Brookes. Will I do?" asked the man, seeming to enjoy the light-hearted banter. Lawrence shifted uncomfortably, knowing he was about to take the conversation in a darker direction.

"Yes. Perfect. You're exactly the right person."

"Well, you're lucky you've caught me. I'm rarely in the shop except on high days and holidays, when there's nobody else to mind the place. I'm too busy in the colliery."

"Perhaps it's fate," mused Lawrence beneath his breath.

"Sorry?"

"Nothing. Look, I'd like to ask you some questions if you don't mind."

Fred stared for a long minute. "Something tells me I won't like this."

"And you'd be right."

"How about you have the apple on the house and walk away?"

"I'd prefer to speak to you."

"Do you have a calling card?" asked Fred perceptively.

Lawrence nodded and removed a small silver case from his jacket pocket. He flipped the lid, extracted the card, and tossed it onto the counter.

Fred picked it up. "Alistair Blatworthy, quantity surveyor," he said appreciatively. "That's interesting. I'm a mining engineer, but I've studied surveying. We can talk shop."

"Ah. Wouldn't you know it?" Lawrence's heart sank. He had been loath to use his alter ego, but with the reverend's insistence on discretion and Martin Newlove cautioning likewise, he'd succumbed to deceit. And it was about to bite him. Sighing, he turned over the card case and took out his actual calling card.

"A private detective too? What a varied career you have had."

"I won't stir up trouble," said Lawrence, watching the young man size him up. Fred Brookes was of average height with a slight build and an unremarkable face. But behind the thick Black Country accent and the slightly hardened hands of a working man, he was intelligent and perceptive. Lawrence instinctively knew that he would resist any more disingenuous behaviour. It was time to come clean.

"I'm researching the Edalji case," said Lawrence. "But I'm not here to cause upset, and I would be grateful if you don't tell anyone."

"I won't," said Fred. "Because you're right. It's still distressing and discussed too often for my liking. Let sleeping dogs lie, for God's sake."

"I would. Only Mr Conan Doyle only got it half right."

Fred nodded. "I agree. Royden Sharp may be a troublemaker and a reprobate. We're not friends and never will be, but he has no reason to harm my family. Or Edalji's, for that matter."

"Then we're on the same side."

"I wouldn't go that far. What's the point of dragging it all up again?"

"To discover who really wrote the letters."

"And slayed the livestock?"

"Do you think they are the same person?"

"No."

"Nor do I. Yet they arrested George Edalji for the hate letters and for slaughtering a horse. I'm surprised there wasn't an outcry in the village over his treatment."

"Well, it wouldn't have come from our direction," said Fred. "My father dislikes the Edaljis intensely."

"And you?"

"I'm not bothered either way. George and I spoke a little when we were younger, but when the two families fell out, we both took sides."

"What happened?"

"Nothing much. They came to blows over the sale of a school property. Dad thought the vicar should have worked harder to save it and been more in tune with the parish, like old Reverend Compson before him."

"So, he didn't approve of an interloper from a different culture?"

Fred frowned. "I won't deny many people felt that way, but not my family. Dad disliked anyone who crossed him. His concerns were for the villagers, especially the children. My elder sister, Lucy, taught at Wyrley School for a time. That's why he took an interest and for no other reason."

"I'm sorry," said Lawrence. "It's been tough on the vicar, but I shouldn't jump to conclusions."

"Apology accepted. We're not against Reverend Edalji, just some of his decisions. But then, none of us are perfect."

"Understood," said Lawrence." I hear some of the earlier letters concerned you. Can you tell me more?"

Fred glanced at his watch. "Edgar will be back in a moment. I won't discuss it in front of him. He'll want to tell Dad, so you'd better be quick."

"Can you remember the first letter?"

"Fairly well. It wasn't so much of a letter as a press announcement. We'd kept well away from the local newspapers, so it was a shock when we ended up in one again."

"Again?"

Fred hung his head. "If anyone asks, we haven't had this conversation. I don't want people to think I'm disloyal. But our family had a bit of trouble a few years before the letters started."

"Trouble?"

"Yes. Don't get the wrong impression, but within six months of each other, both Lucy and my father were cautioned for violence."

Chapter Nineteen

GOSSIP AT THE GROCERY STORE

"YOU DO SURPRISE ME," said Lawrence, leaning against the counter.

"Don't look so worried," said Fred. "I've made it sound worse than it is. We're not talking about a serious assault."

"Then what do you mean?"

"Just a couple of school-related issues. Passions always ran high between our family and the educational establishment. If you scratch around hard enough, you'll discover this yourself, so I may as well tell you. The Wyrley School board hauled my sister Lucy in for a proper dressing down."

"When was this?"

"Years ago, before the letters and long before the livestock crimes."

"Is it relevant?"

"Who knows? Something ticked off the letter writer."

"What did your sister do?"

Fred pursed his lips. "They said she beat the children."

"That's hardly unusual."

"So Dad said. His exact words were *spare the rod and spoil the child*."

"Did Lucy harm them?"

"I don't think so. I can't remember much except Lucy keeping to her room for a few days from the shame of it. I'm not sure if she disciplined the children with a cane or her hand. Either could have left a mark. But several parents complained, and the school board made Lucy promise not to use corporal punishment again."

"Were the children young?"

Fred nodded. "And Lucy was too. She was only a pupil teacher back then."

"And was that the end of it?"

"Yes. Absolutely. Lucy learned her lesson, and that was that."

"And your father?"

"Oddly enough, a similar instance at Wyrley School, this time involving me."

"Go on."

"Father had sent me into the school earlier that day with a message for Mr Lawton. Father must collect Edgar at one o'clock sharp and, under no circumstances, should Edgar be late. I passed on the message and went on my merry way. But when Dad arrived, Edgar was still scribbling on his slate in the corner of the schoolroom. Dad lost his temper and shouted at Lawton. The teacher tried to push Dad outside, but the old man was having none of it and shoved Lawton good and hard in the chest."

"Oh dear," said Lawrence. "I hope it was worth it."

Fred sighed. "Do you know, I can't even remember what we were doing in the middle of the school day, for us to leave so quickly. It was probably something trivial. But

Lawton could never relinquish control, and my father liked his way too. They clashed."

"What was the sentence?"

"Nothing much. A small fine, and he paid Lawton's costs. Another lesson learned."

"So, these events occurred after Elizabeth Forster's conviction and before the second set of letters?"

"Ah. You've heard about Lizzie."

"Did you know her?"

"Only by sight. She was much older than me, somewhere around Lucy's age."

"Understood. And thank you for being so honest. I realise it's unpleasant to talk about your family in this context, but it's always useful to understand how things are. I'm puzzled by the long lull between letters though."

"We were relieved and thought they might have stopped for good. But nothing prepared us for the torrent of abuse that came after."

Lawrence nodded. "You must have been quite young. Can you remember much about it?"

"Oh, yes. The letters were extremely personal and very embarrassing. My school friends teased me remorselessly when they heard about it, and I was ridiculed for years. Lucy was too. She left the village as soon as she could, but I was stuck here until I left school."

"Did the letters continue throughout your education?"

"Yes, and not just for me. The letter writer soon turned his attention to George Edalji. But mud sticks and boys can be cruel. Even when they stopped, the boys still tormented me about it."

"So, your school years were unhappy?"

"Not entirely. Things could have been worse."

"Tell me about the first letters."

Fred Brookes glanced anxiously towards the door. Lawrence checked his watch. They had been alone for ten minutes, and Edgar would soon return.

Fred cleared his throat. "There were many, many letters, more than I remember. The first one that stuck in my mind was a marriage announcement between Maud Edalji and me.

"Surely a prank?"

"Dad thought so, but I was horribly embarrassed. I was only thirteen or fourteen then, and Maud was four years younger. You can imagine how that looked to my school friends."

"I can," said Lawrence.

"Then, a few months later, Dad came storming into the yard with one of the local papers in his hand. He was so angry I thought he might strike me. He thrust the newspaper into my face, and when I read it, I soon realised why. Someone had written to the editor pretending to be us."

"You and your family?"

"No. Me and George Edalji as if we had confessed to writing the offensive letters and were offering to pay damages."

"Yet another prank?"

Fred shook his head. "Not this time. A youngster could easily have written the marriage announcement, but this was entirely different in style. The grammar school gave me a decent education, but I still had to ask my father what some of it meant. Especially some accusations about Sergeant Upton and Elizabeth Foster."

"Elizabeth Foster again. What had you to do with her trial?"

"Absolutely nothing. I told you; I barely knew the girl. Neither did my family. She must have come into the shop from time to time, but none of us would have exchanged more than a few words with her. And the same with Sergeant Upton. We knew him by sight, but he was a police-man, and we stayed well away."

"How strange that they appeared in a newspaper article about you."

"You don't know the half of it, Mr Harpham," said Fred Brookes, glancing at Lawrence's card to refresh his memory. "The marriage announcement was silly, the confession was troublesome, but what followed after was downright cruel."

"What happened?"

"More marriage announcements, followed by notif-ication of my death at my residence in Wyrley."

Lawrence gasped. "Shocking," he said.

Fred shook his head. "It took a while before we heard the news as it appeared in a national newspaper. Fortu-nately, everyone in Great Wyrley knew it was nonsense as they had all seen me. But a friend of my great aunt read it and told her I had died, and she jolly nearly fainted at the shock of it."

"What an unpleasant thing to do."

Fred sighed. "That's how it was for us: one minute a death, the next a marriage. Somewhere along the line, Charlotte Edalji supposedly had another son, and my mother allegedly gave birth to twins, even though they were both past childbearing age. There was no end to it. Back and forth it went, always either the Brookes or Edalji fami-lies and often both together. They must have thought our families spent our lives in each other pockets, but that was never true."

"You were not friends and later became estranged."

"Yes. Much later. And although we had no particular

relationship, Shapurji Edalji still helped our family with church-related matters."

"How?"

"When I was in the church choir, I filled the organ with rags for a prank. The organist sent me home, telling me I was not welcome back. My father was furious and told me I had better find a way back into the choir, or I would feel his wrath. I appealed to the reverend, who intervened and allowed me back at the expense of losing his organist, who resigned in a fit of pique. The vicar didn't have to help me – no love was lost between us, but Shapurji Edalji, for all his faults, is a kind man who supports the underdog. At least that's how it felt to me."

"You should tell him," said Lawrence. "He's suffered a lot and would probably appreciate a few kind words."

Fred Brookes licked his lips. "Perhaps I will one day," he said.

"You've spoken of the announcements, but do you know much about the letters?"

"I'm afraid not. One or two arrived here, but most went to the vicarage. Dad said they were in different hands and styles."

"As were the announcements from what you have told me."

"Yes. Gossip was rife in the village, as you can imagine. And as a teenage boy, I took less interest than most. But I still heard plenty. Some said there were multiple letter writers, all in a gang, taking it in turns to torment our families."

"What do you think?"

"It's too simplistic. I could believe it if the correspondence was all juvenile, but some were childlike, others well-written, and a few were wildly dramatic, either penned by a lunatic or a man in the grip of delusions. There was no consistency to them."

"So, there must be more than one writer of different ages?"

"Exactly. And what are the chances of that? It's impossible."

"Do you have a theory?"

"Not one that fits the facts. I have stopped thinking about it over the years. There was no answer. Nobody has ever satisfactorily explained the inconsistent letters and the many times they have stopped and started. It is like an obsession that never ends."

"Yet it did. The letters stopped."

"Yes, suddenly in 1895. I cannot tell you how relieved we were. And the silence continued for many years."

"Until 1903, I hear."

"Well, yes. I think so."

"Think?"

"Sometime in '98 or '99, someone put my dad's name forward for election on the parish council."

"Fair enough."

"Not really. My father was upset and angry about it."

"Why?"

"He had no wish to be elected to the parish council and considered it a gross liberty that someone had proposed him without asking first."

"A careless gesture, perhaps. But surely that is all."

"That's what we said, but Father was beside himself. That's why I remember the incident so well."

"Do you think he thought there was malicious intent?"

"Yes, in hindsight. If Dad were a few years younger, I'd ask him. He was probably overreacting, and someone thought he would fit the committee well. But it doesn't matter what I think. Dad disagreed and dreaded the resumption of another plague of nasty tricks."

"Understandable," said Lawrence. "It would make anybody jumpy. So, were your family involved when the letters resumed in 1903?"

The door swung open as Fred Brookes opened his mouth to respond.

"Ah, Edgar," he said. "Has Dad settled?"

Edgar nodded. "He sat in his chair and went out like a light."

"Good. Flip the closed sign over while we visit our sister."

"You'll have to go alone. They need me at home. Our youngest is sick."

"Off you go then. I'll see Eliza and drop in on the old man."

Fred extended his hand. "Nice to meet you, Mr Harpham. I think we've covered everything you wanted to discuss. No need to meet up again."

Fred doffed his hat as Lawrence left the shop, wondering what he would do to kill the next three hours before his appointment with Martin Newlove.

Chapter Twenty

ASSASSIN

Major Henry Savage strode from the London Infirmary for Epilepsy and Paralysis and took a large lungful of air, glad to be out of the place. He straightened his tie and walked towards the Maida Vale garage, which Felix Crossley had identified in his curt message a few weeks earlier. The major had raised an eyebrow at Crossley's demand, but as a man in financial ruin, he had been in no position to refuse. But the terse correspondence was nothing compared to the explosive telephone call he had taken after confessing to driving his car into a ditch. Crossley had raged, disregarding the mission's success and elimination of an enemy. Instead, he berated the major for wasting time and money, indignant at the prospect of paying for the vehicle's repair. The major had protested, but Crossley was unmoved. He did not regard Frank Podmore's death as a success; quite the contrary. The major was supposed to extract vital information from him. Not lure the man to a lake in the dead of night, only for him to fall in. To say Crossley had been furious was an understatement. But to give the man his credit, he still paid for the major's services, nonetheless.

The major cast a perfunctory nod at a passing flower girl, remembering the days when he might have purchased a bloom for his wife, Jane. Those days were gone. Jane had upped and left him, joining forces with a male fortune teller, no doubt as crooked as she was. They were living in sin somewhere in North London, probably not far from here. The major grimaced at the thought of bumping into them but comforted himself, knowing it was unlikely in a city as large as London. But the flower girl had stirred up long-repressed memories of his wedding day to a beautiful wife with a military wedding in full regalia. He had been a proud man then, and a good soldier who had steadily risen through the officer ranks. Respected by his men, feared by his servants, and loved by his wife, his life had been good, and he wished he had appreciated it as much as he ought.

Major Savage thrust his hand in his pocket and flipped a coin into the hand of a newspaper seller. He rolled the Gazette and carried it like a baton, marching up the street with a straight back. Standards, Henry, Standards. He might have fallen from grace and been feeding at the table of a man like Felix Crossley, but his life was not all bad. Jane had been a con woman through and through. She could not summon the spirits and had not believed in her own rhetoric for a moment. She had known what she was, but as much as he supported her and enjoyed the lure of filthy lucre, the major had always sought a higher power. He believed in more than earthly bonds and was in awe of the battle between good and evil. He yearned to be part of Crossley's inner circle and wield power that other men could only dream of. If only he could rise through The Order, respect, fortune, and power would surely follow. But it wouldn't be through The Crescent Moon, which, like Crossley, he had abandoned. He had joined Crossley's own hierarchical society – an underground, ritualistic organisation focussed on knowledge and power through any means, good or bad.

The major had clashed with Crossley before, most notably when he had allowed the reptile Harpham to steal the children he had carefully nurtured for Crossley's ritual in Akenham churchyard. And though he hated to admit it, he was at fault and had made mistakes. He should not have allowed Jane to use the children as props for her fake seances. Had they kept to their rooms, no one would have seen William and Millicent. Nobody would have cared. He certainly didn't and had formed no bonds that might have left him unable to watch their sacrifice. Quite the contrary. He had been looking forward to it. Not that he had a particular penchant for bloodlust. But he believed in Crossley's powers and knew the potency of two young children with religious parentage. Major Savage briefly wondered where they were now but pushed the pointless thought from his head. Harpham's cronies had hidden them well and probably changed their names. Crossley had written them off and lined up another prospect, which was where he came in.

After venting his spleen about the damaged car and the premature death of Frank Podmore, Crossley had retreated for a few weeks. But the night before, he had telephoned again, his voice smug as he bragged about his next plan. Still convinced he was on the right path, Crossley had sent a representative to Podmore's funeral. The man had taken a series of photographs using a hidden camera and sent them for development before passing them to Crossley. After careful checking, Crossley had identified Lawrence Harpham, his wife, and Sir Arthur Conan Doyle. And then, to his enormous pleasure, he had seen Aurora's unmistakable face.

Crossley gloated as he described his loathing for his former scarlet woman. The major had nodded politely on the other end of the telephone, wishing he felt the same way about Jane. Instead, he missed her. Knowing that she was living under the roof of a younger, more virile man had not put him off. He would still have forgiven the cuckolding had she come back. But it was not to be. His thoughts drifted until Crossley barked another order, telling him to get down to Maida Vale *for further instructions. The major knew what that meant, and his gut had clenched at the thought.*

It clenched again as he unfurled the newspaper and fanned it against his face, trying to calm the rising nausea. He raised a nervous finger to his temple and wiped the beading sweat into his greying hair. Hospital visits had been the worst of Crossley's orders. He didn't mind most demands, but an audience with Dickie Connelly brought him out in hives. He had only met Dickie a few times before the accident and had not liked him much then. But since Lawerence Harpham had severed his spine with a pitchfork, Connelly had become darker and more vengeful with each passing day. Crossley admired Connelly, and they had formed a weirdly symbiotic relationship, absorbing each other's most evil thoughts. Crossley spent more time with Connelly than was healthy and had paid for his private room on one of the hospital's upper floors. Both men were charming in their various ways and had an inherent ability to get others to do their bidding.

The major's erratic fanning did nothing to dispel his latest memory of Dickie Connelly after the hospital earlier that morning. Forgoing break-fast, the major had arrived too early for visiting hours and had spent thirty minutes waiting in a corridor with an ever-growing sense of dread. The nurses had been in and out of Connelly's room, the last sour-faced redhead marching out as if she could not leave quickly enough before telling him to go in if he must. Keen to get the ordeal over with, he did.

Connelly had been lying in bed, propped up by hospital pillows, one arm hanging limply beside him. He had scowled at the major, an expression of disdain across his once handsome face. Major Savage had dragged the visitor's chair towards the wall, trying to create distance between them. Dickie had noticed, of course, and sneered before flexing his facial muscles into a more benign expression and revealing Cross-ley's plan. The major must return to the garage for another vehicle, which he would drive to Malvern for a second mission. The salient points covered, Dickie had toyed with the major, one minute charming him, the next picking away at his insecurities.

Major Savage was not a stranger to the art of conversation. He had risen in the ranks because he knew how to behave at the commanding officer's dinner table. He could motivate the men and keep the servants in their place. But his grasp of psychology was nothing compared to Dickie's. Even paralysed, Dickie was still one of the most dangerous men he had ever met, able to influence a man to evil merely with the tone of his voice.

Major Savage had feared Dickie Connelly long before that day. Dickie had intimidated him during every previous visit, usually through a request designed to cause maximum discomfort. That day had been no exception. Dickie had allowed Savage the false comfort of sitting at a distance for five minutes. But then, as a punishment for pulling away, he had insisted the major come closer to change a dressing on his leg. The major had naturally refused and opened the door to call for a nurse. But Dickie summoned him back and, with a snake-eyed stare that never faltered, coaxed him back to the bedside. Major Savage shuddered as he walked, trying to dislodge the memory of Dickie's shrivelled body and nakedness between the sheets. No man should have to see another without trousers.

Ten more minutes and the garage would be in sight. Dickie had passed on Crossley's instruction to take possession of a steam-powered vehicle. Though an experienced driver, this would be a first, and Major Savage felt a thrill of excitement about being behind the wheel of a fast car. A sedentary jaunt replaced by a fast-paced mission was another step in his quest for power. A burgeoning sense of pride replaced the wretchedness of his time with Dickie, and he congratulated himself that Crossley had chosen him for the vital task because he trusted him. He would not let the man down again. That had been Dickie's parting *shot as he left the room. Under Crossley's orders, Dickie had spent their last ten minutes together reinforcing the psychology of the individual, explicitly improving his confidence, thereby increasing his chance of success. Odd how Dickie swung from fear to humiliation only to finish by making him feel good. Perhaps that was how he mastered his grip on people, through ever-changing psychological manipulation until they did not know what to expect. Major Savage nodded to himself as he reflected on his thoughts. Crossley used the same technique to great effect, and it was hard to differentiate between the master and the pupil. Both men were equally adept at gaining control.*

The enormous black touring car was on the front of the forecourt when Major Savage arrived, sporting a card reading 'Fred Barber' just as Connelly had told him. After exchanging a few words with the garage owner, he boarded the vehicle and sat up high, feeling lofty and powerful as he prepared for a long wait. Crossley had shown a rare moment of kindness, warning him through Dickie that it would take twenty minutes for the vehicle to fire its boiler to operating temperature. The major opened the newspaper and prepared for the long drive to Malvern.

Chapter Twenty-One

THE ROYAL OAK

LAWRENCE ARRIVED at The Royal Oak three hours before he was due to meet Martin Newlove. It had been a spur-of-the-moment decision brought on by an even heavier rain shower. He could have sheltered in his vehicle, but it would have been cold, draughty, and damp, as would any attempt to dodge the showers by wasting time browsing shops and public buildings.

The barmaid had huffed at the unwanted intrusion when Lawrence returned to an empty bar seldom used at that time of day. She had been busy polishing glasses behind a sparse, functional counter while singing to herself. Lawrence had cautiously approached and asked for a coffee. The barmaid looked up, bemused and, amid peals of laughter, she had reminded him that it was a miner's pub, commonly selling beer. If he wanted a hot beverage, he must go to the cafe at the other end of the village if ale was not to his taste. But with the rain now sheeting, Lawrence elected to stay dry, if not sated, and pulled out his jotter to make some retrospective notes from his earlier visit to the rectory. The girl eventually relented and brought over a coffee pot before directing his attention to the latest local newspaper. It had been one of the longest, least eventful three hours he had spent in a long time, and as five o'clock finally dawned, Lawrence felt relieved that he had not succumbed to sleep.

Martin Newlove was five minutes late. Any longer, and Lawrence would have given up on his new acquaintance. Miners were drifting into the bar on their way back from work, casting suspicious eyes at the stranger in their midst. Then Newlove entered, looked around and sheepishly sidled towards Lawrence with a curt nod before sitting down. "You stand out like a sore thumb," he said.

"It was your idea."

"I didn't think about your clothing."

"What's wrong with it?"

"Nothing. That's the problem."

"You drink here, and you dress well."

"I grew up with these men. They know me."

"I saw another public house. We can always go there."

Martin Newlove cocked his head as if he were considering the proposition. "We're here now," he replied. "Just be careful what you say."

"I was hoping we could talk openly."

"We can if we move tables. What would you like to drink?"

"I'll buy," said Lawrence.

"No."

"A pint of ale then."

Martin Newlove waved to the barmaid, who smiled back. "Your usual?" she asked.

"Make it two."

Lawrence watched as Newlove leaned against the bar,

raising a cheery hand, and nodding to men he had known for a long time. One man tapped him on the shoulder and gestured towards Lawrence. Newlove shrugged noncommittally, and Lawrence wondered how Martin would react if he knew he had already revealed his identity to the Edaljis and Fred Brookes.

The barmaid pulled the requested pints, and Newlove returned. "Follow me," he said, leading Lawrence into a back area containing two chairs and a small table, barely fit for purpose, set into a tiny gap. "This will be a little more private," said Newlove.

"Now we both look suspicious," Lawrence countered.

"Leave it with me. I'll come up with something."

Lawrence took a long draught from his beer, licked his lips, and wished he'd eaten earlier. His stomach grumbled. "Do they serve food?" he asked.

Newlove shook his head. "Liquid only, I'm afraid. Right. What would you like to know?"

"More about the lead players in this saga, if possible."

"It's not some Shakespearean play."

"Accepted. Tell me about Sir Arthur's chief suspect."

"Royden Sharp? There's no proof to speak of. And I'm not saying that because I know the family. Your friend, Conan Doyle, sent handwriting samples for analysis, suggesting that the 1892 and 1903 letter writers matched. He visited Great Wyrley and spoke to a few people in the know who convinced him that Royden wrote the letters out of spite. Conan Doyle said young Sharp loathed George Edalji, but he didn't explain why. I've read one of two of Conan Doyle's letters in the newspaper and listened to more village gossip than I should. But nobody can explain why Royden Sharp might have harboured such an intense dislike that he continued writing letters for years on end."

"Where was Sharp when the letters temporarily stopped?"

Newlove tapped his fingers on the table. "On a ship to America, but don't read too much into that."

"Convenient though, circumstantially."

"I thought that's what you were trying to avoid."

"Point taken. Anything else in Sharp's favour?"

Martin Newlove sipped from his pint, crossed his legs at the ankle and leaned back. "Royden wasn't a bad lad, but he was a handful. I was friendly with his brother Frank. We went to school together, and he often complained about how difficult it was to keep the lad in line."

"In what way?"

"The usual running amok across the countryside with no thought to the consequences. And the odd bit of thievery, not to mention burning down Mr Hatton's hayrick. It was a good thing they had insured it for damage. But I can't see Sharp participating in the animal slayings. He wasn't well-behaved, but neither was he cruel."

"They arrested George Edalji for harming livestock," said Lawrence. "And he was an equally unlikely suspect."

"I know that. And although George's arrest sat uneasily with me, I find it equally hard to believe the same of Royden Sharp. It was a terrible time for the village. Nobody wants to imagine that sort of thing going on at night. But sadly, these things happen in the countryside."

"Are they often announced by letter?"

"No. I've never heard of it before".

"Why are you so certain of Sharp's innocence?"

"Think about it. The boy was only eleven or twelve when the letters began. And if you don't already know, they expelled him from Walsall Grammar School and sent him to the other side of the country."

"Where?"

"Lincolnshire."

"That is a long way. He could still write though?"

"Of course. But a fair few letters arrived by hand, and Royden couldn't possibly have delivered them."

"I see what you mean."

"Exactly. Would you like another beer?" asked Martin, draining his pint.

Lawrence cast an anxious glance towards his still half-full tankard, having no desire for a hard drinking session. "I have a wife to get home to."

"Come on. A second won't hurt."

"Then I'll stand the round."

Lawrence waited until the bar cleared, then purchased two of the same. "Here," he said, passing a pint to the constable.

"Keep up this time," said Martin, winking.

"Violet would not appreciate it if I came home under the influence."

"Now I know why I never married."

Lawrence smiled as he finished his first pint. "Didn't you meet the right girl?"

"You could say that or that the timing was wrong."

"Anyway, were there other letter writing suspects?"

"Yes, a few, mainly schoolboys from Walsall Grammar School."

"Who?"

"Fred Wynne, Wilfred Greatorex, and a boy called Quibell, whose first name I forget."

"Any adults that you know of?"

"Well, Jack Hart, I suppose."

"That's a new name."

"Not to me, it isn't. He's the local butcher."

"Butcher? Then he would have less concern than most about slaughtering animals. Is there any reason why he might target George Edalji?"

Martin Newlove nodded. "Yes. Edalji brought a legal suit against him for defamation of character."

"For himself?"

"No. On behalf of a client. And it cost Hart a pretty penny, I can tell you. But that was a few years before they arrested Edalji and long after the earlier letters."

"But it's the first decent motive I've heard. It's a pity I don't have time to visit him."

"He wouldn't tell you anything."

"Still, I wonder if Sir Arthur considered him as a suspect?"

"I don't know. He didn't take me into his confidence."

"What do you think, Martin? Have you formed any conclusions of your own?"

"None worth pursuing. My work has taken me away from the parish over the years, and I've lost touch with those who might be in the know."

"Such as?"

"Sergeant Upton, for one. He played a part in the earlier years."

"So I hear. He arrested the servant girl."

"I know; a course of action he came to regret."

"Did he say as much?"

Newlove nodded. "Upton said he was too quick to believe the worst of her and in hindsight, he made the wrong decision."

"Interesting. Where is Upton now?"

"I'm not sure. He left the parish five or six years ago."

"Around the same time as Royden Sharp?"

"Probably. Why?"

"No reason. I'd like to have interviewed Upton. But Sharp and Hart are still in Great Wyrley. I must pay another visit."

"One for the road?" asked Martin.

Lawrence shook his head. "No. It's high time I left. You've been very helpful. Thank you. Perhaps we'll meet again."

"You never know," said Newlove as Lawrence made for the door.

Lawrence glanced at his watch as he left The Royal Oak. It was still light, and the rain had petered away, leaving the smell of damp earth behind. After a ten-minute stroll, Lawrence was back near the churchyard and relieved when he spotted his car, knowing that he would soon begin his return journey to Malvern. But his relief was short-lived. The vehicle seemed to be listing to the right. And as he reached it, he saw why. There would be no warm bed or welcome home that night. Someone had destroyed both tyres on the right-hand side.

Chapter Twenty-Two

A DISQUIETING RETURN

Wednesday, August 23, 1910

LAWRENCE APPROACHED Lower Malvern at a snail's pace, limping along on two hastily patched tyres courtesy of a local Wyrley garage earlier that morning. He had returned to the public house as soon as he noticed the damage to his car. Though sympathetic, Martin Newlove could not offer any practical help except to convey that the garage would open early the next day. With few other options, Lawrence had taken a bed for the night at The Royal Oak for an elevated price and had spent sleepless hours fretting that Violet would not know why he hadn't come home. Not that she was a worrier. Violet would pragmatically ponder the matter and settle on the least alarming reason for his absence. She would spare a passing thought to his welfare but would sleep soundly, nonetheless.

Lawrence had tossed and turned all night before leaving for the garage long before it opened. The repair, such as it was, had been quick and adequate for the journey. All that remained was for him to organise two new tyres when he returned to Malvern.

His mood had lightened as his journey went by, even though he had gone almost a day without a proper meal. After greeting Violet, he planned to treat himself to a cooked breakfast with all the trimmings. With luck, Aurora would have one ready to go. But as he drove closer to the cottage, a knot of anxiety gripped him. Already on edge, Lawrence's intuition was on high alert. Someone had gone to great lengths to damage his vehicle, and he was clearly unwelcome in Great Wyrley. It was hardly surprising as the populace had been through enough. If word of his clumsy investigation got out, it had the potential to cause upset. And he had hardly been discreet. But the fear gripping his insides was more than that. He may not be the most logical detective, but Lawrence had a well-honed instinct, and he listened. Every nerve in his body screamed of a looming problem.

He pulled up outside the cottage to find both windows shut against the early morning sun. He heard no murmur of conversation, no sound of life. Lawrence strode up the pathway and wrenched the door handle to find it unmoving, the door locked against the world. He slid his hand under the doormat where Aurora kept the spare key and let himself inside. Lawrence called for Violet but heard no reply, so he ran upstairs, taking them two at a time. The bedclothes lay undisturbed in both Violet's and Aurora's bedrooms. With a thumping heart, Lawrence returned downstairs and into the kitchen, where he spotted a hastily scribbled note in the middle of the table. He tore it open and read a short sentence – *Wait for me. I'll return as soon as I can. Violet.*

Lawrence slumped onto a chair, his mind a mess of

conflicting thoughts as he considered the abrupt message Violet must have written in a hurry. There was no warmth to it, and he wondered if she were angry at his failure to return when scheduled. If so, it was entirely understandable. After all, they were there to protect Aurora, and he had gone swanning off on another adventure to prove a point. On the other hand, Violet might have popped out for milk or other necessary provisions; hopefully, a nice piece of back bacon and a pork sausage. His stomach responded to his imagination with a loud gurgle. Shopping was all well and good but he was hungry now and could not wait another minute. He opened the pantry and hacked off a large slice of bread before spotting a pot of dripping on the marble slab. Slathering it across the bread in a thick layer, Lawrence dug in and soon felt better and more able to face the world. Five minutes passed, and then ten. He ate another slice of bread and made himself a cup of tea. Another half an hour passed, so he took a book and sat on an old iron chair in the garden, constantly fighting the urge to check his watch. He lost the battle an hour later and began pacing the living room, torn between Violet's instruction to stay put and his need to go anywhere that made him feel like he had a purpose.

Finally, after a three-hour wait that felt like an eternity, the door opened, and Violet stepped inside.

Chapter Twenty-Three

THE ACCIDENT

"ARE you a sight for sore eyes? "Lawrence said, striding towards Violet and wrapping her in his arms.

He nuzzled into her hair, relief coursing through him before he realised something was wrong. Violet hadn't responded to him, her body stiff and affectionless. Lawrence stepped back and gazed at her. "What's up, old girl?" he asked, but the words trailed away as he regarded her pale face and red-rimmed eyes.

Violet shook her head wordlessly.

"Sit down," said Lawrence, pulling out a kitchen chair and taking charge. He pushed Violet gently on the shoulders, and she sat down with her hands clasped over her mouth.

Lawrence planted a gentle kiss on her head, then busied himself on the range, saying nothing as he brewed a pot of tea. He did not speak again until he had poured a cup of the steaming liquid and placed it into her hand.

"Drink up," he said.

Violet obeyed, gently sipping while trying to steady the china cup with trembling hands.

"Have you eaten?"

Violet shook her head. Lawrence prepared another slice of bread and dripping and placed it next to Violet.

"I couldn't," she said.

"You must," Lawrence insisted as he cut the slice into quarters and offered the plate again.

Violet sighed and took a piece, nibbling it with little enthusiasm.

Lawrence waited until she had finished. "What happened?" he asked.

Violet closed her eyes as she tried to compose herself. "I shouldn't be here. We must return to Cheltenham right away."

"What's wrong? Is Daisy ill?"

"No. Not Daisy. Oh, Lawrence. This last day has been awful; the worst possible experience."

"Where have you been, and where is Aurora?"

"In Cheltenham?"

"Good Lord. How shocking. She's avoided anywhere she might be recognised."

"It was the lesser of two evils. She had a choice between Cheltenham General and Worcester Hospital, and Aurora thought Worcester would be more dangerous."

"A hospital! Why?"

"Because Worcester is closer to Malvern. Crossley might not immediately think of Cheltenham, although I'm sure it won't take long before he does."

"Slow down, Violet. You're not making any sense."

Violet inhaled and squeezed her eyes shut again, counting under her breath as she calmed herself. Snapping her eyes open, she drained the rest of her tea. "That's better," she said. "I'm sorry. I've been travelling on a bus since dawn, trying to think my way out of this awful situation."

"Start from the beginning," said Lawrence.

Violet nodded. "Aurora and I walked Luna to the school yesterday, as we have done for the last few days."

"Isn't it shut?"

"For lessons, yes. But they have opened for other activities and Luna enjoys them. We left the house and took our usual route along the road. But something wasn't right. I noticed a large black automobile when I left the cottage. It followed slowly behind as we walked along the road. At first, I thought the driver might be lost, and sure enough, he slowed down to ask for directions. He wore goggles and a leather motoring helmet, which should have given us pause for thought. But something about him seemed familiar even though I could hardly see his face. I tried to direct him but didn't recognise his intended destination. Aurora did, and she approached the car with Luna. Well, Lawrence. Something dreadful happened."

"What?"

"The driver opened the car door as if trying to get closer to hear her directions. Suddenly, without warning, he grabbed little Luna by the arm and pulled her into the car. Then he slammed the door shut and accelerated away. Aurora and I ran up the road behind him. Luna screamed and wriggled free. She struggled into the back seat and managed to open the door, but her leg got caught as she tried to escape. She fell and hit her head and rolled into the road."

"Oh my God! Is she alright?"

Violet licked her lips and tried to compose herself. "Luna has a concussion and a broken hip. The car mangled her poor little leg, and they don't know if she will walk again."

"That's dreadful news." Lawrence sat heavily on a chair next to his wife. "But she's alive?"

Violet nodded.

"And awake?"

"Yes. That's why I felt I could leave. But Lawrence, Luna can't remember anything."

"That's just as well."

"I don't mean about the accident. She can't remember who she is or anything about her life. Luna can't even recognise her own mother. Aurora is devastated."

"We should be there with her."

"I know. I only came to find you and pack our bags. Aurora's too. She won't be returning to Malvern."

"No. Of course not. It isn't safe. Well, Aurora must stay at our house."

"I don't think she will."

"At least until Luna has recovered."

"Aurora thinks she's a sitting duck. If Luna weren't so poorly, she'd have taken off immediately."

"Has she told Michael?"

"No. And there isn't much chance of it either. Look, we can't sit around talking about this. Pack up the cottage while I visit the letting agent and settle the rent. Our time in Malvern is well and truly over."

Chapter Twenty-Four

CHELTENHAM GENERAL HOSPITAL

Thursday, August 24, 1910

SETTLING Aurora's affairs had taken longer than expected. Violet had hoped to be back in Cheltenham within the day, but by the time they returned, it was after ten in the evening and too late to visit the hospital. Vera and Daisy were in bed when they arrived. They quietly unlocked their front door and tiptoed in, but the ever-alert Vera Ponsonby had heard the stairs squeak beneath their weight as they climbed towards the bedroom. She met them on the first-floor landing, where they exchanged whispered explanations to avoid waking Daisy. Vera sprang into action and helped them unpack the car. They stood outside in the chill night air, describing the horrific attack. Vera bristled with rage at Luna's suffering and insisted on waking at dawn the next day to telephone Cora Cream. Unsure what lay ahead and with Aurora a flight risk, Lawrence agreed that more hands could only help. They finally got to bed after midnight and woke the next morning to a knock on the door and a half-hearted greeting from Daisy.

Vera took Daisy to school while Lawrence and Violet headed for the hospital. The matron, a stickler for the rules, would only allow them inside once breakfast was finished and the ward spotlessly tidy. So, they waited in the foyer for half an hour, Lawrence pacing in frustration.

A good night's sleep had settled Violet, who was back to her usual calm demeanour. While Lawrence huffed as he strode in ever-decreasing circles, Violet scribbled notes in her book as she planned possible strategies for Aurora's future safety. By the time the doors opened for visiting, Violet was confident in at least one of her plans.

They walked down the corridor, Violet leading the way and arrived at Luna's ward, where she lay in a bed halfway down on the left-hand side, her mother's head resting on the covers where she had fallen asleep.

Violet advanced towards Aurora and gently shook her awake. Aurora opened weary eyes, rubbing them as she tried to remember where she was. Her eyes widened as she reached for her sleeping daughter, and she sighed with relief at the gentle rise and fall of Luna's chest.

"Have you eaten?" asked Violet.

"Yes. They gave me something earlier. I must have fallen asleep afterwards. I've been awake all night and tried so hard not to drop off in case that awful man attacked Luna again. But I couldn't help it. I'm exhausted."

"You must rest," said Violet. "You'll be no good to Luna if you're too tired to function."

"It's only a matter of time until he follows me here."

"Who?" asked Lawrence.

"Felix Crossley." Aurora's eyes filled with tears, but she stared at Lawrence with a steely determination.

"How do you know it was him?"

"Who else could it have been? Crossley killed Frank because of me."

"You don't know that," said Violet, patting her shoulder.

Aurora shrugged Violet's hand away. "What other explanation could there be? He must have known I was in Malvern but could not find me. How many people must die before Crossley leaves me alone? We'll never be safe anywhere."

"You will, I promise," said Violet optimistically. "I spent last night strategising."

"It's pointless. If we're not safe in a provincial town, then we're not safe anywhere."

"Please let us help you," said Lawrence.

"It's not worth the risk. Just look at Luna. Look at her. She'll never be the same again."

Lawrence watched the sleeping child, her innocent face swathed in bandages. "What's her prognosis?" he asked.

Aurora's eyes filled with tears again. "Luna will live," she said, "which is something. And they've set her leg and hip as best they can. But she will be in a wheelchair for a long time and may never walk again."

"That's truly awful," Lawrence replied, his voice choked with empathy. "I'm very sorry. Thank God she's alive, and you still have your child."

"I don't. She doesn't recognise me."

Violet reached for a jug, poured a glass of water, and handed it to Aurora. "I thought her memory might return after a good night's sleep."

"Well, it hasn't. Luna doesn't know me from the ward nurse," said Aurora bitterly.

"Most patients recover from amnesia eventually," said Lawrence.

"I hope she doesn't," said Aurora, her eyes distant and sad. "It would be better for Luna if her memory never returned."

"You don't mean that," said Violet.

"I do."

The bed curtain twitched open, and a cheery nurse appeared. "Doctor's on his way."

"You'd better go," said Aurora. "They won't appreciate too many people at the bedside."

"We'll come back," promised Violet. "You won't be alone for long."

"As you wish."

Lawrence and Violet left the ward and returned to the foyer, where they purchased two cups of tea from a jolly, shiny-faced woman standing behind a large urn. Lawrence grimaced as he sipped the heavily stewed tea with barely a dash of milk, but anything was a welcome distraction from his inadequately filled stomach.

"Aurora has changed, and not for the better," he said as they returned to the ward and sat outside while waiting for the doctor to finish.

"What do you mean?"

"When we first met her, she was timid and afraid of her own shadow."

"Having a child changes you."

"Like a mother tiger?"

Violet nodded. "What do you expect? The attack on Luna was truly shocking. The man is a maniac. No wonder Aurora is too frightened to close her eyes."

"But she seemed hostile to us, Violet. Aurora is distant and bitter."

"I'm not surprised. She's traumatised and probably blames us for forcing her from the workhouse."

Lawrence sighed. "I regret it now. We interfered, and it almost cost Luna her life."

"You're wrong. If we found them in the workhouse, then Crossley could have too."

"But he didn't. We shouldn't have left Aurora in Malvern knowing we have connections there."

"It's nothing to do with us."

"Come now. You've known Frank for years, and so has Crossley. Frank regularly holidays in Malvern."

"Hindsight is a wonderful thing, Lawrence. But we need to stay positive."

"I doubt Aurora will let us help this time, Violet. She's lost faith."

"The poor girl is upset. She's barely slept and is worried sick."

They looked up as the doctor left the ward. He breezed past as Lawrence deposited his empty teacup on a nearby radiator.

"Let's see if we can persuade Aurora to take a break," said Violet as they opened the ward door. "Perhaps she'll let us watch Luna while she rests."

Lawrence pulled Violet back as they approached the bedside. Aurora was leaning into her daughter, clutching her hand as if she would never let her go.

They watched for a moment, the waves of maternal love almost tangible.

"Come on," whispered Violet.

Lawrence approached Aurora. "What did the doctor say?"

She sighed and shook her head. "The same thing as yesterday."

"No improvement?"

"Not with Luna's memory. Her physical injuries may improve with time, but he couldn't say when."

"Why don't you take a rest?" asked Violet. "We'll sit with Luna."

"No. I want to make the most of our time together."

Violet laughed nervously. "Luna has turned the corner, hasn't she? You'll have plenty of opportunities to visit, and it won't be long before she can leave the hospital."

"Not if Crossley gets his hands on her."

"We won't let him," said Lawrence.

Aurora turned away and stroked her daughter's hand. She didn't speak for a long time, then composed herself. "There's only one way to help Luna, but I'll need your support," said Aurora, her voice trembling with the weight of the decision she was about to make.

"Anything. Just tell us what you need," Lawrence replied, his voice steady and calm.

Aurora choked back a sob, her lips quivering as she fought to get the words out. "The only way I can keep my darling daughter safe... is to give her up."

Chapter Twenty-Five

SWEET SORROW

Friday, August 25, 1910

LAWRENCE AND VIOLET sat alone in their drawing room with heavy hearts, pondering the circumstances that had brought them to the horrible course of action being considered.

"Thank goodness we don't need to worry about Daisy," said Lawrence as Violet frenziedly sketched to take her mind off the looming ordeal. Daisy had been in good spirits when she returned and remained so until leaving that morning. Though still on summer holidays, Daisy had spent almost as much time at school as she had out of it. And they were thankful their daughter had not detected the melancholic atmosphere pervading the house.

"Do you think she knows?" asked Lawrence, unnecessarily stirring his tea for the umpteenth time.

"No, dear. Daisy is oblivious. You know how teenagers are – only interested in themselves."

"She barely speaks to me now," said Lawrence.

"Don't take it personally. Daisy would rather be with her friends. Heather Mullins is at a loose end since her folks returned to India. It's a shame that they haven't sent for her. I couldn't bear the thought of Daisy languishing alone at school while all the other girls went home. I'm sure her parents have their reasons, but I'm proud of Daisy for keeping her company."

"Surely Heather isn't the only girl still left at school?"

"I doubt it. But Daisy doesn't say very much about the others. It's Heather this, Heather that, at the moment."

"Like a schoolgirl crush?"

"In a manner of speaking. We're lucky they are so friendly. I'd hate to think of Daisy worrying about the situation here."

"Have you discussed it with her?"

"No. Have you?"

"No."

Lawrence sighed and stirred moodily, rattling the spoon on the china cup.

"Oh, please stop," snapped Violet. "Things are bad enough."

"Aurora won't go through with it, will she?" asked Lawrence, his voice uncertain.

Violet shrugged. "I think she might. She's desperate."

"But what about Michael?"

"I wish I knew what to do for the best. Part of me thinks I should warn him. But he might tell Francis. You haven't tried to contact Michael, have you?"

"Not for a while. And it was like speaking with a stranger. Michael is angry with us, and I understand why. But he has changed every bit as much as Aurora. I expect it's from his brother's baleful influence."

"I'm surprised Francis is still alive," said Violet. "I had

hoped that nature would take its course. Then Aurora and Luna could go home."

"That will never happen. Aurora thinks Crossley would find them there, whether Francis helps him or not."

"Yet Michael allows Francis to stay. He loves his family, and this situation can't be easy. The solution is obvious to us. Why can't Michael see it?" asked Violet, her voice heavy with regret.

"He's behaving like a bloody fool," snapped Lawrence. "I can't rustle up any sympathy."

"I know. But Michael is in a terrible position. Life isn't black and white."

"It is for me."

Violet shook her head in exasperation. Though Lawrence was intuitive and Violet logical, she still operated in shades of grey. Lawrence tended towards fixed opinions that rarely changed, and Violet found his intransigence wearing at times.

"I'll pour you another," said Violet, tipping the teapot into Lawrence's cup before he could protest. She stirred the brew and removed the teaspoon a safe distance away.

Lawrence sipped his drink." It's lukewarm," he grumbled.

"Just drink it."

Lawrence took the cup and walked towards the large sash window overlooking Cambray Church. "It looks like they're preparing for a wedding," he said, watching two young girls trimming the cast-iron railings with flowers and bows.

"Life goes on," murmured Violet.

Lawrence turned away. The black dog was on the prowl and lowering his mood. He was coping with life's difficulties, but the sight of people preparing for festivities was creating an uneasy combination of sadness and guilt. Lawrence drew the heavy velvet drapes to block the view. It was not the right time to watch a joyful event.

"Now it's dark," sighed Violet, pushing her sketch pad to one side. She rose and lit the gas mantle.

Lawrence glanced at his watch. "Where the hell are they?" he snapped.

Violet glared. "That's not helping. Calm down."

"Sorry. I want to get this over with."

"We all do. Perhaps the train was late?"

"That's all we need."

"You can trust Vera. She will collect Cora, and they will arrive as soon as possible."

"But they should have been here twenty minutes ago. Oh, Lord... what if Aurora has taken off? That might have caused the delay."

"Whatever has got into you, Lawrence? Aurora has asked for our help. And she's hardly likely to flee with Luna still in hospital."

"Well, something has held them up."

"Just be patient."

Lawrence strode towards the uncurtained side window, neatly avoiding the view over the church. "Hold on. There's a vehicle idling outside. Perhaps they are here, after all."

"Good. Now sit down and stop fidgeting."

By the time Vera Ponsonby let herself in and reached the drawing room, Lawrence was casually sitting in his favourite chair reading a newspaper.

"Hello, Vera, lovely to see you, Cora," said Violet. She uttered nothing to Aurora, who trailed behind the two older ladies but waited until they passed and enveloped her in a bear hug. Aurora tensed and stepped back. Violet wordlessly squeezed her hands, gazing into Aurora's pale face and red-rimmed eyes. Aurora gave a half smile that swiftly vanished.

"Sit down, ladies," said Lawrence as a pall of gloom settled over the room.

"Don't be so stuffy," said Cora. "Come here." She breezed towards him and pecked his cheek. "Lovely to see you again," she said.

Lawrence tried to ignore the creeping blush settling over his face. "You too," he replied awkwardly.

"This is all very nice, but can we get to it," said Aurora.

"Of course. Would you like some tea first?" said Violet, unoffended by Aurora's abruptness.

"Not for me. I need to get this over with before I change my mind." Aurora stared distantly through pain-filled eyes, her face heavy with stifled emotion. But her voice held firm, her intentions steadfast.

"How can we help?" asked Lawrence.

"I must make a plan. Let me tell you what I want to do, and you can suggest how best to achieve it."

"Go on," said Lawrence.

"I'm sending Luna away. She's still suffering from amnesia and doesn't know me. If we part, she'll suffer no distress, and there will never be a better time than this."

"You can't," said Violet.

"I must. There is no other way."

"But we will do anything. Are you sure we can't help?"

"Certain," said Aurora. "I owe it to my daughter. Crossley will find me no matter where I go. But he's never seen Luna. He won't recognise her without me. She can start a new life under a new name where she will be safe. Can it be done?"

Vera Ponsonby gazed towards Cora as if seeking assurance. "Theoretically, yes."

"I could speak to Isabel. She could find a foster parent," said Cora.

"No. Nothing official. There would be paperwork and signatures; it might lead back to me."

"I agree," said Lawrence. "This must be informal. But who would you trust to have Luna?"

Aurora lowered her eyes. "That's the problem. I have few friends, but I couldn't ask them even if I did. Crossley could use them to find me. That's the flaw in my plan and the problem I hoped you would help me with."

"I know people, good people," said Violet. "My friend in Swaffham might take Luna in."

"No. Crossley might find her through you."

"We could have Luna," said Lawrence.

"Of course," Violet replied. "I'm glad you said that. I considered it myself."

Aurora sighed. "I know you mean well, and I trust you to do your utmost to protect Luna. But Crossley would find you in a heartbeat. It wouldn't work, however well-intentioned."

"And I'm not much use now that I'm getting married," said Cora. I mean, I'd take her if it weren't for Andrew. But he's a high-flying politician with children from a previous marriage. He's already told me he doesn't want more children, which suits me down to the ground. Sorry, I didn't mean to sound harsh or unmaternal. It's a pity as nobody knows we are friends, and Crossley couldn't easily find me."

"Don't be silly. Have you forgotten that you infiltrated The Order?" asked Vera.

"I wore a mask, which I didn't remove."

"Not that it matters if you can't take Luna anyway," said Lawrence. "We should consult Isabel Smith."

"There is another way," said Vera Ponsonby, uncrossing her trousered legs and leaning forward.

"What?" asked Violet.

"Cora and I are closing the agency when she marries in the autumn. And things have already quietened down. Could you manage on your own for the last few months, my dear?"

Cora nodded. "I suppose so."

"Good. I have been wondering what to do with myself when we finish. My father died when I was very young. I'm an only child, and I lost my mother last year. I'll be at a loose end when the agency closes. I could take Luna."

"Could you, really?" Aurora chewed her lip as she scrutinised the woman before her.

"Well, yes. If you want me to."

"It's a big decision," said Lawrence. "You'd put Luna in danger if you saw anyone from your past life."

"I have very few relatives left."

"What about your friends?" asked Cora.

"I'll tell them I'm emigrating."

"But you won't be able to write to them, or they'd discover where you live. It would mean giving up everything," said Violet.

"Including us." Cora edged towards Vera on the settee. "You couldn't attend the wedding, and I'd never see you again. I'm starting a new life, and you'd be giving up your old one."

"I understand the risks and how it must be."

"But, Vera," said Lawrence, pacing towards her, "you must think this through. We've known each other for many years, and I never considered you the maternal kind."

"With good reason," said Vera. "I never expected to have a child."

"How do you know you could give Luna what she needs?"

Vera paused; her brow furrowed as if she were processing the question. "How does anybody?" she replied.

"Luna has only known love and kindness," said Aurora. "Even while we were in the workhouse. It's important that she feels cared for and wanted."

Vera chewed her lip. "I don't know what to say to reassure you. I have no child-rearing experience, and my parents were rather remote and not given to excessive displays of affection. But I grew up with my cousins, and we all got along. I think I can give Luna what she needs. Besides, she must have felt neglected in the workhouse. You can't have been with her all the time. One does what one must when protecting a child, and I would do my best to meet her needs."

"You're right," sighed Aurora. "I tried to keep Luna with me as much as possible in the workhouse, but we slept apart sometimes. Though young, she accepted the situation. But this would be forever."

Vera shrugged. "Luna has amnesia. She won't know any better until her memory returns."

"If it ever does," said Violet.

"Exactly. I can give her as good a life as anyone else. And frankly, Aurora. You have few options."

"And," said Cora, brightly. "You can take Luna from Vera when things are back to normal. A more formal arrangement might make that impossible."

Aurora shook her head. "I told you; this is a permanent decision unless Crossley dies."

"Which he might," continued Cora, ever the optimist.

"I must assume he won't. Vera, you're right. You've been good to me and kind to Luna. We have no known connection, and Crossley is unlikely to find you. But if you agree to this, we must never meet again."

"I understand."

"There's just one thing," said Cora.

"What is it?" Vera frowned.

"How will you ever afford it?"

"Oh." Vera and Aurora exchanged glances.

"I'll take care of that," said Lawrence.

"I can't ask that of you," Aurora replied.

"You're not. I'm offering. I have the means to settle a generous sum for Luna's upkeep. Please accept it. I can't provide a monthly allowance in case Crossley traces it back to me. But I will pay a capital sum into your account, Vera. Move it to another and invest it wisely. It will last until Luna reaches her majority."

"I'm very grateful," said Aurora.

"It's the least I can do."

"Then that's settled," said Vera. "The plan is in place."

"What will you do now?" asked Aurora.

"Return to London and pack my belongings. I'll rent a property and collect Luna as soon as you are ready."

Aurora drew a deep, shaky breath. "I've said my good-byes to Luna and won't return to the hospital. Please don't leave her alone for too long. The doctor has agreed to discharge her."

Vera chewed her lip. "I need to return to London for my things."

"I'll pack them and send them on," said Cora.

"No. You can't have direct contact from this moment forward," snapped Aurora. "I thought you understood."

Cora nodded. "Then I'll take your possessions to the left luggage office at Kings Cross Station. I'll use box number one three six. Remember that. You can arrange for their collection."

"I will," murmured Vera.

Violet turned towards Aurora. "And what will you do?"

"Go home," said Aurora.

"Back to Netherwood?" exclaimed Lawrence.

Aurora nodded.

"You'll be putting yourself in grave danger."

"It doesn't matter," said Aurora, her lips trembling. "I don't care what happens to me. I have just given Michael's daughter away. The least I can do is tell him to his face."

Violet closed her eyes, waiting for the pricking tears to pass before opening them again. "What about Francis? What about Crossley?"

"I don't know or care," said Aurora. "I have brought this danger to Michael's door. He isn't himself and hasn't been for a while. There is more going on than we know. I will go to my husband and make him understand the danger he is in."

"Now?" asked Lawrence.

"Yes, immediately. The cab is waiting outside with my luggage. I will call another one for Vera when I get to the station."

"Will we see you again?" asked Lawrence.

"If you come to Netherwood, although I would advise you not to."

Lawrence took Aurora's hand and pressed it to his lips. "Be safe," he said.

Violet embraced her in a hug. "I will call you every day."

"Goodbye, ladies," said Aurora, untangling herself. She walked through the door without a backward glance and was gone.

Lawrence approached the window as Aurora entered the vehicle. She wiped her eyes with a lace-gloved hand. Moments later, the car sped away.

"Are you sure about this?" asked Cora Cream as Vera rose and paced towards the window, her brows knitted, and square-jawed face drained of colour.

"Not really. But someone must, and I am in the best position."

"You can always change your mind."

"No. It is my duty. I will care for Luna."

They waited silently, not knowing what to say as a wall clock ticked sonorously in the background. Not a word, not even a cough, nothing but Lawrence's nails tapping against the side table until the thrum of an engine announced the second vehicle's arrival.

Vera stooped and collected her handbag from the floor. "Well, I'll be off to the hospital. It was nice knowing you." She offered a hand to Lawrence and again to Violet, her features set stoically.

"I don't know what to say," said Violet.

"Then don't. Cora. Have a wonderful marriage. I'll be thinking of you."

Cora Cream flung her arms around her friend and planted a kiss on her cheek. She tried to smile, but for once, her happy-go-lucky demeanour deserted her, and tears spilt down her face.

"Don't blub, dear," said Vera. "This is the right thing to do."

"I'll miss you forever."

"Likewise," said Vera, turning her back as she walked away.

Chapter Twenty-Six

THE INVESTIGATION CONTINUES

Monday, August 28, 1910

"WHERE IS AUNTIE VERA?" asked Daisy as she perched on the arm of the chair, swinging her legs backwards and forwards.

Violet gazed at Lawrence as he closed his notebook and furtively slipped it into his jacket pocket.

"What are you doing?" asked Violet.

"Nothing, dear."

"Why are you ignoring me? Have I become invisible? Where is Auntie Vera?" repeated Daisy.

"She's gone back to London," said Lawrence.

"When?"

"On Friday."

"You might have told me."

"What's the point? It's taken you two days to notice."

Daisy huffed. "She promised we'd go to the theatre. So much for that."

"I'll take you," said Violet.

"Don't bother. I'm too busy this week and won't have any time until school starts."

"Really? Why?"

"Heather asked if I could board for a while. She's fed up with being alone at night. The other girls don't speak to her. They're all in different years or too stuck up to bother. I said I would keep her company."

Lawrence looked up. "You do realise that staying at school costs money?"

Daisy shrugged. "I've already said yes."

"Well, you can unsay it."

"Don't you care that Heather will be alone?"

"Probably more than her parents do."

"Daddy, you are so unkind and unfeeling."

"Your father has a point," said Violet. "And anyway, the teachers might refuse you."

"Miss Faithfull has already agreed," said Daisy triumphantly.

"Sorry, sweetheart. It's not the right time," said Violet.

"Mummy, you always take Daddy's side."

"Hang on a minute," said Lawrence, fingering the note-book through his jacket lining. "How long would you be boarding for?"

"A little less than two weeks."

"Hmmm. Perhaps we've been a little harsh. It might be nice for your friend to have some company."

Violet looked up and scowled. "Not right now, Lawrence, given the circumstances."

"But the school caters for royalty. It has an excellent security system, more so than our home."

"Why does that matter?" asked Daisy.

"Never mind," replied Violet, unusually stuck for an answer.

"Is it because Daddy is rich?"

"If you like," said Lawrence. "But it's nice of you to be so kind to Heather. Why don't we follow Daisy's plan and let her be with her friend?"

"I'm not keen."

"Please, Mummy. Just this once?"

Violet sighed. "Very well, dear."

"Super," said Daisy. "I'll get packing. Can you drive me up there before lunch?"

"Of course, my little flower," said Lawrence.

Daisy hugged him and kissed her mother on the cheek before rushing from the room.

"What was all that about?" asked Violet suspiciously.

"How lovely to see our daughter so happy. Goodness me, but it's been a while since Daisy me showed any affection."

"That's not what I meant. Why did you suddenly relent and let her go?"

"It's good for her to have a little independence."

"But it isn't safe."

"At the risk of repeating myself, security at the Ladies College is top-notch."

"I remember a time when you felt otherwise."

"That was before my little chat with the headmistress last year."

"Regardless, you never do anything without a reason."

"I'm simply making our little girl happy."

"Lawrence." Violet stared into his eyes, determined to get to the truth.

"Alright. The last few days have been hell. Aurora's heading into certain danger, and we'll never see Vera again. I'm going mad confined to these four walls. I want to get out and do something."

"Such as?"

"Go back to Great Wyrley and try to make some progress with the case."

"No, Lawrence. We already know that someone means you harm."

"Not me. My car. And it only suffered a couple of deflated tyres."

"Someone slashed them with a knife. It's hardly trivial."

"Perhaps, but that might mean I'm on track and have ruffled some feathers. A bit more work, and I might root the culprit out."

"You were supposed to be discreet."

"Easier said than done. But whatever I did has paid dividends. And the letter writer can't be poor old George Edalji, who is currently living in London."

"Just as Sir Arthur said. I still can't see the point in you continuing this farce when Mr Conan Doyle has already secured his release."

Lawrence scowled. "You know why. Arthur's rotten circumstantial case is pure speculation."

"And for yours to be any better, you would need to catch the perpetrator in the act, which is unlikely five years down the line."

"Seven, actually. But we've investigated crimes decades older than that. Come on, Violet. Where's your spirit of adventure?"

"Now is not the time for levity."

"I know, Vi, but what will we do if we stay here other than rattle around the house feeling depressed?"

Violet sighed. "I'm keeping tabs on Aurora. I rang her last night and have promised to call every day. I'm so worried about her."

"With good reason, though I'm surprised she has taken your calls."

"I think she is afraid. It's better if I stay here so I can keep in touch."

"I expect there are telephones in Wyrley," said Lawrence.

"I suppose so."

"Then let's drop Daisy at the school and head off north. You never know, it might cheer us up a bit."

Chapter Twenty-Seven

THE VILLAGE BUTCHER

"OH DEAR," said Violet, standing outside a dilapidated red brick building on Walsall Road while looking at a paint-chipped sign marked 'Guest House'.

"Cheer up," said Lawrence. "It may be nicer inside."

"I'd prefer a hotel. Where did you stay?"

"At The Royal Oak," said Lawrence. "Trust me when I tell you this will be more comfortable."

"Why?"

"Because there are no guest rooms at The Royal Oak. I slept on an old camp bed in a windowless boxroom with mice in the wall."

"I wouldn't want that."

"Exactly."

"Although it might come to it if they don't take us here."

"Let's be optimistic. I'll see if someone's around."

Lawrence strode to the red-painted door and rapped the door knocker. Flecks of paint floated gently to the ground.

They waited for a moment before hearing a shuffling sound coming from within. The door opened to reveal a woman of robust proportions wearing an oversized pair of slippers.

"Good afternoon. Do you have a room?" asked Lawrence.

"I do, sir. Two if you like."

"One is ample."

"One night or two?" she continued.

"Just the one, for now."

"But maybe two?"

"Perhaps."

The woman held out her hand. "Money first," she said. "You don't look the type to run off without paying, but it wouldn't be the first time."

"How much?"

The woman named her price, and Lawrence handed over payment, adding a few small coins for good measure. She nodded and slipped them into her pocket. "Follow me," she said, leading them upstairs.

Lawrence had been right. Unlike its exterior, the house was clean and tidy, with recently painted walls. Though small and minimally furnished, their room was pleasant, though the view over Walsall Road left Lawrence feeling exposed and a little depressed.

"I'm hungry," said Violet as they packed their few possessions into the wardrobe.

"As ever."

"Where shall we eat?"

"Not the pub."

"Then where?"

"Stay here. I'll be back in a moment."

Lawrence vanished from sight and reappeared moments later, wearing a smug expression. "How do lamb chops, potatoes and peas sound?"

"Perfect," said Violet.

"Right. Let's rest for half an hour, and the lady of the house will serve us in the dining room."

An hour later, replete and having gleaned some helpful information from Mrs Edna Mallet, who turned out to be an excellent cook, they made their way towards The Royal Oak.

"I don't know how you do it," said Violet admiringly. "Edna wouldn't shut up. Getting people to talk is usually my forte."

"It was the extra change I gave her," said Lawrence. "Money talks. She'll be lining us up for another night's stay."

"I hope that won't be necessary."

"Oh, I don't know. I want to tie this up, and I still think I might."

"I can't understand why this case is such a draw. It's not as if anyone has died. So far, we've learned of some rather nasty anonymous letters and an unfortunate succession of slain livestock."

"And an innocent man imprisoned for three years while the crimes continued unabated with the lawmakers ignoring the inconvenient truth that he couldn't have done it."

"Yes, but if you think, as I do, that the livestock issue is completely separate, then did the crimes continue?"

"If you are asking if the letters kept coming, then yes," said Lawrence hesitantly. "Although they were in a different hand and style."

"You mean no, then. The original letters stopped in 1903."

"If you put it like that."

"It's all about detail. Now, what is the plan?"

"Let's catch up with Martin in The Royal Oak."

"Will he be there?"

"Hopefully. He said he's a regular visitor."

Violet glanced at her watch. "It's too early for a drink."

"Then let's take a stroll around the village first."

Lawrence took Violet's arm, and they wandered into the heart of Great Wyrley.

"It doesn't feel right," said Violet.

"The village? Well, it's not exactly picturesque."

"No, it's more than that. I'm getting the same feeling I had in Swaffham."

"I wouldn't know," said Lawrence curtly.

Violet ignored the pointed barb, referring to their years apart. "Like someone was watching me," she continued.

"They were."

"Exactly."

"Nobody knows we're here, Violet. Please don't worry. Try to think nice thoughts."

"What a wonderfully pleasant evening," said Violet sarcastically, but her mood lifted as they strode past a neatly tended lawn, inhaling the smell of cut grass. They crossed the road and took a narrow lane, passing a row of cottages where hollyhocks and foxgloves spilt across a low brick wall, and eventually found themselves back on the Walsall Road.

"Ah, look," said Lawrence, pointing to a sign.

"Fresh meat," read Violet.

"We must find our way back here tomorrow. I want to speak to the butcher."

"Why don't you knock on the door now?"

"He'll be closed at this time of day."

"Or not," said Violet, pointing to the window where a pair of hands gently moved a tray of offal from the display.

"Let's try," said Lawrence, advancing to the door.

He knocked, and a gruff-voiced man barked at them to enter.

Clad in a blood-streaked apron and reeking of an unsettling metallic odour, the butcher stood with a chunk of meat in one hand and a cleaver in the other. He slapped the joint onto a wood block and neatly cut it in two.

"What do you want?" he growled in a surprisingly high-pitched, Black Country accent.

"Are you Jack Hart?"

"I am. Who's asking?"

"Lawrence Harpham. Edna sent us down for a pound of kidneys."

"Edna Mallet?"

"Yes."

"Blimey. She got through that last lot quickly." He paused and stroked his chin, leaving a bloody mark. "Must be psychic, that one."

"Why?"

"Knowing I'd be open this late. If it weren't for that bloody fool, Bert, I'd be home by now."

Lawrence opened his mouth to speak, but Violet quietly prodded his side, a sign that he was about to overcomplicate his story. There was every chance that Hart would mention the encounter to Edna, who had not asked them to fetch kidneys or any other meat product.

"That steak looks nice and fresh," said Violet.

"That's because it is. Cut from a freshly slaughtered cow this morning."

"Do you run an abattoir?"

"Nothing so fancy. But if you're asking if I kill my livestock, then yes. And the meat inspectors gave me a clean bill of health last time they visited. Why are you interested?"

"I'm fussy about where I buy meat," said Violet. "But yours seems rather good."

The butcher grinned and flopped a bowl of kidneys

onto the scales, adding weights until they balanced. Then he smiled at Violet and added a few extra pieces.

"Why, thank you," said Violet.

"Give Edna my best," said Hart.

"We will after we've seen the reverend."

Jack Hart's face darkened. "Edalji?" he asked.

"Yes, why?"

"I'd stay away from that lot," he growled.

"Why?"

"Bloody foreigners."

"That's not a reason," said Violet, her eyes narrowing as she stood with her hands on her hips.

"Alright. Bloody lying foreigners."

This time, Lawrence flashed Violet a glare. Violet despised intolerance and might destroy their carefully contrived dialogue with a few ill-chosen words.

"I've met the reverend before, and I wasn't altogether sure if he was truthful," said Lawrence.

"He's shifty, like his son."

"I rather got that impression." Lawrence cast a wary glance towards Violet, whose cheeks were now burning with barely suppressed rage as he pretended to side with the butcher.

Jack Hart snorted. "If you want my advice, I'd stay away."

"I haven't met his son," said Lawrence. "Though I've heard a great deal about him."

"Haven't we all," said Hart, picking up the cleaver and slamming it into the wood block. It stuck there, quivering. "Bloody man," said Hart.

"Well, he brings out the worst in you," Lawrence observed.

"That's because that rotter Conan Doyle dragged me all the way to London to rat out Royden Sharp."

"Oh," said Lawrence, taken aback. "Do you know Sharp?"

"Barely. I don't know where Conan Doyle got his information from, but he was wrong. I couldn't help. Not even for a fat reward. The most I know about Royden Sharp is that he burned down old man Hatton's hayrick."

"Who?"

"Hatton. The local landowner. His son Christopher was a close friend of Horace Edalji. But what's it to do with you, anyway?"

"I'm just interested. And you seem passionate about your encounter with Conan Doyle. But if you couldn't help, then why go to London?"

"Captain Anson said I should."

"Anson? How did he know?"

"Because I told him. I telephoned the police as soon as Conan Doyle made the offer."

"Which was after George Edalji's arrest?"

"Of course. Conan Doyle was trying to get him freed, and he thought there was a plot between the police and some of us."

"Who?"

"Me, Fred Brookes, a couple of chaps called Thomas and Grinsell, and Royden Sharp, who he suspected of being the livestock killer and letter writer. He said it was my duty to break the plot and tell the others that they could turn King's evidence against Sharp."

"What utter nonsense."

"I'm telling the truth. Ask Anson."

"Sorry. I trust your word. I mean the concept of a plot between the police and the villagers is ludicrous."

"That's what I thought, so I called into the police station, and a day later, Captain Anson turned up in my shop. He said that any offer or reward would count as an inducement and affect the reliability of my statement."

"Yet he thought you should go to London?"

"Only to find out what Conan Doyle was up to. They'd been at loggerheads, much like me and that shady son of a street dog."

"You mean George Edalji?" asked Lawrence, trying to stay neutral.

"That's the one."

"I'll wait outside," said Violet in disgust as Jack Hart finished his tirade.

"I won't be long," Lawrence replied, watching her stomp towards the doorway, the tips of her ears an angry red.

"What's wrong with your missus?" asked Jack Hart.

"No patience," said Lawrence.

"She's probably thinking the better of your visit to old man Edalji."

"Who knows?" shrugged Lawrence. "Tell me, why do you dislike George Edalji so much?"

"He cost me a lot of money."

"Why?"

"He said I'd been speaking ill of someone. An alleged defamation case, which I didn't, at least not in the way he tried to make it."

"Did it go to court?"

"No, but I had to pay Edalji to get his client off my back."

"He acted for your accuser?"

"Exactly."

"But you didn't do it?"

Hart scratched his nose. "Not exactly. I don't want to

talk about it except to say that Edalji knew the case wasn't sound, but he hounded me anyway. And I paid up because it was affecting my reputation."

"Good for you," said Lawrence.

"Can we get off the subject?" Hart glanced at an old oak clock hanging perilously from the wall. "You should join your good wife," he said.

"I will. Just one more thing."

"What?"

"Did you see Conan Doyle in London?"

"I did. He was there with his brother, and guess who else turned up?"

"No idea?"

"George Edalji – as if that would change my mind."

"Awkward," said Lawrence.

"More for him than me."

"What did you tell Conan Doyle?"

"Nothing. What could I say? I told you, I barely knew Royden Sharp. Conan Doyle wanted to know about my friend Harry Green and one of his horses. He couldn't question Harry as he'd left for South Africa. So, I made a few general comments about the lad and left. I foolishly reported back to Anson, but I learned my lesson soon after. Apparently, Anson said I wasn't trustworthy, so I stayed away from the whole bloody lot of them after that."

"I don't blame you," said Lawrence. "Well, thank you for talking to me. I will be careful who I speak to."

"Good man," said Jack Hart.

Lawrence turned to leave.

"Hold on. Haven't you forgotten something?"

"Ah, yes. How kind," said Lawrence, reaching for a pound of unwanted kidneys.

Chapter Twenty-Eight

A TALE OF TWO COPPERS

"WHAT A REPULSIVE MAN," said Violet. "Full of prejudice and hatred. I couldn't stay in his shop a moment longer."

"But quite a good suspect, don't you think? Your friend Arthur summoned him to London."

"Perhaps as a candidate for the livestock slaying, but that man lacks the finesse to write poison pen letters."

"He'd be alright for some of the earlier ones. You've seen the newspaper clippings. A teenage boy could easily have written them."

"I wonder why the letters are so very different."

"Multiple authors, Violet. It's the only answer. And our butcher might have been one of them."

"I disagree," said Violet. "But let's move on. I don't want to run into Hart again. I might not be able to restrain myself."

"Good. I could murder a pint. Let's do it."

Violet cleared her throat as Lawrence linked his arm through hers. "I thought you'd gone off beer."

"Me? Goodness no. I could never. Joining the wine association doesn't change anything. Grapes and hops are different animals. And this is not the kind of public house that would serve a glass of wine to a gentleman without comment. Here we are," said Lawrence, gesturing forward.

Violet nervously eyed the building as they entered. The Royal Oak was quiet with only a few miners drinking inside. But there were enough of them to cause a sudden still in the atmosphere as they surveyed the newcomers with suspicious eyes. Lawrence was typically well dressed, with a smart jacket and well-tailored trousers. He looked out of place on his own, but Violet added another dimension, standing out by dress and gender. The bar girl stared at Violet, her eyes darting from top to bottom. "La-di-da," she muttered beneath her breath. Violet cast an impervious gaze towards the girl. If she cared, she did not show it and walked purposefully to the bar with Lawrence.

A casually dressed man turned as he heard their footsteps.

"Ah, Martin," said Lawrence. "Are you off duty?"

"Good God. Could you be any more obvious?"

Lawrence ignored him. "This is my wife. Violet, meet Martin Newlove."

Violet offered her hand and muttered an appropriate greeting.

Newlove smiled at Violet but rolled his eyes at Lawrence. "Over there," he sighed, pointing to the same small space at the back of the room they had occupied a few days before.

The three squeezed around the tiny table, which rocked as Lawrence propped the bag of kidneys against it.

"How are you?" asked Lawrence conversationally.

"I hoped for a relaxing evening after being roped in to paint mother's fence earlier. Not much chance of that now."

"We won't keep you for long," said Lawrence.

"What are you doing back here?" asked Newlove.

"You said I should talk to Jack Hart and Royden Sharp.

"Yes, I did. Good luck with that. Jack hands over to his assistant on a Tuesday. I mentioned your interest in the case to Royden Sharp yesterday in passing. He flatly refused to have anything to do with it."

"We've just caught up with Mr Hart," said Violet, lifting the bag of kidneys.

Martin wrinkled his nose. "That smells awful. What is it?"

"Rather more kidneys that we can manage."

"Disgusting. Put it out of my sight. I wouldn't eat offal if I were starving, and I've been feeling slightly peaky all day."

"That explains the lack of uniform."

"I wasn't on the sick. I knocked off early, that's all. I was up with the larks painting before duty today and called it quits about three o'clock. I'm good for work but not for contemplating offal." Newlove visibly shuddered, and Violet kicked the bag a little farther away.

"Anyway, what do you want? Or are you here for some other poor unsuspecting copper?"

"Don't be like that," said Lawrence. "Anyone would think you didn't want to help."

"A little discretion would go a long way. Too many people know who you are and why you are here. I thought you meant to keep it quiet?"

" I did," said Lawrence. "But the more I ask around, the more I hear. And if that method was good enough for Sir Arthur, then it's good enough for me."

"Except that he was trying to achieve something. I may have disagreed with the man; God knows we only want to be left alone, but at least he was trying to do some good."

"Come on, Martin. All the problems will disappear when I discover the letter writer or the livestock slayer."

"If you say so. Now, did you get that car of yours sorted out?"

"Yes. But let's not get into that just yet, although I may pick your brains for possible culprits later."

"It would be quite a list. What do you want to talk about?"

"Over to you, Violet."

"Lawrence and I have been discussing this case, and I'd like to look at it from a different perspective. The letters are important," said Violet. "But so are the people. I need to know more about the policemen involved and why they were so firm in their suspicions."

"Which ones?"

"Captain Anson and Sergeant Upton."

"I see."

"I take it you know them?"

"He does," said Lawrence before Newlove could reply.

"Good. Then why was Anson so convinced of George Edalji's guilt?"

"Two reasons," said Martin. "The first is good old-fashioned prejudice."

"You mean the colour of his skin?"

"Exactly. I wasn't on the case, but I encountered Anson a few times and heard him talk about the Edaljis more than once. He spoke disrespectfully about the family."

"How?" asked Violet.

"Mostly in his intonation. He was sarcastic and rude when mentioning the vicar's faith."

"But Reverend Edalji is a Christian," said Lawrence.

"Exactly. Anson deliberately referred to him as Hindu and ignored the respect normally reserved for a vicar."

"But the reverend can be quite forceful," said Lawrence. "Could is personality have upset Anson?"

"Possibly," said Martin. "But Anson never liked George, and however hard the family tried, it did not alter his view."

"So, George was a scapegoat from the start?" asked Violet.

"Not really. Fred Brookes bore the worst of it in the early days."

"Yes, from the letter writer. But I'm trying to understand Anson's motives. He left Fred Brookes alone for the most part and fixed his suspicions on George."

"That's a fair assessment."

"Tell me about Sergeant Upton?"

Martin frowned. "I didn't serve with him. I worked in Birmingham much of the time, but I still had family here. My mother, sister, and nephew lived in the village. Both women had lost their husbands, and times were hard, so I visited as often as I could. I'd see Upton in the pub occasionally, and as we were both serving policemen, we discussed our jobs and put the world to rights."

"Upton first arrived in 1888," said Lawrence.

"If you say so."

"Yes. When they arrested Elizabeth Foster."

"I remember."

"But Upton couldn't have shared the same prejudice as Captain Anson," said Lawrence.

"Why?" Newlove and Violet asked the question as one.

"Because he arrested Elizabeth Foster when the vicar asked him to with little fuss. He must have thought her guilty and was happy to act on Reverend Edalji's instructions."

"True," said Newlove. "But he deeply regretted it after and thought he had acted too hastily."

"Did Upton tell you that?" asked Violet.

Newlove nodded. "Yes. We got talking over a pint one day, and he came over all maudlin and said that it had been a bad decision."

"I'm surprised he gave it much thought," said Lawrence.

"Well, you wouldn't understand as you're not part of this community," said Newlove. "Upton's decision affected a lot of people. Elizabeth had many friends and relatives."

"Perhaps one of them had it in for Reverend Edalji." Lawrence's voice rose at precisely the same time as the volume of the pub chatter lowered. Several pairs of narrowing eyes fell upon him.

"For heaven's sake," hissed Newlove.

"Sorry for the indiscretion. But putting the cat among the pigeons won't do any harm."

"These people are tired, and they've had quite enough scandal in recent decades."

"And I have a good working theory about that," said Lawrence, still deliberately raising his voice.

"Enough," warned Violet.

Lawrence conceded the point and changed the subject. "Did Upton speak of George Edalji?" he asked.

Martin finished his drink and stifled a belch. Sweat prickled his forehead, and Lawrence felt momentarily guilty for putting him in a tricky situation among his community.

"Occasionally. But only when he wasn't banging on about Captain Anson. They were as thick as thieves, you know," said Newlove.

"Odd, with such a difference in rank," said Violet.

"I wouldn't risk it," said Newlove. "Fraternising with the higher ranks is fraught with uncertainty. One minute, they're all over you. The next, you're facing disciplinary action for stepping out of line."

"You sound as if you speak from experience," said Lawrence.

"Not mine, just what I've observed in others. Either way, Upton was treading a fine line."

"But he must have had some influence," said Violet.

"Exactly. That's why Anson believed him when Upton said he saw George Edalji post one of the letters."

"That would have ignited the rumours," said Lawrence.

"It did. Especially as Upton claimed it a long time after the fact."

"Interesting," said Violet. "So, Upton was in the thick of things for a while?"

"Yes. I was away during the worst of it, but I heard that Upton was summoned to the vicarage in the early nineties after a flood of hand-delivered letters, this time with objects. The vicar ignored them at first, but when someone left a bag of shit on the doorstep, he called them in again. Oh, excuse me, ma'am, I meant excrement." Colour flooded across Martin's cheeks as he squirmed in discomfort.

"Don't worry. I have heard the word before," said Violet.

"Even so. I forgot myself. It won't happen again."

"Do go on," said Violet.

"Well, his boss, not Anson, was a superintendent. Now who was it?"

"Does it matter?" asked Lawrence.

"No, but it's annoying that I can't think of it. A pompous man, we gave him a nickname. I wish I could remember."

"What happened?" asked Lawrence abruptly.

"Upton and a constable were called in to watch over the vicarage. Well, it should have been impossible for anything to happen under that amount of scrutiny. But someone dropped a dirty great iron key on the doorstep right under their noses."

"Perhaps they were not as observant as they should have been," said Violet.

"It's possible. And a few nights later, someone smeared faeces on the outside of the upstairs window. Now that would have been a mean feat with two policemen watching."

"Let me guess. Sergeant Upton assumed that George had done it," said Violet witheringly.

"So I heard, second hand, of course. But that was the general gist. He took the information straight back to Anson, and from that point on, they took George Edalji's guilt for granted."

"How ridiculous," said Violet.

"You can see their point," Lawrence interjected. "After all, moving undetected in the house is easier than taking a ladder to an outside window."

"But a competent observer would see both actions," said Violet. "Even an insider would need to open the window and wipe the excreta on it. And as you used the plural, there must have been at least two such attempts. Someone should have seen it. Which windows did they watch? How close to George's room were they?"

"Don't shoot the messenger," said Martin, holding green paint-speckled hands out in front of him defensively. I heard it from a relative who heard it from goodness knows where. I can't be sure the police ever checked."

"I guarantee they didn't," said Violet. "The whole investigation sounds second-rate."

Martin sighed as if he had taken her comments to heart.

"Sorry," said Violet. "I don't mean to cast aspersions on the entire police force. I apologise."

"Accepted," said Martin. "Why don't I buy you a drink?"

"No. We must go," said Lawrence, or Edna will lock us out."

"Edna? You're not staying with Edna Mallett, are you?"

"Yes. And so far, we're enjoying it. She's a damn fine cook."

"And a shocking gossip. Don't listen to a word she says."

Lawrence smiled. "Yes, Edna is good for a story or two, that's for sure."

"Lower your voice," said Violet through gritted teeth. "Hart, the butcher has just walked in."

They said goodbye to Martin Newlove and waited just long enough for Hart to get to the bar before leaving without being seen. Only when they were halfway up the road did they realise they'd left the bag of kidneys behind them.

Chapter Twenty-Nine

THE FOUNT OF ALL KNOWLEDGE

Tuesday, August 29, 1910

LAWRENCE AND VIOLET awoke the following day to a rumble of thunder outside. Lawrence opened his eyes to the sight of sheets of rain lashing against the windowpane and promptly closed them again. But his attempts to go back to sleep failed, and he reluctantly woke, washed, and dressed before going downstairs. Violet lay slumbering in bed until the smell of coffee roused her.

"Did you fetch that?" she asked as Lawrence set a cup on her bedside table.

"I couldn't sleep," he replied. "Not for want of trying. So, I went downstairs on the off chance. Mrs Mallett is up and about, and if you stir your stumps, she'll be serving a cooked breakfast in half an hour."

"Wonderful," said Violet. "Let me drink this before it gets cold, and I'll get ready. But let's not take too long. I must find a telephone and call Aurora."

"I'll see you downstairs," said Lawrence. "Mrs Mallett has set a fire, and I'd like to chat to her."

"A fire? In August?"

"Have you seen the weather? It's stormy and several degrees cooler than yesterday. I don't care whether it's August or December. When it's cold, it's cold."

"Whatever you say, dear. I'll see you shortly."

By the time Lawrence returned to the kitchen, the fire had taken effect, casting a warm glow over the room. He approached the range to take full advantage.

"Sit down," said Edna Mallett, pulling a kitchen chair closer to the comforting fire. "Would you like another coffee?"

"Please."

Edna poured from a pan on the range and took the cup to Lawrence. She pulled up a second chair and sat beside him, cradling her drink.

"You must think I'm made of money lighting a fire in the summer months. My Ernie would have torn me off a strip. But I've stacked some old papers to burn after breakfast. I hate throwing things away. You never know who might come across them. And who doesn't like to be warm, anyway? Whoever would have imagined such a horrible day in the middle of summer?"

"The weather's grim," said Lawrence. Fortunately, Violet and I managed a lovely stroll last night in the late evening sun. I'd have made more of it if I'd have known today would be a washout."

"I'm not sure how you would have found time," said Edna." You were late back as it was. A good thing I left the front door on the latch."

"We dropped into The Royal Oak."

"Goodness me. That's a strange choice for a gentleman."

"I was looking for someone. And the beer isn't bad."

"I wouldn't know," said Edna. "I've never been near the place. Not that I drink, except for a sloe gin at Christmas."

"Good choice. I haven't tried that in years."

"My sister, Mildred, makes it for me. She often brings a bottle on Christmas Day. Oh, and talking of gifts, you'll never guess what I found on the doorstep this morning."

Lawrence raised his eyebrows. "A milk delivery?" he suggested lamely. "Or the morning post?"

"No. Something wholly unexpected and quite mysterious."

"I couldn't say."

"No. And it isn't fair to ask you, as you wouldn't guess, in a month of Sundays."

"Then please tell."

"Several pounds of kidneys in a paper bag," said Edna. "I could hardly believe my eyes. The butcher must think I'm short of money. That's assuming it came from him."

"Ah," muttered Lawrence, his face colouring slightly from guilt. For a passing second, he considered owning up to the offal, which someone in the pub must have returned. But trying to explain himself was too much to bear, so he settled on silence and tried to ignore his nagging conscience.

"Well, it was a chilly night," Edna continued. "And the meat hadn't spoiled, so I thought I might as well use it. I've got some stewing steak in the pantry. How do you fancy a nice steak and kidney pie for your tea tonight?"

"Wonderful," said Lawrence, salivating at the thought of a hearty meal with piping hot gravy.

"Then I shall make one this afternoon. You'll be staying for one more night, won't you?"

"It looks that way. And especially if your pies are as tasty as your lamb chops."

Edna Mallett beamed. "I love cooking, but making a meal for one is no fun."

"Do you have many guests?"

"Yes, mostly during the summer. It's unusually quiet this week, and Mr Woodward, my other paying guest, left yesterday. But it's so close to September now that I'll only get the odd one or two people staying this side of Christmas."

"That's a shame," said Lawrence.

"Isn't it? I enjoy having guests. I miss my Ernie when I'm here alone. I remember when we couldn't wait for our residents to leave so we could spend our time together. That's when dear Ernie was alive. Now I'm alone so often that I yearn for people to stay longer."

"Have you lived in Great Wyrley for a long time?"

"Oh yes. I went to school here."

"And your children?"

"We didn't have any."

"Ah. So, you were a schoolgirl long before Lucy Brookes became a teacher?"

"Oh, yes. Many years before Miss Lucy. But my youngest sister Polly knew her."

"Did she now? I heard Lucy was rather strict."

Edna Mallett paused for a while. "More immature than strict, I would say. She used corporal punishment too readily. But not because she was cruel. I think she'd learned a rough-handed approach at home."

"Her father seems to have been a rather forceful man."

"William Brookes never minced his words, that's for sure. But age is a great leveller. He's not the man he once was, and I suspect he's not long for this world. Do you know the Brookes family?"

"I know of them," said Lawrence. "And I saw Fred Brookes a few days ago."

"He was a nice boy," said Edna. "Such a shame to see his name slandered in the newspapers."

"And George Edalji's too."

"Not to mention several other young boys from the grammar school. I doubt we will ever know what happened, but I never blamed Fred and assumed Master George was guilty. I was astonished to hear that they had released him from prison."

"Why did you suspect George Edalji?"

"Family prejudice, I suppose. My Ernie was kin to the Fosters. Have you heard of Elizabeth Foster?"

"Yes," said Lawrence.

"Then you'll know Reverend Edalji treated her abominably when he accused her of writing those awful letters. The poor girl lost her job and ended up in court."

"I heard she ran away from the rectory."

"That's right. Elizabeth fled to the house of one of Ernie's cousins, who took her in. But Elizabeth was so upset she never fully recovered. She sank into a dark depression, and no one could get through to her – not her family or her young man. Elizabeth left all her friends and returned to her mother in Norton Canes, a broken woman."

"Didn't she marry?"

"Yes, eventually, but not to her first love, who she abandoned when she left the village. She met another young man a few years later. They married and had children. But the accusation took a terrible toll on Elizabeth's health. She suffered a lifelong illness and died a few years ago."

"She must have died young."

"Yes. In her mid-thirties. It was a terrible waste. Elizabeth grieved for her lost reputation, which affected her health."

"Do you mind if I ask a direct question?"

"No. But I may not answer it."

Lawrence rubbed his nose, pondering whether it was worth upsetting his warm-natured, cooperative host, but curiosity won. "Do you think Elizabeth was innocent of writing the letters?"

"Undoubtedly, and I'll tell you why. Though I saw very little of Elizabeth after she left Great Wyrley, I paid my respects at her funeral. I spoke to her mother, who told me about Elizabeth's final weeks. Elizabeth knew she was dying and swore to her husband that she was innocent of all charges laid against her. Elizabeth didn't attend church regularly, but she believed in God and the afterlife. She would never have risked meeting her maker without confessing her sins. She did the opposite and swore her innocence."

"Did Elizabeth come from a big family?"

"Very large. She had many brothers and sisters, uncles and aunts."

"So, any of them might hold a grudge?"

"They might. Why do you want to know?"

Violet's arrival saved Lawrence from having to answer the awkward question.

"Oh dear. You've caught me gossiping," said Edna. "I'm a long way behind with my chores."

"Don't rush," Lawrence replied. But Edna jumped up.

"Shall I set the table?" offered Violet.

"Thank you, dear."

"It's steak and kidney pie tonight," said Lawrence. Violet

pulled a face, then clicked her fingers as she remembered her next task.

"Is there a telephone in the village?" she asked.

Edna's brow furrowed as she juggled the components of a cooked breakfast. When her tasks became more orderly, she took a breath and gave Violet directions to the nearest phone.

Ten minutes later, they enjoyed a delicious, carefree breakfast in a warm house. But within the hour, they were shivering in a phone box on the outskirts of Walsall.

Chapter Thirty

UNDER SIEGE

LAWRENCE RAISED his raincoat collar and stared grumpily at the device before him. The kiosk was uncomfortably narrow and not improved by Violet squeezing against him while she tried to contact the operator.

"I don't think it's working," she said.

"It had better be. I'm not driving anywhere else," Lawrence snapped.

"We must reach Aurora. I promised."

"She'd rather be left alone."

"No. We can't contact Luna, but we must stay in touch with Aurora."

Lawrence huffed a sigh and leaned against the wall, watching his wife as she stared nervously at the telephone.

"Go on then," he said.

Violet rubbed condensation from the glass and peered outside.

"What's wrong?" asked Lawrence.

"I feel like a caged tiger," she replied.

"I don't like these new-fangled kiosks any more than you

do. But if you want to call Aurora, you must get used to feeling claustrophobic."

"That's not what I mean. I can't shake the feeling that someone is watching me." Violet shuddered as she spoke.

"Wait," said Lawrence protectively. "I'll take another look outside."

Lawrence disappeared momentarily, then returned with rivulets of rain running down his back. "This road is as empty as the proverbial miser's purse. Not a soul for miles. They are too sensible to come out in this weather."

"And no cars?"

"One or two, Violet, and I can't do much about that. Look, old girl. I know you had a bad experience but try to stop worrying. I would never willingly put you in danger," he said reassuringly.

"I know. But Crossley seems to get everywhere."

"He's a man, not a supernatural entity. Crossley would have to put serious time and trouble into tracking us down. And why would he when there are easier targets?"

Violet's face paled. She picked up the receiver for a second time and repeatedly tapped the switch hook. "Operator," she said after the tenth press. Her face relaxed when a friendly voice replied, asking for a number. Violet rattled it off and waited while the operator connected, crossing her fingers tightly, hoping Aurora would answer. But the booming voice on the other end of the phone was male.

"I'd like to speak to the lady of the house," said Violet officiously, trying to disguise her voice.

"Who shall I say is calling?" asked the man. Violet listened intently and immediately discounted Michael or Francis as the owner of the voice. For a moment, she wondered if she had reached the wrong number.

"I said, who is calling, madam."

"Angela Jones," said Violet, summoning a name from her imagination.

"Regarding?"

"A purchase Mrs Farrow made from my store."

"Very well. Please wait."

Violet placed her hand over the receiver. "They must have a butler."

"I doubt it. The last I heard; Michael was cutting down on staff."

"He's gone to fetch Aurora."

"So I heard."

"I wasn't sure."

"Violet, we're crammed together like sardines. I can hear as much as you can."

"Shh." Violet raised her finger to her lips as someone coughed on the line.

"Mrs Farrow speaking."

"Oh, Aurora. Thank goodness you're safe. I have been so worried."

"Out of stock, you say. Oh dear. How very inconvenient."

"Can you talk?"

"No. That won't do at all."

"Shall I call back?"

"That won't be necessary. I'll take a note of your details. One moment. I'll be straight back when I've found a pen."

"Something's wrong," Violet said, anxiously glancing at Lawrence.

"I expect someone is in earshot. She'll be looking for privacy."

"Of course."

"Don't worry." Lawrence squeezed Violet's hand, then kissed her cheek.

"Stop it," whispered Violet, edging away. "Someone might see us."

"We're married," said Lawrence. "And no one in their right mind would queue outside a telephone kiosk in this weather.

"True." Violet returned the kiss, this time full on Lawrence's lips.

"Mrs Harpham, I love you more than ever. And especially when you care nothing for propriety."

Violet smiled and touched his cheek as they heard a slamming door on the other end of the phone.

"Awful timing," said Lawrence as the moment was lost.

"Aurora. Are you alright?"

"Sorry, Violet. I was relocating to the drawing room and shut the door too hard."

"Can you speak privately?"

"Yes, I've stretched the wire as far as it will go. But Stephens is hovering near the study, and I don't trust him. The security staff rarely use the drawing room, so I should be able to talk freely."

"Who is Stephens?"

"Michael's latest employee, supposedly here to keep the premises safe and keep an eye on Francis. But with Francis ensconced at Netherwood and more like a master than a guest, it's like closing the stable door after the horse has bolted."

"Then why bother?"

"I don't know."

"Did you ask?"

"Yes. But Michael was elusive. He's not been well and has taken to his bed. I suspect there's much he isn't telling me."

"Oh dear. But was Michael pleased to see you?"

Aurora audibly sighed. "He said he was."

"But?"

"But he doesn't trust me. And I can't blame him. I've taken his daughter away, and he wasn't expecting me to return alone. I've told Michael that Luna is safe. He thinks she is coming home in a few weeks, and I can't bring myself to reveal that he'll never see her again."

Aurora's voice trembled.

"Oh, Aurora. You must be feeling dreadful."

"I'm devastated. Nothing will ever be the same again."

"You can always change your mind."

"Never. Not when evil is afoot."

"At Netherwood?"

"Yes. I can feel it all around me. The atmosphere is fraught with tension. I walk around the place with butterflies in my stomach and the ever-nagging feeling of impending doom. Like someone is standing behind me with an unsheathed weapon waiting to plunge it into my back."

"Michael is still your husband. He will protect you."

"I don't think so," said Aurora softly.

"Why?" barked Lawrence, grabbing the handset.

Silence.

"I said why?"

"Sorry, Lawrence. You caught me unawares."

Violet snatched the telephone back again. "I'm so sorry. I should have said that Lawrence is with me."

"Where are you calling from?" asked Aurora warily.

"A public telephone box."

"Ask her why?" said Lawrence, impatiently.

"Don't bother repeating yourself, Lawrence. It's because Michael has changed. He looks the same and speaks the old way. But he's a shadow of his former self. Michael lacks emotion. He says the right things, but he doesn't feel them.

He seemed upset and confused when I told him about Luna. But he should be furious. He hasn't seen his little girl for months. And I come home without her, refusing to say where she is. If it were the other way around, I'd be livid and consulting my solicitor."

"Perhaps he's afraid you will leave again."

"I doubt he'd react if I did."

"But Michael loves you. His behaviour doesn't make sense."

"Violet, Michael is a pale imitation of the man I married. If I didn't know better, I'd say he was under a spell."

"And who has cast this spell?" asked Lawrence.

"Francis, I suppose. When I was last here, Michael was at his beck and call. Now, my husband barely leaves his bedroom."

"Is Francis still dying?" asked Lawrence, raising a sceptical eyebrow.

"Yes. He's lost more weight and is in a chair. He can't walk anymore."

"I bet he was surprised to see you."

"If so, it didn't register. Francis spoke as if I had just returned from the shops."

"Are you feeling safer?" asked Violet.

"I should be, but I'm not."

"But if Francis is dying, you have less to fear."

"Felix Crossley wants my daughter. Has she left Cheltenham yet?"

"Yes, dear."

"Good. Then I don't know where she is and can't give her location away."

"But Crossley doesn't know that," said Lawrence softly.

"Exactly. I will never be safe."

"You should leave," said Violet. "Go abroad. Change your name. Do anything you can to get away."

"I will," said Aurora. "But only when I know Michael is safe."

"He's hosting Francis. Surely Crossley will consider him an ally?"

"Felix Crossley has no friends. He takes advantage of people until they outlive their use. Crossley barely tolerates Francis, from what I hear. I'll tell you what I think."

"What?"

"Francis may be dying but still wants a way back into the fold."

"He's got one. Michael may not have welcomed him back with open arms, but he has extended brotherly love well beyond anything Francis deserves."

"Not that fold. The order. Francis has never come to terms with being banished to the outskirts. He would like to be back in the thick of it."

"Surely not in his condition?" said Violet.

"The Order is full of powerful men." Aurora paused and composed herself.

"Are you still there?"

"Yes. And when I say powerful, I don't mean in strength, although they are a force to be reckoned with. There are several thousand, I believe."

"Strength in numbers?"

"No. It's more than that."

"Ask her to explain," said Lawrence, pressing his cheek against Violet's as he fought for control of the conversation.

"If I told you everything that occurred in The Order, you wouldn't believe me. Human nature does not accept what it cannot see. And the higher an adherent climbs, the more possibilities are open."

"I don't know what she means. Ask her to be explicit." Lawrence frowned and drummed his fingers in frustration.

"I can hear you, Lawrence. Felix Crossley is powerful because he has the strength to make people obey him."

Lawrence sighed. "Like one of those dreadful charlatans. You know what I mean, a snake-eyed hypnotist?"

"In a manner of speaking. You must remember what Dickie Connelly did to Michael."

An unwelcome memory flashed through Lawrence's mind as he recalled throwing himself into Richmond Lake to rescue a drowning Michael. Had he been a moment later, Michael would have died, succumbing to Dickie Connelly's evil will. "I remember," murmured Lawrence.

"Dickie Connelly studied psychology. He learned how to manipulate the human condition. And he learned from the best. Crossley's greatest skill is to have mastered the art of convincing someone to act against their principles."

"How does Francis fit into that?"

"I can only guess, but knowing Crossley as I do, he will have something Francis wants."

"Such as?"

"The elixir of life."

"Oh really," snorted Lawrence.

"Not literally," said Aurora. "There's no such thing. But Crossley's powerful magic may give the illusion of good health. A placebo effect that could have a real impact on Farrow."

"No amount of wishful thinking can cure a cancer."

"Belief is a powerful thing, Lawrence. And Crossley's powers extend beyond anything you could rationalise."

"Now you are asking me to believe in the supernatural."

"I know you better than that. But I have seen things, even done things that you could only imagine. The power of the mind is an untapped resource. Farrow understands Crossley's abilities better than most. If he can deliver Felix Crossley's greatest desire, then Crossley may be benevolent towards him."

"You mean Luna."

"I do."

"Then you shouldn't be near Netherwood," said Violet, displacing Lawrence again.

"I can't abandon Michael."

"I love Michael like a brother, but he made a bad choice," said Violet. "You must keep safe, for Luna's sake."

"She'll never know," said Aurora. "And it's better this way. I will work to regain my influence over Michael. And encourage him to leave Netherwood."

"Where will you go?"

"Anywhere. I don't care about myself. My life is nothing without my darling girl. I thought I had steeled myself to a future of misery, but if I can't be with Luna, then perhaps I can have my husband back in the fullness of time. That is, if he can ever forgive me."

"You are so brave," said Violet.

"Not really. Francis Farrow still terrifies me, even though he is half the man he was. His eyes are sunken, his hair hangs in wisps, and his cheekbones stand out like ridges under parchment. I could snap his arm in two if the mood took me. Yet a few words from him, and I am a quivering wreck. Especially when he mentions Luna."

"Did he ask after her?"

"In the nicest possible way. And why wouldn't he? After all, I am her mother and came home without her."

"What did he ask? How did you reply?"

"He said, 'Where is that charming little girl of yours?' And he spoke gently, with great concern, yet his eyes told another story. He reminded me of a great coiled snake with a flickering tongue watching benevolently but with poisonous hostility nestling inside."

"How did you reply?"

"I said I had left Luna with a school friend until the end of September. I could see he wanted to ask more, but he swallowed the question and is biding his time. Farrow is not as skilled as Crossley. He can't compel me to reveal my secrets. Not yet anyway. And not in such a feeble and emaciated condition. I can only hope he succumbs to the inevitable soon."

"You poor thing," breathed Violet. "We can travel to Netherwood and keep you safe."

"Over my dead body," hissed Lawrence.

Violet clapped her hand over the telephone. "Be quiet. She'll hear you."

"No," said Aurora emotionlessly. "Not yet. If I need you, I will find a way to let you know."

"I'll call every day," said Violet.

"Yes. Please do. I will tell everyone that I have an unresolved problem with my dressmaker. That should satisfy their curiosity for a few more days."

"Very well, dear. Stay safe."

"Take care," said Lawrence, but Aurora had already rung off.

Chapter Thirty-One

CHRISTOPHER HATTON

VIOLET WAS UNCHARACTERISTICALLY quiet during the drive back. Lawrence tried to engage her in conversation, but it wasn't until they reached the outskirts of Great Wyrley that the tension in her face relaxed, and she spilt her innermost thoughts.

"Aurora is playing a dangerous game," she said as Lawrence detoured through the village.

"She knows what she's doing."

"I'm glad you think so. It's foolhardy."

"Aurora thinks she has nothing left to lose."

"Why are we going this way?"

"I wanted to drive past the vicarage."

"Why?"

"Unfinished business."

"What?"

"I don't know exactly, but I can't help feeling we're missing something important."

"And why will driving past the vicarage help?"

"To jog my memory."

Violet sighed. "There are better ways," she said. "Let's go back to our room and work it out logically."

Five minutes later, they had parked the car and entered the lodgings to the welcome smell of baking.

Edna Mallet heard the door go and waved a cheery hand towards them. "That's your steak and kidney pie cooking," she said.

"We're looking forward to it," Lawrence replied before heading upstairs. He tossed his hat onto the dressing table and lounged on the bed, hands behind his head.

Violet poured herself a glass of water and joined him.

"What shall we do until teatime?" asked Lawrence.

"Go for a stroll? Or find a tearoom?"

"I fancy a nap. I didn't sleep very well last night."

"It's only a little after twelve. That would be a terrible waste of a day. Anyway, didn't you say something was bothering you? Let's get that out of the way, and you'll sleep better tonight. Now, what is it, and where did you hear it?"

"I've no idea."

"Come on, Lawrence, try harder."

"If I knew what it was, I wouldn't need a memory jogger."

Violet sighed. "You're not being very helpful."

"Forget it. I'd rather sleep."

"No. It's bothering me now and offending my logical reasoning."

Lawrence sat up and crossed his arms. "Me and my big mouth," he said.

"Don't be like that. You've solved many crimes by listening to your instinct. What's it telling you?" asked Violet.

"That I've overlooked something important."

"Something you heard lately?"

"Yes," said Lawrence uncertainly. "But not today or yesterday. At least, I don't think so."

"This visit, or the last?"

"It must have been when I was alone in Wyrley. Or you'd remember, wouldn't you?"

"I'd like to think so."

Violet raised the glass of water to her lips and stopped mid-sip. "Where's your notebook?"

"In my jacket."

"Did you use it during your last visit?"

"Not always. But I jotted a few things down when I slept at The Royal Oak. God knows I had nothing better to do."

"Good." Violet approached the wardrobe and reached inside Lawrence's jacket.

"Here," she said, handing the jotter to Lawrence. "Your notes. You read it. I don't know what I'm looking for."

"I'd have more enthusiasm for this if I weren't so tired," said Lawrence, stifling a yawn.

"You can sleep after you've found it," said Violet firmly.

Lawrence rolled his eyes and opened the journal, tracing his finger along the page. "Not that or that," he said. "Hmm. Fred Brookes. No. Nothing original there. I've written about Shapurji Edalji's argumentative nature. That's true, but I don't think it's relevant."

"Is he?" asked Violet.

"Quarrelsome? Yes."

"That must upset some people."

"I daresay, but he isn't rude and doesn't set out to offend. It's more that our dear reverend holds his ground on issues he believes in."

"Good for him," said Violet.

"Exactly." Lawrence resumed his reading. "Charlotte Edalji was prickly; Maud stayed upstairs out of the way."

"Maud being the sister?"

"Quite. But I didn't speak to her, and nothing they said about her stands out. We've covered Elizabeth Foster, Sergeant Upton and, of course, saint Conan Doyle."

Violet rolled her eyes. "That again. Are you jealous?"

"Of course not. Anyone can be a pompous old fool."

"Old? He can't be much older than you are. Possibly younger."

"Well, that's what comes of being sanctimonious. It's ageing."

"You're impossible, Lawrence. Arthur is a lovely, compassionate man. Young Mr Edalji would still be behind bars were it not for him."

"Half a job, Arthur, you mean."

Violet shook her head. "Now, hold on a minute. Arthur Conan Doyle secured George Edalji's release. Tell me, exactly what you have achieved?"

Lawrence snapped the notebook shut. "Nothing yet. I'm still working on it."

"Keep going. You won't find what you're looking for by giving up," coaxed Violet.

"Later. I'm having a nap."

Lawrence turned over and closed his eyes. Sighing, Violet took the notebook and leafed through it. Five minutes later, she prodded Lawrence in the side. He ignored her. She poked him again.

"What is it? I'd just dropped off."

"The Edaljis' third child, Horace."

"What of it?"

"You've barely mentioned him."

"He wasn't there. Apparently, he's left home."

"Even so. I'd have expected a little more information about him."

"The Edaljis barely spoke of Horace. And when they did, things were a little strained." Lawrence closed his eyes again, then moments later, opened them with a start.

"That's it," he said.

"Horace?"

"Yes. The Edaljis had plenty to say about George and Maud, but poor old Horace barely got a look in. And when he did, Charlotte Edalji couldn't get off the subject quickly enough. He must be something of a black sheep."

"Well done, Lawrence. Good work."

"I haven't done anything."

"But you will."

"I don't even know how to find Horace."

"You had plenty of help from Fred Brookes. Can you ask him?"

"Fred was on the move last time we spoke. I doubt I'll see him again."

"Then who else could you ask?"

Lawrence snapped his fingers, and Violet jumped. "I don't need any help. Jack Hart has already told me."

"I don't remember that."

"You were angry at the time and not listening. Hart said Royden Sharp burned down Mr Hatton's hayrick. He's a local landowner, and his son Christopher was a good friend of Horace Edalji's."

"Good. A landowner's son shouldn't be too hard to find."

"We can ask the fount of knowledge downstairs. Edna is sure to know. Let's have a chat over tea."

"Or now," said Violet.

"You're not going to let me nap, are you?"

"The sooner we go back to Cheltenham, the better. I'm more worried about Aurora than you are. And it's easier to keep track of her when we're home with the telephone at our disposal. I'm prepared to spend another night here, two at the most. Then we must leave."

"Right. I'll drag my sorry carcass downstairs now. Are you coming?"

"Of course. And take your raincoat."

Edna Mallet was busy topping and tailing runner beans in the kitchen.

"You know everything, Edna," said Lawrence as they entered the room.

"Not everything. But little happens in the village that doesn't come to my attention."

"Perfect. Then do you know a man called Hatton?"

"Squire Hatton?"

"That sounds right. A local landowner."

"I did."

"Good. Then where does he live?"

"Well, that depends on your point of view."

"Sorry?"

"Whether you think he's a saint or a sinner. Personally, I'm on the fence."

Lawrence knitted his brows.

"Oh," said Violet. "You mean he's dead."

"That's right. He's been gone for at least three years now. And I doubt he's with the angels."

"That's alright. As long as his son is still around."

"Squire Hatton had ten children. Which one do you want?"

"Christopher."

"Then you're in luck. He's studying to be a mining engineer. But he's home at the moment. At least he was last Friday. Though how long he'll stay is another matter."

"In that case, we should go now," said Violet. "Where does Christopher live?"

"Brook House Farm, near the Great Hall."

"I know it," said Lawrence. "But what about supper? His eyes rested on the large pie cooling on the range.

"You can have it whenever you like," said Edna. "I was going to join you, but Maggie Rawlings called by while you were upstairs. They're one player short for gin rummy tonight, and I have agreed to join them."

"Good for you," said Violet. "I hope you have a lovely time."

"I'll leave the makings of dinner on the stove," said Edna. "Boiled potatoes and green beans. I'll have mine before I go, so take as much as you want. I shan't expect leftovers."

"And I can assure you there won't be any," said Lawrence. "Right. Let's get to it, wife."

Violet rolled her eyes. "We'll see you later, Mrs Mallett."

Chapter Thirty-Two

BROOK HOUSE

LAWRENCE STOOD at the front of Brook House, pondering his next move. It was one thing engaging the local tradesmen in unsolicited gossip about the greatest scandal ever to hit Great Wyrley and another bothering the local landed gentry. He expressed the thought to Violet, and she replied disparagingly.

"Squire Hatton is dead, dear, and hardly likely to threaten you with a shotgun."

"One of his sons might."

"Only if you are particularly annoying. Be nice, and I'm sure they will help."

"I've run out of plausible stories."

"Then tell the truth and use your friends in high places."

"I don't have any."

"I mean Arthur Conan Doyle, of course. You might have little time for him, but he is very well-regarded in literary circles. Drop his name, and you are sure to succeed."

Lawrence scowled. "I don't want to be associated with

Conan Doyle. He tells a good yarn, but it's another thing doing the legwork."

"Don't start that again. I suggest you open the conversation with Arthur's investigation and use his name to your advantage."

Lawrence sighed. "I will if I must. It worked at the vicarage, so I'll grit my teeth and pretend to admire the man."

"As well you might. Let's get to it then."

Violet clasped Lawrence's hand and strode towards the property.

"You seem unusually forthright," said Lawrence. "Are you alright, old girl?"

"I'm glad of the distraction," Violet admitted. "Between Aurora and a constant feeling of watchful eyes, I'm not feeling quite myself."

"What do you mean?

"Never mind. I'm just being silly," said Violet, rapping firmly on the door. She passed her card to the housemaid, who let them inside and left them on the doormat before seeking her master. Ten minutes passed, and Lawrence shuffled his feet.

"Has she forgotten us?" he grumbled.

"Patience," said Violet, her mind elsewhere.

Another five minutes passed before the housemaid reappeared with a red-faced young man pacing slightly ahead.

"Christopher Hatton," he said, offering his hand first to Lawrence and then Violet. "What can I do for you?"

"I'm a friend of Arthur Conan Doyle," said Lawrence. Violet squeezed his hand encouragingly.

"Really," said Christopher, sounding impressed.

"Yes. Did you meet him when he visited Wyrley?"

"No. I sent a message to his lodgings offering information, but he could not spare the time to come to Brook House."

"Really. I'm surprised."

"I was too."

"Can you give us a few moments now?"

"I can, but wouldn't you be better off getting your facts directly from Conan Doyle if you're such close friends?"

Lawrence glanced at Violet. She gave an imperceptible nod and spoke. "Arthur has asked us to continue his investigation without referring to his previous work. He would like a second opinion on his prime suspect, Royden Sharp. Arthur suggested we speak to several notable people, and here we are. We know very little about your part in the case as Arthur purposely withheld details of his investigation to avoid leading us in a particular direction."

"Your man Conan Doyle showed no interest in what I had to say three years ago, and I can't see why that would change now when he's already achieved his objective."

"Mr Edalji might be free from prison, but the case is far from complete," said Lawrence.

"And who are you to resolve it if the police and Sir Arthur Conan Doyle could not?"

Lawrence appraised the young man standing before them, coolly discussing the case with a maturity beyond his years.

"Violet and I are private investigators."

"I daresay. But your story about collaborating with Sir Arthur is fishy, and I don't like the smell of it. If you want my help, you must offer a convincing reason for me to give it."

"Very well," said Lawrence, accepting defeat. "I don't like Conan Doyle's conclusion. I don't mean regarding

George Edalji's release, but the circumstantial evidence used to cast suspicion on Royden Sharp."

"Why not? Sharp is a reprobate of the first order – a bloody arsonist and all-around bad apple."

"I'm sure he's all those things, but Conan Doyle's reasoning is faulty."

"Why should you care?" asked Christopher Hatton.

"It offends my sense of order."

Violet shook her head at Lawrence's lame excuse for his interest in the case, but his reply seemed to satisfy Hatton.

"Understood. I'm a facts man too. But what use do you think I can be when Sir Arthur Conan Doyle so roundly dismissed my initial offer of help."

"That's a reason in itself," said Violet.

Christopher Hatton nodded. "Correct deduction, for which you now gain admittance. Follow me." He strode apace down the hallway. Lawrence and Violet followed, breaking into a trot to catch up.

"This way," said their host, banging open a door that clattered into a wooden doorstop and slammed back on itself. Lawrence raised the flat of his hand and caught the blow.

Hatton steamed ahead, barking a cursory apology without ever turning around. Presently, they arrived at the back of the house.

"Inside or out?" asked Hatton.

Violet glanced at the overcast sky.

"Inside."

"Fair enough. Take a seat." He gestured through another door, and they found themselves in a small library surrounded by floor-to-ceiling bookcases on three walls.

"Very nice," said Lawrence, admiring a series of bound volumes decorated with gold leaf.

"Not bad for a countryman. I can't claim credit, though. My father stocked the library. He liked to sit here in the evening with a book in one hand and a sherry in the other. Woe betide us if we disturbed him before dinner."

"Reading is one of life's greatest pleasures," said Violet.

"So father said. I prefer the outdoors myself and anything mechanical. Still, I like to spend the occasional hour or two in this room. It's peaceful and rarely used. Now, take a seat, will you? Havers will be along with some drinks in a minute. She was trailing us up the corridor and has no doubt been distracted by some domestic chore or other."

Lawrence smiled as he sat down, crossing his long legs, relaxed and at ease. Now that Christopher Hatton had satisfied his doubts about their motives, he presented an open and accommodating disposition, eager to help and without guile.

Hatton leaned forward. "So, you'll want to know about Horace Edalji."

"Exactly. How did you know?"

Violet interjected. "We were trying to understand why his parents barely mentioned him."

"Dear old Horace," said Hatton. "The poor chap couldn't do right for doing wrong. My mother would say that's what comes of being the middle child, and there's some truth in that."

"Go on," said Lawrence.

"Well. You doubtless know that Horace and I went to school together. We were chums; not bonded by blood or anything dramatic like that. Horace and I built a solid friendship, and we spent a lot of time together. Mostly here as I didn't much like the vicarage."

"Why?"

"Oh, I don't know. The vicar could be prickly. Not so

much with me, but he crossed swords with my father more than a few times. And when that happened, I felt uncomfortable in his home. The Edaljis are a quiet family, and we are not. I grew up with nine siblings, and with that many children under one roof, we were somewhat boisterous. Not rude, you understand, but rowdy and we occasionally forgot our manners. As for father's language, that could be rather ripe. Horace fit better in our domain than I would have with his family."

"Fair enough," said Lawrence.

"What was Horace like?" asked Violet.

"Pleasant," said Christopher.

"That's a very dull word," said Violet.

"Is it? Then I'm not doing him justice. Horace was reasonably bright and fairly outgoing with a decent sense of humour."

Violet raised an eyebrow. "You mean average?"

"I suppose I do, but not in a derogatory way. In context, his elder brother George was highly intelligent but timid and insular, and Horace's sister Maud was quiet too. Horace was on the right side of sociable and smart enough for a robust debate. He didn't take himself too seriously. Horace eventually became a government clerk, which tells you everything you need to know about him: solid and dependable."

"You liked him then?" asked Lawrence.

"Horace was all things to all people and one of the least offensive men I have ever met."

"Then why is he a pariah in his home?" asked Violet.

"And how did he escape the vitriol surrounding George?" added Lawrence. "Or did he?"

Christopher Hatton steepled his hands. "Isn't that the

golden question? Yes. As far as I know, Horace Edalji did not attract a single nasty letter or mention in the paper."

"Could he have penned the letters?" asked Lawrence.

"Hardly," said Hatton, shaking his head. "Horace and I were the same age. The first letters arrived two decades ago when we were only nine years old."

"The early letters were very childlike," said Violet.

"I agree, but still too sophisticated for a boy of such tender years."

"Then why didn't Horace come to the attention of accusers?" asked Lawrence, still persevering.

"Because nobody considered him a suspect. Why would they? He was too young, and unlike his brother, Horace did not roam around the countryside in the dead of night."

"An evening stroll is no reason to vilify someone," said Violet frostily.

"I know. But the village was fraught with rumour and speculation, especially when the livestock killings occurred. Any nocturnal activity garnered suspicion."

"Be that as it may," said Lawrence, swiftly changing the subject before Violet got on her high horse. "It doesn't explain why Horace seems to be *persona non grata* with his family."

"And now we get to the crux of it," said Christopher. "Are you by any chance acquainted with Captain Anson?"

"We have crossed paths," growled Lawrence.

"Anson is, as you will appreciate, an acquired taste. But more effective than your friend Conan Doyle gave him credit for."

"Did you discuss the case with Anson?" asked Lawrence.

"Not exactly. My father and I gave statements to Constable Cooper around the time they arrested George Edalji. I then wrote to Captain Anson because of conversations arising from my statement. To the best of my knowledge, those letters are still in the Home Office.

Violet frowned. "Then they must be important. What persuaded you to write them?"

"Horace did."

"Horace?" echoed Lawrence.

"Yes. He asked me to intervene, and as a longtime friend, I felt obliged."

"But why?"

"Horace was concerned about the more enthusiastic of his brother's supporters. If they pushed too hard for his release, Horace feared things might get out of hand."

"In what way?" asked Lawrence, reaching for his notebook.

"He thought agitating at such a high level might cause more harm than good."

"How can campaigning for George's release be a problem? What's the worst that could have happened? A few bruised egos, some reluctance on the part of the police? I would have tried everything to help if George was my brother," said Violet passionately.

"Not if you had reservations."

Lawrence and Violet exchanged glances. "You mean…?"

"Yes. Horace worried that certain truths might come out."

"You mean he doubted his brother's innocence?" asked Violet.

"No. He outright refuted it."

Lawrence chewed his lip while Violet bowed her head, deep in thought. The clock chimed the half-hour as the silence grew to uncomfortable levels. "Was there some sort of sibling rivalry?" asked Violet, eventually.

"To a certain extent, but that's another matter."

"It would give Horace a reason to lie."

"Except that he didn't. Look. Any rivalry between the Edalji brothers resulted from their somewhat unusual sleeping arrangements. Are you aware of this?"

"I am," said Lawrence. "Perhaps you can explain it to Violet."

Hatton sighed. "Don't take this too far out of context, but it might help you understand why Horace viewed himself as an outsider. Now, when Horace was younger, six or seven perhaps, one of the children became extremely ill. I can't remember if it was Horace or Maud. And it doesn't matter. The point is Charlotte Edalji started sharing a room with her daughter, and the reverend moved into George's room. Horace remained alone. The so-called temporary arrangement became permanent and never changed."

"Even when the boys were adults?" asked Violet.

"No. Never. George still shared a bedroom with his father at the time of his arrest in 1903."

"How extraordinary," said Violet.

"Not to mention lacking in privacy." Lawrence stroked his chin. "Though very useful in terms of an alibi."

"All of those things," said Christopher Hatton. "But from Horace's point of view, he was the solitary child nobody wanted."

"Surely they changed the sleeping arrangements when Horace moved out?" asked Lawrence.

"Not as far as I know."

"They kept an empty bedroom?"

"Yes… in case Horace returned, which he did from time to time at the beginning, though rarely. His visits soon stopped after the big argument."

Lawrence and Violet waited in anticipation of Hatton's

reveal, but Hatton stood and walked to the bookcase, taking out a hefty tome and leafing through the pages.

Lawrence frowned. The man was showboating, biding his time, setting out his stall.

"Go on," he urged.

Hatton cleared his throat. "Horace contacted me because he did not want to be directly involved. At his request, I sent two typewritten copies of letters in George Edalji's handwriting for comparison with the hate letters.

Lawrence curled his lip, disappointed in the revelation. "That would have been old news by then," he said.

"Not when you factor in the content."

"My goodness. Was it one of those letters?" Violet stared her mouth agape.

Hatton nodded. "Two of those letters, to be precise."

"What did they say?"

"Both letters were full of the usual filth, and one was addressed to the servant girl."

"Elizabeth Foster?"

"No. Elizabeth left years before. But this particular letter showed striking similarities to those written previously, inciting the housemaid to random acts of mischief. The writer had it in for the poor old reverend and cursed him roundly."

"There's no evidence that George disliked his father," said Lawrence.

"Probably not. But you shouldn't assume they had a good relationship. George was the classic introvert and kept it all in."

"I'm sorry, but I find this hard to believe." Lawrence rose, stretched his legs, and perched on the back of the settee. Christopher Hatton pursed his lips.

"What's the problem?"

"A steady stream of policemen in and out of the vicarage," said Lawrence. "Surely to goodness, they checked for incriminating letters while searching the property."

"Yes, but Horace found them long before he disclosed their existence. He never intended to betray his brother and stored them for safekeeping."

"Why would he do that if he didn't expect to use them?" asked Violet.

"I don't know. It's not as if he doubted their provenance. Horace saw his brother writing one of the letters. That's how he knew where to look for it."

"Did anyone interview Horace?"

"No," said Hatton. "Ridiculous, isn't it?"

"If it were true, then it would be in Captain Anson's interests to validate the letters."

"Exactly. Anson wrote to me and asked if Horace would agree to an interview. As I'm sure you will appreciate, Horace was reluctant but said he would if necessary. Anson knew he risked partiality problems conducting the interview himself and asked the Home Office to step in. But by then, Conan Doyle had made George Edalji a *cause celebre*. Failure to release him would be fraught with tricky political issues. The government had no stomach for it and refused to get involved. It was easier to release Edalji and avoid inflaming tensions."

"And that's why he missed out on compensation," said Violet.

"Quite."

"And Conan Doyle didn't interact with you or Horace in case he heard something that might ruin his case."

Hatton resumed his seat on the couch. "And there you have it," he said.

"I wonder why this has never come to light?" asked Violet.

"It's not in anybody's interests. Conan Doyle is a hero, George Edalji is free, Horace has left home, and I get to live a quiet life. There's nothing to gain by bringing this to light."

"How did Charlotte and Shapurji find out?"

"Horace told them in anticipation of the Home Office interview. It never happened, and he could have spared himself a lot of heartache. The family didn't believe him and were horrified at his cooperation with Colonel Anson. They didn't turn him out of the vicarage, but it was too uncomfortable for him to remain."

"When did this happen?"

"In 1907, just before George's release. Poor old Horace. I doubt I'll ever see him again. He's married and lives in Hereford now, but his wife's Irish, and he's likely to move across the water."

"Hereford. That's not far," repeated Lawrence.

"Don't waste your time. Horace won't talk to you. He wants to forget the whole sorry business."

Violet drew a deep, disappointed breath. "I thought George Edalji was innocent," she said.

"Don't get me wrong. George didn't harm the livestock. He didn't have it in him. He wrote a few letters in the early years while playing a foolish prank on the vicar, and instead of owning up to it, he kept quiet. George could never have foreseen the trouble it would cause. Subsequent letters were entirely vindictive and designed to damage George's reputation or that of his friends. They bore no resemblance to George's earlier work."

"And you're sure of this?" said Lawrence.

"There's not a single doubt in my mind."

Chapter Thirty-Three

ROTTEN LIVER

"WELL, THAT'S THAT," said Lawrence as they walked away from Brook House.

"Good. Can we go home now? I'm worried about Aurora."

Lawrence glanced at his watch. "Hardly at this time of day. And I wouldn't want Edna's steak and kidney pie to go to waste."

"Don't be silly. She won't mind."

"Why do you think he did it?"

"Who?"

"George. Who else?"

Violet sighed. "For attention, maybe? He was a young boy when it all began."

"Too young?"

"No. And Christopher Hatton has no reason to lie."

"Then why the other letter writers?"

"Revenge on George for bringing the village into disrepute."

"Fair enough, but why were the Brookes family targeted?"

Violet stopped and placed her hands on her hips. "I don't know, Lawrence. Perhaps they suspected Fred Brookes was involved. It doesn't matter now."

"Of course it does. George Edalji didn't end up in jail for writing some harmless letters as a minor."

"I know that," said Violet. "He suffered terrible consequences for what amounts to a childhood prank. But he's out now and probably wants to put it all behind him."

"Leaving other guilty parties free to go about their business."

"As they have been for several decades. It's time to let it go. If not, you risk the truth coming out, just as Horace feared."

Why was Hatton so free with the information?

"He's probably relieved to tell someone. And our code of ethics binds us to secrecy."

"When it suits us."

"You wouldn't?"

"Probably not, but Hatton doesn't know that."

"He struck me as very astute. And he won't suffer any consequences, not even if you tell Arthur, who must keep it to himself or lose all credibility. I doubt he'd believe you anyway."

"Yes. Conan Doyle has a distant relationship with facts that don't suit his theories."

"Whatever you say."

They walked on in silence for a few hundred yards, soon arriving at their lodgings. Lawrence pushed the door, but it did not open.

"Don't worry. Edna is out. She's bound to have left us a key."

"That's right. She said she would."

Lawrence lifted the doormat while Violet groped inside the letterbox for a string. Neither search produced a key. "Damn," said Lawrence. "I'm starving."

"We can try the back door."

"Of a terraced property? That won't be easy."

"Stay here," said Lawrence, turning to walk up the road.

"No. Something's wrong." Violet inched up her skirts and ran towards him, taking his hand.

Lawrence briefly stopped and caressed her cheek. "There's nothing to worry about."

"I know. But where you go, so do I."

"Come on then, wife. Let's trek a path to our dinner."

The route to the rear of Edna's house was via a path leading from the end of the terrace to a narrow alleyway behind the gardens, each serviced by an identical door in the wooden fence.

"Nothing to it," said Lawrence unlatching the gate.

They approached the rear door to find it ajar.

"I thought Edna was out," said Violet uncertainly.

"And it's unusually quiet. Wait here."

Lawrence led the way, pushing the door wider as he entered.

"Stay outside," he barked, turning as Violet stepped towards him.

"What is it?"

"Don't come in."

But Violet, her heart in her mouth, had already gone through. She stood on the kitchen doormat, staring in horror at the sight of Edna Mallet lying prone on the kitchen floor, her mouth agape with vomit splashed on the tiles.

Lawrence crouched beside the stricken woman and

pushed two fingers on her carotid artery. Shaking his head, he looked up. "She's gone."

"Oh no. What happened?"

"Don't touch the body, but if you look around her mouth, you can take an educated guess."

"Oh, my goodness. She's covered in blisters and burns. Someone's poisoned her. But how?"

Lawrence walked towards the nearby table, pulled out the chair and sat down. His eyes rested on a plate of steak and kidney pie, green beans, and boiled potatoes. A knife lay on the plate, but the fork was missing. Lawrence leaned to his side, examined the trajectory of the body, and saw a glint of metal by the range.

"She collapsed from this chair to her position on the floor, dropping her fork as she fell," he said.

Lawrence picked up a glass of water, held it to the light, and sniffed. "Nothing untoward in here."

"Then it's in the pie."

"I'm afraid so."

"We could be lying there too."

"It doesn't bear thinking about," said Lawrence.

"But who would kill Edna? She was a harmless old lady."

"Or a terrible gossip, according to Martin."

"This is our fault," said Violet. "Running around the village with a bag of offal with the butcher's name printed on the side. What were we thinking?"

"Hardly this. And who knew we were staying here?"

"Practically anyone. I had to ask you to lower your voice twice yesterday. One pint of ale, and you're garrulous."

"Oh God. We were talking about it when Jack Hart came in."

"He's hardly likely to poison his own meat in an identifiable bag."

"Then who?"

"There must have been twenty or thirty people surrounding us when Hart arrived, and we hardly know them. Anonymous letter writers don't generally advertise their presence," said Violet.

"But what had they to gain from killing Edna?"

"Perhaps she knew something if she really was a gossip."

"True. But there's something else to consider."

"What?"

"Perhaps we were the targets."

Chapter Thirty-Four

THE OFFICIOUS INSPECTOR GREEN

TWO HOURS LATER, Lawrence was regretting calling the police. Not that there had been any choice in the matter. They couldn't leave Edna's body lying on the floor. But the officious and uncooperative detective in charge was testing Lawrence's patience, and his frustration was palpable.

"You can't stay here tonight," said Detective Inspector Green as he buttoned up his overcoat.

"We've paid for our lodgings," Lawrence replied. "And it's too late to drive home."

The inspector shrugged. "That's your problem," he said. "If you remain, you risk interfering with the evidence."

"I'm a private detective, and I know better."

"An amateur, you mean. All the more reason to move you on."

Lawrence glared scathingly. "Surely you won't leave her here all night?"

"No. The waggon's on its way from the mortuary. But we can't allow intruders until we have collected all the evidence. Off you go and leave the experts to solve the crime."

"Don't you want a statement?"

"Why? You've told me what happened, and I've written it down."

"I thought you might want something more formal?"

The inspector drew himself to his full height. "I have everything I need," he repeated.

The door opened, and Martin Newlove appeared, clad in his uniform. He glanced sympathetically at Lawrence.

"About time," said the inspector. "Take these people away."

"When we've packed," said Violet, her arms crossed over her chest. Lawrence smiled admiringly.

The detective let out a heartfelt sigh. "Do it now," he glowered. "And you go with her," he instructed Newlove.

Lawrence leaned against the range and contemplated the beginnings of rigour mortis in Edna's face.

"Strychnine," he said.

"I beg your pardon?"

"My money's on strychnine."

"Mind your own business," said Green.

"It's very much my concern. The poison was in a pie she made for our supper."

"You've told me that, and I think it's unlikely."

Lawrence stared in disbelief. "Are you serious?"

"Deadly. I suspect food poisoning."

Lawrence glared at the inspector's reddening face and tried to meet his eyes. But Inspector Green's gaze darted across the room, seemingly anywhere but near Lawrence.

"Your evasiveness suggests that even you don't believe that. What are you hiding?" asked Lawrence curtly.

"I'm not discussing this case with you, however much

you push me. We've had nothing but trouble with armchair detectives."

"I take it you had a problem with Conan Doyle?"

The inspector pursed his lips and stared out of the window.

"Ah. Another policeman jumping to the conclusion that because George Edalji looks different, he must have been guilty. Did you find it frustrating when they released him?"

"Damn you, yes I did. And with good reason."

"Did it ever occur to you that there are shades of guilt? I am not an admirer of Arthur Conan Doyle, and Edalji has made mistakes in his life, but not enough to lose his liberty. And if it weren't for the rank prejudice of certain members of the police force, he wouldn't have done."

"Get out," said Inspector Green.

"When my wife finishes."

"Now." The inspector, now incandescent with rage, wagged a furious finger in Lawrence's face.

Lawrence considered retaliating, perhaps even goading him to amuse himself. But Green's florid face suggested a man not entirely in control of his actions. Wisely, Lawrence exited the room and waited on the front doorstep until Violet appeared, closely followed by Newlove.

"Riling the inspector is not a wise move," said Martin.

Lawerence snorted. "It must be hard working for a fool."

"I heard that," yelled Inspector Green. "If I see you within fifty yards of this house, I'll arrest you. Police Constable Newlove, escort these people from the premises."

Violet sighed. "Don't worry, Martin. Lawrence and I will drive home."

Lawrence shook his head. "Not at this time of night."

"But where will we stay?"

"I'll take you to The Oak, and we'll think about it," said Newlove.

Though late, the pub was abuzz with chatter about Edna's death, already widely known in the village. The moment Newlove entered, a cluster of men surrounded him, each pressing him for further information.

"How on earth did they know?" asked Lawrence as they slunk towards their usual table, trying to evade the crowd.

Violet shook her head. "It must have been the neighbour. We didn't tell anyone else."

After five minutes, Newlove pushed through the crowd and headed for their table. "No accommodation here, I'm afraid. The barmaid suggested Mrs Brown's lodging house, but she's full. I've had an idea and sent our lad off to check. You'll be alright to wait here for ten minutes?"

"Your lad?" asked Lawrence.

"Our latest recruit. Only eighteen and wet behind the ears, but a good enough runner. I'm sure he'll be back in no time."

"Back from where?" asked Violet, but an old man with a grizzled beard tapped Martin on the shoulder, demanding to know details of Edna's death. By the time Martin had extricated himself, a fresh-faced, uniformed youth had burst panting into the pub.

"He's agreed," said the boy.

"Good. Off you go, young man. Inspector Green has a job for you. Tell him I'll be right behind.

"Where are we going?" asked Lawrence.

"Reverend Edalji will put you up."

"I don't think that's appropriate."

"I do," said Violet. "We can ask them to confirm Christopher's story."

"They'll deny it, and it would be a terrible liberty to discuss it when they are hosting us."

"Then we'll go home."

"No. We are close to the truth of this mess. Closer than I realised. I think I know what happened and, to a certain extent, why. Assuming Edna was the target and not us, we should be able to work out who."

"Really? You're a few steps ahead of me, for once," said Violet.

"Ready?" asked Martin, returning his attention after yet another inquisitive villager had bombarded him with questions.

"Yes."

"Then I'll leave you to it."

"Right, you are." Lawrence took the suitcase in one hand and linked his other arm through Violet's.

"For better or worse," he said as they took the short walk to the vicarage.

Chapter Thirty-Five

A PLACE OF REFUGE

Wednesday, August 30, 1910

THE REVEREND and his family were all in bed when Lawrence and Violet timidly knocked on the vicarage door. They waited silently, hoping someone would still be awake, when the door creaked open, revealing their house servant, Dora. She offered them a hot drink before showing them to the guest room, where they immediately settled down for the night.

Lawrence woke first and padded down the landing in his pyjamas before returning to the room and gently shaking Violet on the shoulder.

"What is it?" she asked.

"I can't get into the other rooms," grumbled Lawrence.

"I should think not. Why would you?"

"To see how easy it would be to smear excrement on the windows from the inside."

Violet pulled a face. "Does it matter? What time is it?"

"A quarter to seven. Do you think we should show our faces?"

"I suppose so, although I'd welcome another hour in bed. But we must thank the reverend even if we leave soon after."

"Before breakfast?"

"No. I'm starving. Hopefully, their hospitality will extend to a light meal, and it will be useful to talk. But, Lawrence, we really should go home. I must speak to Aurora."

"I know. We'll leave straight after breakfast, I promise."

"Thank you. I thought you might feel tied to Great Wyrley as you seem on the verge of solving this mystery."

"I think I'm close. But without knowing who..." Lawrence's voice trailed away, and his eyes stared mistily into the distance.

"Well, the sooner we dress, the better."

"Damn," said Lawrence, approaching the wardrobe.

"What's wrong?"

"Did you get my hat?"

"When?"

"Last night, from Edna's."

"Oh, my dear, I'm sorry. I had it in my hand, but I don't think I took it downstairs. It must be lying on the bed."

"I'll pop out and get it after breakfast."

"We can go together."

"No. It's quicker if I shoot off alone. And you may disapprove of my actions if they've locked up the house and left it."

"Please don't break in. You'll get arrested."

"I know what I'm doing."

"But it's on the main road. Someone will see you."

"They won't," said Lawrence, confidently. "Besides, they'll likely have left a copper in post."

"Hopefully not Green."

"He's too high ranking. It will be some lowly sap."

"So, what's your theory, Lawrence?"

"Revenge that got out of hand. But I won't know who it is until I can work out why something relatively insignificant has become important enough for someone to kill."

"Have you decided the killer tried to poison Edna rather than us?"

Lawrence nodded.

"You're very short of words, Lawrence. Can you elaborate?"

"Not now, but I will."

Violet sighed. "This is not very collaborative."

"I'm still thinking things over. A little breakfast is bound to help."

Ten minutes later, Lawrence and Violet descended the stairs and followed their noses to the dining room. Reverend Edalji sat at the top of the table, his wife and daughter on either side. Lawrence approached the reverend, his hand outstretched. Edalji stood and returned the gesture.

"Please join us," he said.

Lawrence took a seat by Maud Edalji while Violet sat next to Charlotte. Both women acknowledged their presence but did not speak, and an uncomfortable atmosphere soon developed. After five minutes of excruciating silence, Charlotte picked up a small silver bell and rang apathetically. Dora soon appeared.

"Ma'am?"

"Fetch some tea and toast for our guests," said Charlotte.

"And a fresh pot for me," said Shapurji. "Maud?"

"No. I have things to do. Excuse me," said Maud abruptly before leaving the room.

"Thank you for extending your hospitality," said Lawrence. "We appreciate it."

"Knock, and the door will be opened to you," murmured the reverend.

"You're very kind."

Charlotte raised an eyebrow. "It is our duty," she said coldly.

"You've heard about Edna Mallett?" said Lawrence.

"Yes. Poor woman. I will visit her friends later to offer my condolences. She has no family since Mr Mallett died."

"Did you know that Edna was poisoned?" asked Lawrence.

"I heard she suffered from food poisoning," snapped Charlotte.

"More likely strychnine," said Lawrence firmly.

Charlotte looked searchingly at her husband.

"Surely not," said the reverend. "Has the autopsy confirmed this?"

"Not as far as I know," admitted Lawrence.

"Then it's idle gossip," said Charlotte.

"An educated guess based on evidence." Lawrence steepled his hands and tried to look authoritative.

"I won't believe it until the doctor agrees."

Lawrence opened his mouth to comment, but Violet touched the back of his hand in warning. "Did you know Mrs Mallett?" she asked.

"Yes. I've known Edna for a long time. She's a good woman," Charlotte replied. "And without a shred of malice. You imply that somebody killed her, but why would they?"

"Perhaps she knew something?" said Lawrence.

"About what?" Charlotte glared, steely-eyed.

"You know why we are here," said Lawrence softly.

"Only too well. But nothing connects this death to our troubles. Tell him, Shapurji."

"I'm afraid it does," said Violet. "One way or another."

"As if our lives were not hard enough already. This is too much."

Charlotte Edalji removed a large linen handkerchief from her sleeve and dabbed at her eyes. "I can't go through this again."

"You look ill," said the reverend. "Why not rest in your room?"

Charlotte pushed a plate of half-eaten toast into the centre of the table. "No. But I shall take a moment in the living room. Please do not disturb me." She rose and left, straight-backed and holding herself with forbearance.

"My wife is a remarkable woman," said the reverend. "But sensitive. And it's no wonder with all we have suffered."

"We are sorry to drag up unhappy memories for you," said Violet.

"Then go. And leave poor Mrs Mallett to rest in peace. If the police decide it's food poisoning, it's no bad thing."

"Are you suggesting we turn a blind eye to murder?" asked Lawrence.

"It might have been an accident. You say Edna Mallett ate a poisoned pie? But perhaps the meat was intended for an animal?"

Violet shuddered. "No one uses strychnine for pest control. It's hard to purchase for a reason. Besides, we took the meat directly from the butcher and as much as I disapprove of him, no shopkeeper in their right mind would deliberately contaminate their own produce."

"Why would you want the police, who caused so much harm to your son, to conceal this crime?" asked Lawrence.

The reverend cocked his head and gazed blankly. "You speak as if I should know all the answers. I don't. But you can't begin to understand the suffering in this village after twenty years of scrutiny. The constabulary will investigate the crime correctly if it is one. But I doubt they will reveal any details while things are still uncertain."

"It's too late," said Violet. "There's already widespread speculation."

"And so, it begins again. My poor wife. She cannot endure much more of this."

"I'd like to help her," said Violet. "We spoke unthinkingly. You have offered us refuge, and we thoughtlessly speculated over this business as if we could ever understand your position. Please forgive us and let me go to Mrs Edalji to apologise."

The reverend half-smiled and blinked several times. Violet's heart swelled with pity as she realised, he was holding back tears. The beleaguered reverend had reacted to a rare act of kindness. "You are welcome to try, but she may not speak to you," he said softly.

"I should make an effort. It's the least I can do," said Violet.

Lawrence finished his toast in a few quick bites as he watched Violet walking away. "I must pop out," he said, brushing crumbs from his palms with a serviette.

Reverend Edalji nodded but did not speak, instead raising a hand in farewell. Resisting the urge to ask about Horace, Lawrence buttoned his jacket and set out for the lodging house on Walsall Road.

Chapter Thirty-Six

RUN RABBIT RUN

LAWRENCE WALKED BACKWARDS UP the path from the vicarage, scrutinising the property as he crunched towards the gate. The large front windows were easy to get to. Anyone could reach them from the outside, though the culprits must have been daring to go so close to the living areas beneath. But the side windows were narrow, higher up and more challenging to reach. As Lawrence suspected, the ease of contamination depended on the chosen window. Having learned nothing useful, he turned and strode towards the road but stopped at the sound of a breaking twig.

Lawrence turned and surveyed the garden. Mature trees and shrubs surrounded the house, leaving plenty of areas for mischief makers to conceal themselves. And as an air of unease crept over him, he gained an unwanted insight into the toll taken on the Edaljis with the constant fear of an unknown enemy lurking outside, striking with ease and destroying the quiet enjoyment of their home forever.

Lawrence idly wondered why they had not moved away,

then rolled his eyes at the realisation that they could not. The vicarage was their living, their only means of income. The Edaljis were trapped like rats in a cage, there to be poked and prodded by the evil that had made their lives a misery and destroyed their son's reputation. Lawrence shivered and acknowledged that Arthur Conan Doyle might have been right after all. He had released George Edalji from suffering and given his parents welcome tranquillity. And Lawrence had stirred it all up again in the name of vanity. It was time to walk away and leave them in peace, even against his better judgement.

His mind made up, Lawrence increased his stride before hearing a pop and seeing a puff of sawdust coming from the large oak beside him. He instinctively squatted, listening for further sounds, but the garden was silent. Brushing foliage from his knees, he stood again and examined the tree. Lawrence swept a hand over the damaged trunk, clearing splinters of wood, then stared in puzzlement at the perfectly round hole in the trunk with a glint of metal beneath. Then his brain caught up with the evidence of his eyes, and he dropped to the floor as a second shot rang out. Heart pounding, he glanced towards the rectory, expecting to see the reverend or a curious housemaid searching for the source of the noise. But the door remained firmly shut. Nobody had heard it. And come to think of it, for all the damage to the tree, there was little noise to match. But someone was taking potshots at him, and he had been lucky to escape injury.

Lawrence's heart thudded in his chest. He had been in danger before but never from a hidden assailant with a lethal weapon at distant quarters. The shooter could have concealed himself anywhere.

Lawrence considered running back to the safety of the

rectory, but he might end up with a bullet in his back. Would running forward be any better? Lawrence panted, his breath ragged as fear overtook him. He wiped his moist forehead and considered his options. Violet was in the rectory, and he must be careful not to lure danger towards her, leaving him only one option. He must sprint towards the brick wall and conceal himself immediately before the shooter had a chance to aim and extinguish his life. As Lawrence sprang from his haunches, another shot whistled through the bushes. But he was already in motion, running towards the road. He reached the wall, flattened himself against it, and searched eagle-eyed for a vantage point where a marksman might hide. Lawrence placed a shaking hand to his forehead, trying to see past the glint of the rising morning sun. But the brick garden walls impeded his view. The shooter must be higher. Could he see him? The lack of fire suggested not. He was safe for now. But that would change if his assailant moved. He stuck his head out and sneaked a glimpse beyond the gate, seeing nothing but a black car idling in the lane too far down for a shooter to conceal himself. Clenching his fists in frustration, Lawrence tried to make sense of the silent garden. How could he steer clear of his enemy if he couldn't hear him? And why the silence? In Lawrence's experience, gunshots came with loud explosions. He had heard of firearm silencers, but they were a recent invention and largely uncommon. Still, it was the most likely explanation for the deadly silence of the bullets. But silent guns and shady assassins made leaving through the gate unwise. He should take another route and be quick about it. Pondering his situation further would not help. Lawrence needed to move, and soon. Taking a deep breath, he doubled back and plunged through the undergrowth at the back of the garden, hoping it would take him to familiar territory.

Lawrence emerged and wiped a hand across his bloodied face, shredded by concealed thorns in the bushes, and took a moment to survey the landscape. The tall church spire gave him all the clues he needed about where best to find cover, and he risked a run across the flat ground to reach the sanctuary. But after only moments of sprinting, another shot whistled past, and Lawrence realised his enemy was in close pursuit. He fell forward on his front and crawled across the furrowed field, dirt and dust coating his face. Another shot sent debris flying inches from his side. He'd been lucky so far, but he was making himself a target. Lawrence stood and ran for his life, swerving unpredictably from side to side across the last few yards as he hurled himself towards the safety of the church wall. The shooter was in hot pursuit and would corner Lawrence if he went inside. He must find a hiding place where he would stand a fighting chance of escape if discovered. Now drenched with bloodied sweat, Lawrence made for the safety of the rear of the church where gravestones stood sentry over the dead, some erect, others listing and neglected. He considered taking cover by a large square tomb, but it was too obvious. Though it would give him the cover he needed, Lawrence ignored it, kneeling behind a freshly inscribed stone with a bush immediately behind.

He waited nervously, hoping against hope that the shooter had gone away. But a swish of grass and plod of footsteps suggested otherwise. Lawrence shivered as the approaching steps grew louder and tried to still his trembling limbs. But the sudden sharp shock of hearing the crisp metallic click of a rifle bolt sliding metal to metal sent his nerves spinning. He almost lost control, nearly bolted from his hiding place. But reason prevailed, and he crouched shivering, hoping Violet wouldn't find herself a widow in the coming moments. The gunman prowled the churchyard in ever-decreasing circles, all of them close to Lawrence. Cursing through whispered breath, the unknown assailant uttered an expletive and loosed a shot above his head. The sound of the bullet was unmistakable, but the silent delivery spoke of sinister intent – a rifle with a silencer for sure.

The man was close now, so close that Lawrence could hear the rustle of grass beneath his feet. He chanced a glimpse and snapped back his head at the sight of a pair of shiny paint-speckled boots. The man lingered, the position of his legs suggesting silent scrutinisation of the churchyard like an owl searching for prey. A single movement, a cough or splutter, would mean Lawrence would face the full force of an armed enemy bent on his destruction. He heard a sigh, another expletive, the clatter of a rifle unwisely slammed against a tombstone in temper. Then the footsteps moved on, growing quieter as the gunman walked away. Lawrence waited with bated breath, head down, quietly contemplating the ground beneath his feet. He must not move a muscle. He might still be under scrutiny. Patience was the order of the day. By the time Lawrence dared to move half an hour later, he almost tumbled to the ground as his stiff legs buckled beneath him. But he was alive, and better still, he had the answer. He knew everything: the perpetrator and, more importantly, the reason.

Chapter Thirty-Seven

NEXT STEPS

LAWRENCE CUT through every minor lane, dodging people and traffic until he located his car. Forgoing the opportunity to reclaim his lost hat, he sped towards the vicarage, hunching low in the driving seat. He screeched to a halt directly outside the door, leaving the engine running, and entered without pausing to knock.

Violet heard the door and ran to meet him. "Where were you? I've been worried sick." She paused, cocked her head, and examined his face. "Lawrence. What happened?" she asked, tracing her fingers down the scratches on his cheek.

"Get your things, Violet. We're leaving at once."

"But why?"

"Please. Just humour me."

Violet turned and left without a word, returning moments later with her handbag.

"I'll get the suitcase," said Lawrence. "Don't set a foot outside this house."

He grabbed the baggage and ran back downstairs. "Let's go."

"What about the reverend? This is terribly rude."

"No time," said Lawrence. "I've parked the car with the passenger side facing the door. Run straight inside and duck down as low as you can."

"Why? You're frightening me now."

"For your safety and mine. Ready?"

Violet nodded. Lawrence pulled open the door and cast a cursory glance outside. "Now," he said.

They ran to the car. Lawrence hurled the suitcase into the back and pushed Violet's head lower as he drove away. He took a hasty glance up the road, then drove furiously towards Walsall.

They returned to the outskirts of Great Wyrley six hours later.

"Well, that was a waste of time," said Lawrence.

"You tried."

"Not hard enough, it appears."

"The sergeant might have listened if you'd told him the name of your suspect."

"I don't trust the police to act on it."

"Then why did you spend most of the afternoon trying to convince them to come to the village?"

"You know why."

"No, I don't. You've carefully curated all the details you want me to hear without parting with any factual information."

Lawrence sighed. Violet, wise as usual, knew when he was prevaricating. Once they were safely away from the village, he had played down his concern for their safety, not to mention his terrifying earlier encounter. And he still hadn't told Violet what he suspected and why. Increasingly annoyed at his reticence, she had stubbornly stopped asking. And now he was in a quandary. Violet desperately wanted to go home while he knew enough to risk attempting to provoke a confession. He needed to get Violet to a place of safety, knowing full well that she wouldn't go if she thought he was in danger. What to do?

"You've made a wrong turn. Cheltenham is that way," said Violet.

"I know."

"We need to go home. You promised."

"Please indulge me. Just one more time."

"No. I told Charlotte that we were leaving the village. They have suffered enough. It's time to draw a line under the whole affair. Besides, you said we were in danger. Were you exaggerating?"

"No. We are. That's why I'd like to take you back to the vicarage while I deal with this once and for all."

"Well, I'm not going."

"Please, Violet. I can't guarantee your safety or mine, and this is the last throw of the dice."

"Do you think I'm the kind of woman to sit at home while you walk into the lion's den alone?"

"I hoped you might."

Violet frowned. "You should know better. I'm coming with you, and that's the end of it."

"Right. Then we'll need to do this publicly for our own protection. The culprit won't strike if all eyes are on us. That's if they turn up at all, which is a major flaw in my plan. I don't know who will be there. This could all go very wrong."

"Where will this be?"

"At The Royal Oak."

"It's usually busy," said Violet. "You must stand a good chance."

"Let's hope so," said Lawrence. "If it's too quiet, I must insist you stay behind. There's safety in numbers."

"And I must remind you I am an independent woman and will do as I choose. And I'd like to return to Cheltenham, so if I tolerate this brief interlude, you must allow me to decide on matters of safety."

Lawrence sighed, knowing he had met his match. He had tried to do the husbandly thing many times over the years, protecting his wife as best he could. But Violet wasn't accommodating in that regard. And she had been even less pliable since joining the suffragist movement. Violet had firm views on husbands asserting their authority, and he stood no chance of changing her mind. He must factor Violet's safety into the night's proceedings and hope for a hefty dose of luck.

Lawrence glanced at his watch. "It's too soon, but we can't hang around in the car. Anything could happen."

"Will it be any better in The Royal Oak if it's empty?"

"It's marginally better than being outside. We're as safe there as anywhere."

"Then let's go inside and wait."

They entered the public house expecting customers to be thin on the ground but were pleasantly surprised by the low buzz of noise as they opened the exterior door. Over a dozen men stood chatting in a cluster around the bar. Lawrence accompanied Violet to a more prominent table than previously, and she sat uneasily feeling their eyes upon her as Lawrence approached the bar to order drinks. He returned to find a balding man with a scar across his face leaning against a low wall, chatting to Violet as if he knew her. The man glanced at Lawrence with evident irritation at the interruption to his ignoble intentions. He winked suggestively at Violet as he walked away.

"What did he want?" growled Lawrence.

"Nothing. He greeted me, and I took advantage of his presence to ask a few questions."

"Such as?"

"The names of the men at the bar."

"Anything useful?"

"Yes. See that young man loitering over there? That's Royden Sharp."

Lawrence followed her eyeline to see a short, light-haired man in overalls deep in conversation with a man whose dirt-laden clothes suggested he had come straight to the pub from the coal mine.

"Interesting," said Lawrence.

"Oh, and look what the cat dragged in," said Violet.

"Jack Hart, excellent."

Violet's eyes narrowed. "Will you let me in on your theory now?"

"Ultimately, yes. But I want to see how this plays out."

They sat for another ten minutes, silently sipping drinks neither had much appetite for. Then, half a dozen men arrived, including Edgar Brookes and Christopher Hatton.

"That's a surprise," said Violet. "I thought young Mr Hatton was a cut above this type of drinking estab-lishment."

"It gets better and better," said Lawrence, reaching into his pocket for his notebook.

"What are we waiting for?"

"Me to marshal my thoughts as much as anything," said Lawrence. He pulled up his sleeve, glanced at his watch, and tapped the glass face twice as if it might make time go faster. "Will you be alright while I go to the men's room?" he asked.

Violet nodded. "It's so busy, there's barely room for another person. I'll be perfectly safe."

Lawrence emerged from his ablutions to find Violet sipping her drink while waving across the room. He nodded as he saw the familiar form of Martin Newlove entering the pub in civilian clothing.

"Ah, good. Martin is off duty. I bet that young man is his nephew. Perhaps he'll join us for a drink, and we'll find out," said Violet. "I'm sure he is as eager to hear your theory as I am."

"Hold that thought. I'm about to let loose. But before I do, I'd like to ask you a favour. It's up to you whether you agree, and I'm not asserting myself or taking your cooperation for granted. But I love you very much, Violet, and there may be a reaction to what I am about to say. Please don't leave these premises if anything happens to me or place yourself in a situation where you are alone. Will you cooperate?"

Violet nodded her head. "I'll try."

"Good." Lawrence cupped her face and drew her close before planting a kiss on her forehead. "I love you, Mrs Harpham."

"I love you too."

"Right. Here goes nothing."

Chapter Thirty-Eight

A LOGICAL CONCLUSION

LAWRENCE STOOD and cleared his throat, struggling to make himself heard above the buzz of noise. He tried again before grabbing an empty tankard from the adjoining table and slamming it down three times in quick succession. The conversation ceased, and a swathe of faces turned towards him.

"Your attention, please?" demanded Lawrence.

"What for?" asked a burly man.

"I won't keep you long."

"You can sod off, whoever you are. We're here for a quiet drink, aren't we, lads?"

"Too right," said a pock-marked miner with a streak of white in his otherwise dark hair.

"Give the man a chance," growled Jack Hart.

"Who died and made you the gaffer?"

Hart narrowed his eyes, and the man sat down, scowling as he nursed his ale.

"The floor's all yours," said Hart.

Lawrence licked his lips. "My name is Lawrence Harpham. I'm a private detective."

"Are you here about the old lady?" asked a red-coated man.

"Edna Mallett? In a manner of speaking. We were there the day she died."

"Is this a confession?" Red Coat's friend nudged him in the ribs and cackled.

"No. But I'm hoping one might follow, though it won't come from me."

"Then what do you want?" asked Red Coat.

"Sir Arthur Conan Doyle righted a grave injustice," said Lawrence.

"If you say so." A bearded man standing next to Martin Newlove took a step forward and glared at Lawrence.

"A grave injustice," repeated Lawrence. "And nothing will persuade me otherwise."

"Some might say he got what he deserved," said the bearded man.

"So I've heard. And it's a common point of view. But you're wrong. The Edalji family did not deserve the years of mental torture forced upon them. I wonder if they would have suffered the same if they looked more appealing."

"Careful," warned Christopher Hatton.

"Seconded," said Edgar Brookes. "Our family did not escape the wrath of the letter writers. We were in their sights for years, so it's not all about race."

"Accepted," said Lawrence. "To a certain extent. But however you dress it up, people victimised the Edaljis for being different. And it's impossible to understand the depths of their despair without standing in their shoes."

"So why drag it up again?" asked Jack Hart.

"Because no one ever solved the crime. You," said

Lawrence, pointing to the man in overalls. "Is your name Royden Sharp?"

"Yes. Why?"

"How do you feel about being Conan Doyle's prime suspect?"

Sharp shrugged. "I don't care."

"Then why are you leaving the country?"

"None of your business." Sharp's face reddened as he passed a hand around his neck and loosened his collar.

"Your position can't be comfortable," said Lawrence.

"We all know he didn't do it," said Jack Hart. "So what's the problem?"

"Well, that's the difference, isn't it? Mr Sharp has friends to advocate on his behalf."

Half a dozen men muttered their affirmation.

"Ironic," said Lawrence. "For what it's worth, I think the evidence against Mr Sharp is poor to non-existent, just as it was with George Edalji. And if George had the support you enjoy, the outcome might have been different. But they threw him to the wolves, sacrificed on the altar of indifference. Nobody cared. Nobody but Conan Doyle."

"And your point?" The burly man slammed his glass on the table and spat out the words.

"I don't believe Sharp did it any more than George. So, nobody has faced justice for decades of poison pen letters, slain animals and now the death of poor Edna Mallett. Someone should pay. And if they don't, well-meaning individuals like me will pick the case apart for decades to come. Better to lance the wound now and unmask the perpetrator."

"Good luck with that," said Red Coat, smirking.

"I've had all the luck I need," said Lawrence. "You see, I know who did it. And I know why. Who wants to hear?"

"Tell us if you're so clever. I won't believe it, though," said Red Coat.

"That's up to you. Listen and then tell me what you think."

Lawrence picked up his tankard and gulped the last of the ale before clearing his throat. "Innocence means being free from guilt, pure and blameless, if you will. But that definition crates a binary choice, implying the wrongdoer is entirely guilty or completely innocent. But what if the truth lies somewhere in between? What if one is largely innocent of a crime but blameworthy in some other small regard? Should that person then suffer in perpetuity?"

"What are you talking about?" growled the bearded man. "Speak clearly or shut up."

"I'll put it another way. Should a silly youthful prank lead to three years in prison?"

Lawrence stopped talking and glanced around the room. Silence fell. Nobody spoke. He waited, letting his words sink in.

"Well, should it?"

Christopher Hatton spoke up. "I know what you're getting at. A silly prank should not spoil someone's life, but that goes both ways. The prank, for all its innocence, might have serious consequences for somebody else."

"Thank you," said Lawrence. "You have put it well. That is exactly what happened, my friends, but I think you already know that."

"We're not your friends," growled the burly man.

"And we don't know what you're talking about," said Red Coat. "Sling your hook, why don't you?"

A grey-haired man stepped away from the bar and approached Lawrence. "Are you referring to Elizabeth?"

"Yes. Did you know her?"

"She was my niece."

"Then I'm sorry for your loss."

"The hell you are."

Lawrence blinked, unprepared for the venom in the man's low-pitched voice.

"Why don't you tell me about it?"

"Why don't you find another place to drink?"

"Very well. I will explain myself. The first poison pen letters arrived at the vicarage in August 1898. They were simplistic letters, initially harmless and somewhat juvenile. But things soon turned sinister after damage to the rectory, followed by a series of unpleasant letters sent to Elizabeth Foster, the maid. Crude graffiti appeared inside and outside the property, and letters arrived written on the flyleaves from books in the children's playroom. Whoever penned the letters must have had access to the inside of the vicarage."

"Tell us something we don't know." Red Coat scowled.

Lawrence ignored him. "We can rule out the vicar and his wife, who were unlikely to write vitriolic letters to themselves. And the younger children were too small to be worthy of consideration. Horace was nine and barely out of short trousers, while little Maud was only six. The only other residents were George Edalji and Elizabeth Foster. Elizabeth, though older, was not well educated, while George, though only thirteen, was smart. He attended the local grammar school and excelled intellectually. Now, no parent wants to consider their child misbehaving, especially given the disturbing sentiments expressed in the letters. I'm not suggesting that Reverend Edalji deliberately overlooked the possibility that George might be the culprit, but subconsciously or otherwise, the prospect of Elizabeth being guilty suited them better. They called upon Sergeant Upton and accused Elizabeth of the crime."

The burly man jumped to his feet, knocking over his pint. "Stop boring us with your history lesson. We all know this. For God's sake, let it be."

"Wait," said Elizabeth's uncle solemnly. "Hear him out."

"Thank you," said Lawrence. "And you're right. You are more familiar with these events than I am, but it helps to summarise. They prosecuted poor Elizabeth, who fled the vicarage in shame, before returning to her parents' house."

"Where she kept to herself for several years," said her uncle. "She lost her good reputation and all desire to leave the house. She was a poor, broken thing until she met Arthur."

"Elizabeth was innocent, and Sergeant Upton regretted his part in her conviction," said Lawrence. "I hear she died protesting her innocence."

The uncle nodded. "Elizabeth knew she was dying, and she swore to the end that she had not sent the letters."

"But you all knew that," said Lawrence. "Because in the summer of 1892, someone gave George a taste of his own medicine and decided to punish him for his childhood folly. But remember this. George, by all accounts, was very fond of Elizabeth. He never intended her to suffer for his youthful indiscretion."

"Then why did he do it?" asked Red Coat. "And more importantly, why didn't he confess?"

"George was only thirteen, and for all his intelligence, he was still a child learning his place in the world. I understand the anger from Elizabeth's friends and their desire for revenge, but the punishment was cruel and did not fit the crime. The Edalji family suffered unbearably. Their punishment was too much, too long, and extremely unkind. You should all be ashamed."

"Don't include me in it," said Edgar Brookes.

"I don't. Your family suffered too. You were not involved in the quiet conspiracy to prolong the Edalji family's torture. But others were. Several others who took it in turns to torment them."

"Who were they?" asked Red Coat.

Lawrence stared pointedly at Elizabeth's uncle, who shifted uncomfortably from foot to foot. "I wasn't part of it. Not personally. I can't speak for Elizabeth's brothers."

"No matter," said Lawrence. "I am sure they, like others, jumped on the band waggon. But they did not instigate the letters. Someone else started this, but who and why?"

Lawrence paused for effect. "Elizabeth attended court in 1889, yet the first letters arrived two and a half years later. Why?"

"I thought you had all the answers," said the pock-faced man.

Lawrence pursed his lips. "I believe I do," he replied. "But perhaps Elizabeth's uncle can confirm my theory."

"Go on."

"Elizabeth took to her room for a long time and kept to the house for years. But at some point, she recovered her confidence and started going outside again. I know from my research that she married in 1894. But when did she meet her husband?"

Elizabeth's uncle cocked his head. "A few years before."

"Around the summer of 1892?"

"Possibly."

"I think it is more than likely."

"Big deal," said the burly man.

"It is a big deal. And I didn't realise to what extent until Edna Mallett mentioned in passing that Elizabeth had a sweetheart."

"Did she?" Elizabeth's uncle grimaced, scratching his chin as he considered Lawrence's words.

"It was a fledgling romance and not well known. I can't say how Edna found out, but she did. And she told me that Elizabeth walked away from everything she knew, including her sweetheart."

"Did he write the letters?"

"Not necessarily, and certainly not all of them. But Elizabeth's lover stirred the pot, fostered disharmony and grievance within the community and provoked hostility and distrust towards the Edaljis. He used a young member of his own family to write the earlier letters before penning some of the later ones. In between, without ever directly asking anyone to do it, he manipulated others to carry on the intimidation until George Edalji went to prison."

"For killing a horse. He deserved it."

"George was incapable of harming an animal. He didn't commit the slayings. Neither did the letter writers. As my good wife says, the psychology is wrong, and they are completely different crimes. I don't know what sick individual took pleasure or revenge by attacking the livestock, but it was not the letter writer. They simply took advantage and linked their letters to the killings."

"Then why the secrecy?" asked Christopher Hatton.

"Another good question," said Lawrence. "In the early days, if caught, the letter writer would have suffered a similar prosecution to Elizabeth. Reputationally damaging, but unlikely to result in imprisonment. The crimes became more serious over time, with death threats to the Edaljis, which would have attracted a longer sentence. And Edna's death makes it a capital crime."

"But that would only affect the letter writer, not the man that instigated them," said Hatton.

"And there you've hit the nail on the head. Strictly speaking, he hadn't committed a crime, only aided and abetted one."

"Then he could afford to be caught."

"But what if he couldn't?" Lawrence opened his arms, palms facing the ceiling, as he asked the rhetorical question. A sea of blank faces stared back.

"Go on," said Violet impatiently.

"I'll come back to that," said Lawrence. He faced the crowd again, encouraged by their silence and rapt interest. "Earlier today, someone tried to shoot me. I hid well enough to stay out of sight, but the gunman came within feet of me, and I saw his boots. Paint-speckled boots." Lawrence looked up. "Green paint," he continued, aiming his words towards the back of the room. But the recipient of his pointed glance had melted away into the background. "Damn it," said Lawrence. "He's gone."

"Who?" asked Violet.

"The one person who would lose everything if discovered."

Violet frowned. "Who?" she repeated.

But Lawrence sprang up, running towards the door. "Stay here," he commanded, turning to face her. And then he was gone.

Chapter Thirty-Nine

CATCHING THE KILLER

LAWRENCE RAN into the darkness and pulled up short beneath a streetlight. He waited momentarily, eyes focussed, trying to detect his quarry. Only when he heard the faint sound of running feet did he pick a direction and sprint towards the sound. Huffing heavily, Lawrence powered forward, but his quarry was well ahead. After two hundred yards, Lawrence pulled up and bent over, trying to catch his breath. A few seconds passed as he considered his options. He guessed the bolthole where the man would likely head but did not know its location. Cursing, he returned to the pub, halting as he saw a young man running towards him. Lawrence backed into the shadows and waited until the boy was close enough to touch, then he lunged towards him, spinning him around and forcing his arm up his back.

"What the hell are you doing?" asked the lad.

"Where is he?" snarled Lawrence.

"Who?"

"Your uncle."

"I don't know."

"What's your name?" hissed Lawrence.

"Leslie."

"Well, Leslie. I have little time, and you have even less. Tell me where he's gone or I will start breaking bones."

"I don't think so."

Lawrence roughly shoved the arm farther up Leslie's back. He screamed. "Stop. It's breaking."

"I told you that. Now talk."

"My uncle has gone home. It's over there."

"Take me," said Lawrence.

"I will if you release my bloody arm."

Lawrence lightened his grip fractionally and shoved Leslie up the road while maintaining a firm grip. "Off you go and make it snappy."

"Alright. Stop pushing."

They walked for a couple of minutes as a waxing moon glowed high in the sky. "This is it," said Leslie, nodding towards an end-terraced house backing onto fields.

"He'd better be there or you'll regret it when I find you."

"Do your worst."

"Oh, I will, Leslie. I'll make sure you serve time for your part in this. Don't think you've escaped justice for the filthy letters you wrote for your uncle."

"He made me. I was only a boy."

"Perhaps at the beginning. But George Edalji was young too, and you didn't care about him like I don't care about you. And as for your uncle. What a bitter disappointment he's turned out to be."

Leslie Newlove opened his mouth to speak, but the sound of a squeaking garden gate reminded Lawrence of his primary task.

"Stay here and be quiet, or it will be the worse for you."

Lawrence tiptoed through the gate, listening for signs

of life. He passed the only downstairs window, peering inside to see an elderly woman with her head lolled back in quiet repose, gently swaying on a rocking chair. But the sounds Lawrence had heard came from outside. He glanced around the garden, noticing a large wooden structure along the rear brick wall. Lawrence strode quietly towards it, grimacing at the dusty window with myriad spider webs obscuring the view. He reached into his pocket and used his handkerchief to wipe the worst of it away. Pressing his nose to the glass, he squinted at the dark interior, spying plant pots and garden tools in front. But the light was too poor, with the edges and corners of the shed too obscured for any useful view. Lawrence waited quietly, contemplating his next move, then slowly and deliberately crunched up the garden path, making as much noise as possible.

Lawrence ducked behind the coal house, signalling to Leslie to stay quiet and remain beyond the gate at the front of the house. Then he settled on his haunches and waited. Five minutes passed, then another few, before a creak from the shed door rewarded his patience. He peered around the corner to see a shotgun emerging a few seconds ahead of Martin Newlove's face. Lawrence stifled a sigh and squeezed close to the coal house, his mind frantically calculating how to extricate himself from the situation. Gravel surrounded the outhouse. If he moved, Martin would hear him. If he stayed, he would be in full sight as soon as Newlove approached the house. He had no choice but to bluff his way out.

Lawrence cleared his throat. "Hands in the air, Martin."

An audible gasp hissed through the night air as Lawrence's words caught Martin Newlove unaware.

"Where are you, Harpham?"

"Never you mind. I'm armed, and you had better stand still. Don't move a muscle."

"I don't believe you. Where would you get a gun from?"

"That's not your concern. But if you step farther forward, you'll soon feel its effect."

Lawrence recoiled at the jarring sound of metal on metal as Martin Newlove drew back the bolt of his rifle.

"Just making sure I have enough ammunition to finish this," he said.

"There's no point. The game's up. Why don't you tell me all about it?"

"Why bother? You have it figured out."

"Was I right?"

Newlove huffed a sigh audibly across the garden. "More or less," he said.

"So, you were Elizabeth's betrothed?"

"Not quite that. We were both young. But it would have developed. I hoped she would come back to me, but then she married someone else, and I couldn't bear it. Elizabeth was the love of my life, and George Edalji ruined it."

"But why all the letters? Creating them must have occupied your every waking moment?"

"It's all I had outside of work. I never met another woman. No wife, no love, no family. No room for anything except the bitterness that man fostered inside me."

"But why bring the Brookes family into it?"

"They were just as bad. Anyone who tolerated the Edaljis was my enemy. I started with the Brookes to drive a wedge between the families. It took a while, but it worked."

"And the livestock killings? Was I right about that?"

"Yes. It had nothing to do with me. I don't know who started it, and I don't want to know. But using it in the letters was too good an opportunity to miss. I dropped a link between the two things in casual conversation and it soon spread."

"It's hard to believe two simultaneous crimes had no connection. Who would harm animals for the sake of it."

"Don't be naïve. It's more common than you think in the countryside. You can go anywhere in England and hear similar reports of livestock damage. Farmers are not sentimental, and the creatures are not pets. They are a valuable commodity."

"So why slay them?"

"I don't know. Revenge, possibly pleasure. Either way, I didn't do it, even if the timing was beneficial. It certainly upped the ante and fixed eyes more firmly on the Edalji boy."

"Did you write any letters?"

"No. Not one. You were wrong about that. I didn't need to. Don't blame Leslie. He's always been willing to please and let others influence him."

"Who else?"

"Mostly impressionable schoolboys. Some knew George Edalji, but others did not. It wasn't difficult to drop an insinuation here and a sweetener there, usually by an anonymous bribe. I found it even easier to get the adults involved. The right word in the right ear would soon direct resentment towards the family. Everyone knew about the letters and could easily pick up the task. But when the adults began, the tone of the letters changed. I didn't know who or how many writers there were at any time. I was safe and encouraged it to continue, but then they arrested George Edalji."

Lawrence waited for Newlove to continue, but an uneasy silence fell. He wondered if Newlove was creeping forward, gun in hand, about to pounce, and his heart thudded as a clammy dread settled on his skin. Almost without thinking, Lawrence removed his silver calling card holder from his pocket and clunked it against the steel door of the coal cellar as if cocking a weapon.

"You're making me nervous," Lawrence growled, projecting a confidence he didn't feel. "And that makes me trigger happy. Where are you?"

"Still here," said Newlove softly, his voice a healthy distance away.

"Edalji's arrest must have made you happy," Lawrence said, shifting his weight off a leg prickling with the beginnings of pins and needles.

"In some ways," said Newlove. "That damned creature got what he deserved, but it increased the risk to me. Sergeant Upton and Captain Anson never looked much further than Edalji for the crime. But things tightened up when they arrested him. Other members of the constabulary started questioning the locals. And I wasn't sure who was writing letters by then. I had been careful in my prompting, but it would only take a few loose lips to mention me, especially if they spoke to Leslie. He wouldn't have stood up well to their interrogation."

"But you never wrote the letters. What's the worst that could have happened?"

"By then, there were regular livestock slayings, and I'd spread the idea of a connection within the community. Inevitably, it appeared in print, more so as time went on and the letter writers got into their stride. It suited me to see George Edalji under increasing suspicion of more serious crimes. But, if anyone discovered my part in it, they would think I'd slaughtered the animals which was criminal. It gave me sleepless nights, and I started pulling away."

"Your constant stirring may have encouraged the livestock killings."

"Unintentionally."

"Nevertheless."

"Shut up. I'd never hurt an animal. But I'd lost control of the situation, and the village had turned against the Edalji family. If anyone had investigated properly, discovering my influence wouldn't have taken long. I might have kept my police career with the letters alone, which could have been difficult to prove. But an accusation of damaging another man's livelihood, whether true or not, would have finished me."

"So, you got away with it. George Edalji went to jail while you satisfied your urge for revenge and continued with your career. I bet you had a hairy moment when Conan Doyle arrived on the scene?"

"For a while. Conan Doyle convinced himself of Royden Sharpe's guilt, which was a major sticking point. I had stoked up Royden good and proper, and he was likely heavily involved in the letter writing."

"Then why were you so adamant he was innocent?"

"I didn't want you talking to him. He might have mentioned my name in passing. It would only take one or two people to do the same. Leslie would cave. He knew everything."

"So, my arrival put the cat among the pigeons."

"Yes. It did. I slashed your tyres; in case you were wondering."

"How? We were drinking together. You had no time."

Newlove exhaled. "I knew you were trouble from the start and dealt with your car before coming to the pub. I hoped it might put you off."

"That sort of thing stiffens my resolve. It's left you with a dilemma. You should come quietly."

"No. My career is my life. There's only one way this is going."

Lawrence heard a crunch as Martin Newlove took a slow step forward. "Wait," said Lawrence. "What about the offal?"

"What about it?"

"Were you trying to kill Edna or me when you poisoned the kidneys?"

"What?"

"You put something in the bag of meat we left."

"I did not."

"You must have. You were the only one who knew where we were staying. Don't deny bringing it to Edna's house."

"I wouldn't. You left that disgusting bag of offal at the public house and thought I'd bring it to you."

"Then who put poison in the bag?"

"I don't know. I saw you'd forgotten it, so I dropped it around when I had finished drinking. The house was dark, so I hung the bag on the doorknob."

"I don't believe you."

"No, and neither will anyone else now they know about me and Elizabeth. I realised I'd be a suspect as soon as Edna died. That's why I went after you with the shotgun. With you gone, no one would know I'd touched the bag of kidneys. But you should know it wasn't me. Why would I use poison when I have a gun? I'm finished, Harpham, and it's your fault. If only one of those shots had hit you, we wouldn't be here now. Or if I hadn't tried to do a good deed. But anyone could have seen me carrying that damned bag of meat and thought I killed Edna. The fact remains, I don't have any poison, and I wouldn't know where to get it."

"It doesn't wash, Martin. Edna knew you were Elizabeth's sweetheart."

"I didn't know that until you mentioned it tonight."

"It's ironic. I would never have suspected you until I saw your boots. You'd probably have got away with it if you'd left me alone."

"I should have thrown them away when the paint wouldn't come off, but it doesn't matter. This mess has gone on long enough." The sound of Newlove readying the shotgun cracked through the night air.

Lawrence shrank back.

"Don't do this, Martin. If you kill me, you'll spend your life behind bars. And you know what they'll do to a convicted copper."

"I will serve time, regardless. The police won't tolerate a lawbreaker, and I've already lost everything that mattered. I'm damned if I'm going to jail."

"Then put the gun down and walk away. Don't make me try to stop you."

"As if you could. You don't have a weapon. You're bluffing."

Newlove moved again, short stepping to one side, making a barely audible groan as metal hit enamel.

Lawrence prepared to bolt. He might outpace Martin and dodge the bullet if he ran for it now. But he would endanger Leslie as he ran towards him. Surely Newlove, however unhinged, wouldn't injure his nephew.

"God save me," muttered Newlove as an explosion screeched across the garden.

Lawrence dropped to his belly, his ears ringing at the sudden, unexpected blast, his nose twitching at the smell of cordite.

"No," screamed Leslie, darting through the gate. "What have you done?"

Lawrence jumped to his feet. "Nothing," he said, holding his hands in the air. "I'm unarmed."

"Uncle?"

"Stay still," barked Lawrence.

Both turned their heads at a sudden tap on the window as Martin's grey-haired mother pressed her face to the glass, looking bemused. Lawrence stood directly in front of her. "Get inside. Get her away from the window," he commanded.

Only when Leslie Newlove had reached the living room did Lawrence turn and walk towards the rear of the garden. Martin had fallen back on the path, still clutching the short-barrelled shotgun, but now minus the top of his skull. Blood and brain matter spattered the wooden shed. Lawrence turned to go. There was nothing left for him to do now but fetch an officer. Trembling in shock, he made his way towards the pub, sickened at the sight he had seen. Lawrence blanched at the prospect of explaining it to the local constabulary. Worse still was the chilling thought that someone other than Martin Newlove had deliberately tried to poison him.

Chapter Forty

CAPTURED

"THERE YOU ARE," said Violet as Lawrence stepped through the door of The Royal Oak. "Did you find him?"

Lawrence nodded.

"Who was it?"

"Martin Newlove."

"I thought so but I wasn't certain at first. It should have been obvious when Martin slipped away. I wanted to follow you but stayed as you asked. And young Mr Hatton insisted on keeping me company. He's only just left."

"I'm glad you weren't with me," said Lawrence. "Thank you for keeping safe." Lawrence lowered his head and covered his face with his hands.

"Are you alright?"

"Not really. There's no easy way to say this, Violet, but Martin Newlove is dead."

"Oh my God. What happened?"

"He blew his brains out."

"Why?"

"For all his faults, Martin was a dedicated policeman. He knew he'd lose his job and couldn't face the disgrace."

"I should think so too. He killed Edna."

"Martin denied having anything to do with her death. And I believe him. He seemed puzzled at the suggestion."

Violet snorted. "Nonsense. Who else could it be? There can't be two people in the village who mean Edna harm. Martin Newlove inflicted years of torment on the Edaljis and must answer for his crimes. It serves him right that justice prevailed."

"That's a little harsh."

"I don't mean he deserved to die, but imprisonment would have been just. Nobody is above the law, especially not a policeman."

"Well, the only place he'll be going is the morgue."

"Does anybody else know?"

"Yes. I met Jack Hart and friends when leaving Newlove's garden. They heard the shot and came to investigate. Hart offered to fetch the authorities. I should have hung around, but I was happy for someone else to take responsibility.

"They'll want a statement from you."

"Not if they think it's an unexplained suicide."

"That's unlikely after your long denouement in the pub."

"I didn't name Newlove. Did anyone see him leave?"

"Yes, his nephew Leslie."

"Who I left at the front gate. Leslie won't volunteer any information. It's not in his interest to talk about it."

"But what about everyone listening here tonight?"

"They may put two and two together, but where's the evidence? They'll think I'm another interfering busybody who bit off more than he could chew."

Violet frowned. "I don't understand you, Lawrence. You've just solved the investigation that baffled Sir Arthur, and instead of proclaiming your success, you want to slink off into the night and let Newlove off the hook."

"I'm not worried about Newlove. It's the others."

"Who?"

"Reverend and Mrs Edalji. They've been through enough. Tomorrow's newspapers could contain a small paragraph about the unexplained suicide of a local policeman or a front-page news article dragging up the whole sorry matter yet again. Then, the fingers will start pointing at anyone who may have written a letter in anger. Leslie Newlove is a penny short of a shilling and heavily influenced by an uncle who should have known better. Martin's mother is grieving for her dead son, and George Edalji has been quietly living without scandal since his release from prison. The residents of Great Wyrley have had enough. It's time to leave and let life return to normal."

"You'll have to eat humble pie next time you see Arthur."

"I don't care. I should never have got involved. Let's drive home and pick up Daisy."

Violet's face lit up with a beaming smile. "That would be perfect. If we leave straight away, I can call Aurora first thing tomorrow."

"Exactly."

Lawrence offered his arm as Violet rose from her seat. She buttoned her coat and edged closer to him as they walked past the bar.

"You won't mind driving in the dark?" she asked.

"Not if it means waking up in Cheltenham."

They exited The Royal Oak and headed towards Walsall Road, now shrouded in darkness. They had only walked twenty yards when they heard a faint rustle, and a man stepped out of the shadows and into the glare of the streetlamp, his collar high and a hat shoved firmly over his head. Lawrence smiled as they passed, glancing at the ground then he heard the clink of metal as the man walked by. Lawrence clutched Violet's arm as his brain caught up with his eyes, and he recognised a sleek metallic bullet casing.

"Quick," he whispered, pulling Violet ahead. But the warning came too late, and he felt a cold, hard metal object against the nape of his neck.

"Don't move a muscle, dear boy," came a familiar voice.

Violet turned around.

"Eyes forward," snapped the man. "Or your husband gets it."

"What do you want?"

"See that car ahead?"

Lawrence glanced up the road to a black vehicle parked on the pavement.

"I see it."

"Put your hands in the air, open the rear door and get inside."

Lawrence looked towards Violet. She stole a sideways glance, saw the weapon, and shook her head. Lawrence unclenched his jaw and sighed. With a gun in his back and his wife close by, this was no time for heroics. Lawrence acquiesced and approached the door, lowering himself onto the leather upholstery with his arms aloft. Their captor snaked his arm around Violet's waist and grasped her wrist before sliding the gun into his pocket. He removed a pair of handcuffs and handed them to Violet.

"Cuff your husband," he commanded, grabbing the gun

which he held against Violet's temple. Lawrence lowered his arms and offered his wrists.

"Do it," he echoed.

"But, Lawrence."

"Do it, my darling."

Violet snapped the handcuffs shut and moved away while the man slammed the door. He forced her roughly to the other side, produced a second set of cuffs, and applied them to her wrists before sliding into the front seat.

"Well?" asked Lawrence.

The man grinned, lowered his collar and removed his hat, then peered at his captives in the back seat.

"Oh God. You again," said Lawrence as Major Savage leered back.

"That's right," said the major cheerfully. "What a stroke of luck meeting you here."

"Was it?"

"Of course not. I've been following you for several days, waiting for the right opportunity. You're a lucky man," said the major. "My first thought was to kill you, but you'll be just as effective as a prisoner. Perhaps even more so. Especially with the lovely Mrs Harpham in tow."

"Don't touch my wife. Don't even look at her."

"You're not in any position to stop me. Haven't you worked it out yet? Felix Crossley is everywhere. You can't escape us. Not until he's got his hands on the child. He won't forgive you. Not now and not ever. And I'm sure he will be just as pleased to see you in handcuffs as he would to cast eyes on your sad, rotting corpses."

"Did you kill Edna?" asked Violet.

Lawrence frowned. "You did. You poisoned the offal."

The major chuckled. "Far be it for me to turn my back on a lucky opportunity. I tracked you down to your lodgings, only to find your dinner hanging on the doorknob for anyone to interfere with."

"And you just happened to have poison."

The major opened a square box nestling in the front foot well. He removed a rope, a spanner, and a large brown bottle with a glass stopper. "Tools of the trade," he said wolfishly.

"You're nothing more than a common criminal," said Lawrence. "So much for swearing allegiance to the king."

"I took my oath during Queen Victoria's reign," said the major.

"That's no excuse. You're the lowest of the low."

"My military career was in another life. And don't think you're above criticism. You stole the children I carefully groomed for Crossley and turned him against me. I lost my wife and my home, and all I had left were my friends in The Order. Now that I have captured you, I can redeem myself with Crossley and give him what he wants."

"Which is?"

"A replacement child.

"And that's why you tried to kill us?"

"Yes. I would have shot you had the opportunity presented itself. But a slow poisoning would have been more satisfying, if the old woman hadn't got in the way. No matter. You'll be just as good alive as dead. I would have enjoyed seeing the look on Aurora Farrow's face when she heard of your demise, but now I can let her watch as I do my worst to you while she spills her secrets, trying in vain to save your worthless lives."

"Where are you taking us?" demanded Lawrence.

"To Netherwood, of course. Now shut up, there's a good chap. I need to concentrate, and it's rather a long drive."

Chapter Forty-One

IMPRISONED

Wednesday, August 30, 1910

LAWRENCE WATCHED the sun peep from the horizon through purple and orange-hued clouds, wishing he could wipe the sleep from his eyes. But the short chain securing the handcuffs to the armrests allowed little movement. He had slept fitfully for the last hour, having given up any thoughts of escape, but had spent the previous five hours in an adrenaline-fuelled state of anticipation. The major had not stopped, and the vehicle must have been low on fuel, but he had driven on regardless, allowing no possibility for Lawrence to raise the alarm. As dawn broke, the car slowed and tackled the bumpy driveway leading to Netherwood. Every hair on Lawrence's skin stood to attention as they approached the house, knowing he would soon be in Francis Farrow's presence. He reluctantly whispered Violet's name, wishing he could let her sleep in blissful peace. But as he spoke, her eyes fluttered open. She smiled as she glimpsed his face, and her eyes widened at the sight of his handcuffs as she remembered what had gone before. Violet flexed her fingers and rubbed her wrists beneath the metal cuffs.

"Are we here?" she asked.

Lawrence nodded. "For better or worse."

"At least we'll see Aurora, but I'm worried about Daisy."

"Shhh. Try not to mention her. She's safer at school than anywhere."

"Are you sure?"

Lawrence tried to dismiss his clawing disquiet at being so far from his daughter. "She'll be fine," he said, showing confidence he did not feel.

The major yanked the brake, and the vehicle ground to a halt. He approached Violet's side of the car and unlocked her cuffs.

"Wait here," he said to Lawrence as he marched Violet towards the front door.

"Leave her alone," shouted Lawrence, but the major ignored him. Ten minutes later, he returned and frog-marched Lawrence inside.

"Where are you taking me?" asked Lawrence.

"Never you mind," hissed the major. "Get down there." He pointed to the basement stairs, and Lawrence descended with the revolver poking into his back.

"Why the whispers?" asked Lawrence. "Are you hiding something?"

Lawrence's vision momentarily blurred as the butt of the gun cracked against his head. Nausea rose in his stomach, and for a moment, he thought he might pass out.

"Shut up," repeated the major as he propelled Lawrence to the end of a corridor. Slamming Lawrence against the wall, Major Savage reached for a chunky key hanging to the side of a door and unlocked it before shoving Lawrence inside. He fell to the floor, clutching his head.

"Lawrence," cried Violet, rushing to her husband and kneeling beside him.

"I'm alright," said Lawrence. "As long as we're together."

"How very heartwarming," said the major, his words dripping with sarcasm.

Lawrence brushed the dust from his trousers. "At least I have someone who cares. How is Mrs Savage?"

The major slammed the metal cover over a grill set into the door, momentarily plunging the room into darkness.

"Damn," said Lawrence.

"Wait." Violet approached the opposite wall and wrenched a piece of plywood from a small, barred window; the plywood clattered to the floor.

They waited quietly for the major to reappear, but he must have been out of earshot. Lawrence glanced around the room.

"At least we can see," he said. "I hope we're not here for too long. There's no heat, nothing to sit on and no water closet. It doesn't make for a comfortable stay."

"Michael won't allow him to hold us against our will."

"If he knows we are here. I doubt they'd risk telling him."

"What's that?" asked Violet, nodding towards the door.

Lawerence cocked his head. "Footsteps and a godawful squeak," he whispered. "Someone's coming." He moved towards Violet and held her hand as the door grille opened again, and an unfamiliar face appeared.

"Who are you?" asked Lawrence, staring into a pair of deep-set eyes below a low-browed forehead.

"Mind your own business."

"Unless you're about to release us, it is my business."

"I'll be the judge of that. Now behave yourselves. You

have a visitor. Any trouble, and you'll answer to me." The man waved a meaty fist towards Lawrence as he spoke.

Lawrence stared at the floor, trying to resist the urge to roll his eyes at the thug before him.

"I'm opening the door. One move from you, and you'll live to regret it. Stand back."

The key turned, and the door opened. Lawrence's jaw dropped at the sight of an emaciated Francis Farrow sitting in a wheelchair, pushed by his thuggish minder. Violet edged closer to Lawrence.

"My dear friends," said Farrow.

"Not in this lifetime. Lawrence stepped forward, and Farrow's minder jabbed a warning finger.

"Stand back and shut up," he said. "I told you, no trouble." Leering at Violet, he placed his hand inside his jacket and removed a switchblade. Then he mimed drawing it across his throat. "Or she'll get that," he said.

Violet gazed calmly towards him. She did not flinch or fuss and maintained an impassive expression. Lawrence swallowed an angry retort and, following suit, nodded as he spoke to Francis Farrow.

"You look like the living dead," he said.

Farrow's smile slid from his face. "I have a few months left, all being well."

"Shame," said Lawrence.

"You still can't forgive me?"

"Never. You are a lying, manipulative hound, and I wouldn't trust you if you were the last man alive."

"How about you, dear Violet? Can you spare a kind thought for a dying man?"

"Perhaps, if you release us."

Farrow lowered his head and shook it sadly. "If only I could. Unfortunately, you are not my prisoners. As much as

I would like to interfere in Major Savage's plans, I'd be upsetting the master. And I need him. But I will arrange some refreshments. And anything else that would make your stay more comfortable."

"A key would be helpful," said Lawrence.

"Ah. The old Harpham humour. Some things never change."

Lawrence scowled. "Yes. Sadly, you're alive and breathing."

"Are you still disappointed in me?"

"Far from it. What's a murdered wife and daughter between friends?"

Francis Farrow covered his face with his hand. "Enough. It was an accident. Let's not go over old ground. I came here to help you."

"Then free us," said Violet.

"I can't. Crossley will have my guts for garters."

"And you need him," said Lawrence. "Has he promised some snake oil miracle cure?"

Francis Farrow's head jerked up as he looked Lawrence straight in the eye. "Felix Crossley's powers are genuine. He can save me if he wishes. And he has pots of money should he choose the hospital route."

"Then why hasn't he cured you? Have you had a little fight?"

"Crossley doesn't gift his favours like sweets," muttered Farrow feebly. "One must earn them."

"So, he'll watch you die like the dog you are."

"Crossley will save me. But I won't take a chance on his benevolence. Savage has got it all wrong. He thinks Aurora will cave if he threatens you. But I know her from old. She's suffered far worse and is strong and determined despite her helpless appearance. I have a far better plan."

"What's that? Boring her into submission?"

"Shut up," said the minder, baring his teeth. "Show some respect to your elders."

"What will you do?" asked Violet, speaking to Farrow in a conciliatory tone.

"Hypnotise her, of course."

"Do you know how?"

"Don't you remember?" asked Farrow, his tongue darting lasciviously from his mouth.

Violet shrank towards Lawrence. "No, I don't."

"Hypnotism made you more amenable to my approaches when we were in Swaffham," he replied. "You didn't want to enter my little parlour, but I soon persuaded you. Tell me, Violet, did you care nothing for me?"

"I loved you as a friend."

"Not good enough. But never mind. I am too old and ill to care for romance. But I learned with the best, and I still have it in me to persuade Aurora to part with her secrets. The major has no such skills. I will find the child's where-abouts using my greater intelligence. And the poor old major will have to go crawling to Crossley to confess his failings."

"Leave her alone, Francis, please," begged Violet.

"Sorry. No can do."

"I knew it," said Lawrence. "You never cared a fig for redemption. You just wanted to slime your way back into our lives. What the hell have you done with Michael?"

"Nothing," said Francis, looking offended. "He's my brother and perfectly safe in his room."

"Does he know we are here?"

"Of course not. He may want to do something about it. Even *my* hypnotic powers don't extend to full control."

"You've been mesmerising Michael?" asked Violet.

"Only when necessary. He is generally compliant. It's easy to manipulate a man with a conscience like Michael's."

"You're rotten to the core, Farrow," snarled Lawrence.

"I'll take that as a compliment. Now, do excuse me. I must try to gain access to Aurora if I can get past Major Savage. Stephens, wheel me away."

"Don't worry about Savage," said the minder, cracking an unpleasant smile.

"Capital. Be good, and I may see both of you again."

The door slammed shut as Farrow and Stephens left.

"What a thoroughly disagreeable pair," said Violet. "I thought he was here to keep an eye on Farrow, not cooperate with him."

"He's turned traitor by the sound of things. Thank goodness this hypnotism idea is a load of nonsense. At least he won't get to Aurora that way."

"It isn't," said Violet, her brow knitted in concern. "Frank studied it for years. You've experienced the power of psychology yourself. It's effective and disturbing."

Lawrence thumped his hand against the grille. "We need to get out of here."

"I know. And I badly need to see Aurora."

"She won't have any influence over our situation."

"I know that, but I must warn her and check she's well. Aurora has made the ultimate sacrifice to protect her child. She must be reeling at Luna's loss and is highly vulnerable to Farrow's approach."

"We should be careful ourselves," said Lawrence. "God knows how they would react if they discovered we know as much about Luna's disappearance as Aurora. Their surveillance must have been faulty to think capturing us would influence Aurora to talk. Thankfully, our Cheltenham meeting seems to have gone unobserved. I think we can confidently assume they know nothing about Vera."

"But that puts Aurora under terrible pressure," said Violet, shaking her head.

"I know. We must get out of here and help her."

"How? Look at this room. It's like a prison."

Lawrence approached the window and tugged at the bars. They did not give an inch. He walked around the small room, sweeping his hand against the walls as he moved. "Solid as a rock," he muttered.

"Why would Francis build a prison in Netherwood?" asked Violet.

"He didn't. This was always a storeroom. Not sure why they fitted bars. Oh, hello." Lawrence stopped as a small chunk of red stone clattered to the floor, dislodged by his fingers.

"What is it?" asked Violet.

"Just a crumbling and badly made brick," Lawrence replied disappointedly. "Damn it." He pushed his fingers into the indentation. Nothing moved.

"Try this," said Violet, handing him the plywood.

"It's not very strong. Still, I'll give it a go."

Lawrence snapped the wooden sheet over his knee, creating a long section. Then he plunged it into the wall and turned. A few flakes of red dust fell to the floor. "This will never work," he muttered, trying again.

Five minutes later, they heard a faint sound from the other side of the wall, as if something small had fallen to the floor.

"Ah, daylight," said Lawrence. "For all the good it will do from an internal wall."

"What can you see?" asked Violet.

Lawrence placed his eye against the tiny hole. "Nothing. It's too small."

"Stand aside." Violet removed her shoes, took one and examined the small square heel.

"This might be sturdy enough," said Violet, whacking it onto the brick. A crack appeared on the right-hand side. Violet brandished the shoe and slammed it once more. A one-inch piece of brick splintered into dust.

"Well done," said Lawrence admiringly before squinting into the hole again.

"What do you see?" asked Violet, but Lawrence sprang back and shoved her towards the opposite wall.

"What is it?" she asked.

"I c-can't b-believe it," stuttered Lawrence, his hands shaking.

Violet raised her hand to his cheek and moved his face towards hers. "What is it?" she repeated.

"We're sitting on a time bomb," said Lawrence. "There's a case and a half of blasting dynamite, only feet from this room."

Chapter Forty-Two

AURORA TO THE RESCUE

VIOLET CLUNKED her shoe on the iron door for the forty-second time. Nobody heard. Nobody came.

Sitting on the floor with his back against the far wall, Lawrence stared moodily ahead. "What the hell are we going to do now?" he asked.

"Nothing until somebody comes for us."

"And then what?"

"Let me think."

"Well, don't take too long about it."

"How dangerous is the explosive? Are we really in danger?" asked Violet, still pounding on the door.

"It depends." Lawrence put his hands over his ears. "Please stop making that diabolical noise. It's giving me a headache."

Violet sighed and put her shoe back on. "Depends on what?" she asked.

"Whether the explosive is unstable," said Lawrence. "I take that back. Dynamite is inherently unstable, but you can safely store it under the right conditions. Thankfully, it needs a blasting cap to ignite. But we don't know how old it is or whether they've bothered to treat it correctly. Unfortunately, dynamite tends to sweat."

"And has it?"

"I can't tell from this distance. It's not easy to see, anyway. Nitroglycerine leaches from an ageing stick of dynamite over time, which eventually crystalises."

"And might explode if exposed to a naked flame?"

"Violet… a slight bump could ignite it."

"Why would Michael risk storing dangerous explosives?"

"He wouldn't. Michael doesn't know they're there. Something nefarious is afoot. God only knows who hid explosives at Netherwood and what malicious intentions are behind it."

"We must warn Michael and Aurora."

"How?"

"One of us must get out of here."

"Again, how?"

"I'll feign sickness. It's worked before."

"Yes. At Major Savage's house, and he won't fall for that again."

Violet's face fell. "I forgot about that. Alright. Savage will bring Aurora here at some point, surely? She won't believe they've captured us if she doesn't see it for herself."

"And then what? We can't speak freely in front of the major."

"Then I don't know what to suggest except wait."

"Perfect," said Lawrence. "Like two rats in a trap."

"They won't be long. Major Savage will want to get to Aurora before Francis does."

"You may be right. I hear footsteps. Stand by."

The grille opened, and Major Savage appeared, flashing a sly smile before stepping aside.

"Come inside, my dear Mrs Farrow. Here are your friends, just as I promised."

"Oh, my dear," cried Violet as Aurora's pale face appeared.

"Oh, it's you," said Aurora disinterestedly. "What are you doing here?"

"Lawrence stood and dusted himself down. Violet caught his confused look and spoke before he had the chance.

"We're here against our will."

Aurora shrugged. "That's too bad."

"I beg your pardon?" said Lawrence angrily.

"What are you playing at?" asked the major. "I thought they were your friends?"

"Not lately."

"Then you won't care if I rough them up a bit?"

"Not particularly," said Aurora. "I have better things to think about."

"I don't believe you," said the major. "Let's find out, shall we?"

He thrust the key into the lock and barrelled through the door, brandishing his gun. "Harpham. Get over there," he said, gesturing to the back of the room.

"Not on your life."

The major pointed the revolver directly at Violet. "Get over there and kneel."

"You wouldn't," said Lawrence.

"Try me."

Lawrence backed towards the window and knelt. The major approached Violet and snaked an arm around her neck, standing behind her with the gun pointing to her temple.

"There's a room full of dynamite next door, you damned fool," shouted Lawrence.

"So there is," said the major. "A good thing you mentioned it. Stay there while I remove your wife to a safer location."

"No," said Lawrence. "Take me."

"I don't want you. I have plans for dear Mrs Harpham that don't concern you."

Major Savage backed towards the door, dragging Violet with him. She did not resist and kept a calm head. Lawrence watched as Aurora looked on impassively."

"Oy, what's going on?" shouted a brutish voice from down the corridor.

The major blanched and released Violet. "Blast it," he said. "That damned man won't leave me alone for a second."

Steps thundered towards them, and Stephens appeared, his florid face displaying barely concealed anger. "Mr Farrow is looking for you, ma'am," he said.

Aurora visibly shuddered. "I'm currently occupied with Major Savage."

"Not anymore. Off you go."

Stephens burst through the door just as the major slipped his revolver into his jacket pocket. "What are you doing here?" he demanded.

"Having a word with my prisoners," said the major.

"Well, keep Mrs Farrow out of it."

"I'll do as I please."

"I don't think so."

Stephens walked menacingly towards the major, towering over him. "Out," he said.

The major fingered the lump in his jacket but thought the better of it.

"I'm taking Aurora."

"No, you are not. You can get upstairs until Crossley arrives. Then it's up to him."

The door slammed shut, leaving Lawrence and Violet alone.

"Blast it. They're leaving. Are you alright, Violet?"

"Yes."

"What the hell was wrong with Aurora? Have they got to her? She doesn't seem to give a damn about us."

"She's behaving strategically. The less Aurora appears to care, the safer she is."

"Never mind us."

"Who would you choose to protect, Aurora or Daisy?"

Lawrence sighed. "I take your point."

"Hush. I hear footsteps." Violet pressed her face to the grille, listening as a soft footfall came down the corridor.

"Aurora," she whispered.

"Violet. Listen. There's barely any time. Stephens and Savage are arguing. They didn't see me double back."

"It's so good to see you," said Violet.

Lawrence grimaced. "I suppose it takes our minds off the roomful of dynamite next door."

"I heard you mention it earlier," said Aurora. "Try to forget it for now. Things are desperate. Everything has changed over the last day. Francis has shown his true colours. Felix Crossley is on his way to Netherwood. He wants Luna at all costs, and if not her, he'll take me instead."

"Surely Michael wouldn't allow it?" asked Lawrence, approaching the door.

"They've drugged him. He hasn't been right for a long time, and now I know why. Francis must have been slipping something into his food for a while."

"Yet he boasted he'd hypnotised him."

"Perhaps he has. But the drugs have made Michael more compliant. Lawrence, do you remember where my husband sleeps?"

"Yes."

"Good. I'm not under lock and key. Not yet anyway. I'll create a distraction somehow and release you later. Savage and Stephens are too close to chance it now, and I must get the key from the major. You must find Michael and get him out of here. Crossley won't tolerate any more resistance from me. They'll use Michael to get my cooperation."

"What about you?"

"I don't care anymore. Crossley will pursue me forever. You will never meet a more ruthless man than he is. When you've got Michael, leave. Not just Netherwood, but your home in Cheltenham. Take Daisy and anything else you care for, and go far away, preferably alone."

"How can things have got this bad so quickly?"

"I overheard Francis and Stephens talking. Crossley is facing another coup from inside the cult by some fool who thinks they are strong enough to take him on and challenge his authority. He plans another ritual like the one he tried at Akenham, but he needs a child of God and is determined to find Luna."

"But she isn't Michael's."

"Crossley doesn't know that, and she'd be in just as much danger if he did. Trust me. This is the only way. Promise me you'll get Michael out of this house."

"And then we'll return for you," said Lawrence.

"Just get Michael to safety. Swear it."

"We do," said Violet.

"Goodbye and thank you."

They watched as Aurora turned and ran softly down the

corridor. As she opened the door, they could still hear Major Savage and Stephens arguing.

"Do you think she'll come good?" asked Lawrence.

"I hope so. This is the worst scrape we've ever been in."

Lawrence hugged her tightly. "We'll be alright, old girl."

"Not this time. Felix Crossley will kill us. He's unhinged, and we don't stand a chance. Crossley killed poor Frank."

"More likely the major."

"But by Crossley's command. If we're not careful, we may never see Daisy again."

"Bear up. Of course we will."

Violet pulled away. "Now is not the time for platitudes. We're in grave danger, don't you understand?"

Lawrence took her hands and gently pulled her towards him. "Of course I do. Everything is coming to a head. It's only ever been a matter of time. But I do believe we'll get out of here."

"And then what?"

"I think we both know," said Lawrence softly.

They lay quietly in each other's arms as the hours ticked away, the scant light from the window dwindling into dusky indigo hues.

Lawrence pretended not to notice Violet stifling a sob while thinking of Daisy. He lay preoccupied, making plans to keep his family safe if they ever escaped. Lawrence sighed as his stomach growled. They hadn't eaten for over a day, not that he was hungry. But if they needed to move quickly, some form of sustenance would be necessary. Just as he began to doubt Aurora's reliability, they heard familiar, gentle footsteps in the corridor, and the door creaked open.

"Thank God," said Lawrence, springing to his feet.

Aurora ducked inside the room and closed the door. "Wait," she said, listening carefully for noises outside. "No one has followed me. Thank goodness. It's taken all day to steal the key from Major Savage, and we're running out of time. Crossley will arrive at nine o'clock. It's eight thirty now. You have half an hour. That's all. And I can't stress enough how important it is that you have gone by the time he arrives. Please help my darling Michael, but if you can't get him away by nine o'clock, then leave."

"We can't go without him," said Violet.

"I have a plan. Do your best to get him out, but I will take care of things if you can't."

"Come with us," said Lawrence. "If we leave now, we can all escape."

Aurora shook her head. "This will never end if we don't act decisively. Stephens, Savage, and Farrow are in the drawing room, still hostile, each unwilling to let the other out of their sight. I let Farrow think he'd hypnotised me and fed him a false location for Luna. Crossley will realise as soon as he arrives. I gave a different location to the major, who also thinks he wore me down."

Aurora stroked a bruise on her temple, and a surge of anger burgeoned in Lawrence's throat.

"The brute," he raged.

"Never mind. It did the trick and gave me the opportunity to feed him a story. Both men think of themselves as victorious. Now, there are three guards with dogs in the garden and a maid upstairs. She will be close to Michael and may also look in on me, but I've dressed the bed to make it look like I'm asleep. The major gave me a drink earlier with a suspicious powdery residue. He thinks he's subdued me, but I suspected he might try to, and I haven't eaten or drunk anything all day to be on the safe side."

"Likewise," murmured Lawrence.

"I'm sorry how things have turned out. You deserve

better. I should have acted a long time ago instead of running away. I wasted time hiding in the workhouse when I should have left the country. More fool me. Still, what will be, will be."

"I'm worried about you," said Violet, her eyes soft and sad.

"Don't be. I have chosen my path."

"Please tell us what you intend to do."

Aurora clasped Violet's hands. "Just trust me," she said. "Now go. Time is precious. Good luck,"

"God bless," said Lawrence. "We will see you later. Come on," Lawrence ushered Violet through the door.

"Wait," said Violet, turning back to Aurora, but Lawrence grasped her hand and pulled her along. "Stay close," he whispered. "There's no time to lose."

Chapter Forty-Three

ESCAPE

LAWRENCE AND VIOLET climbed the short flight of stairs to the ground floor and pushed the half-open door, closing it gently behind them. They tiptoed quickly along the corridor, trying to ignore the buzz of conversation in the drawing room. A glance to their right would tell them if the door was open, but they were exposed and even a split-second delay might leave them in sight. Instead, they slunk towards the stairs, flattening themselves against the wall and waited with bated breath.

The conversation continued before escalating into a heated exchange, the words drowned out by a sea of noise as three voices vied to compete. Satisfied, they crept up the stairs, treading lightly and trying to avoid the familiar squeaky floorboard just beyond the dogleg. As they approached the top, Lawrence turned and pressed his finger to his lips before jabbing his finger ahead and making walking motions. Violet understood his gesture and stopped dead, waiting quietly for further instruction. Seconds ticked by, and Lawrence clenched his jaw in frustration. Violet squeezed his hand and gently stepped past him, snatching a glimpse down the landing.

Violet jerked her head back at the sight of the house-maid, slipped a hand in her pocket, retrieved a penny, and held it towards Lawrence while pointing to the opposite corridor. She took off her shoes, and Lawrence did likewise.

Violet glanced anxiously at Lawrence. He nodded, and she hurled the penny down the corridor. They took two swift steps backwards and ducked out of sight before hearing faltering, uncertain footsteps coming towards them. They waited until they saw the maid tiptoe towards the source of the sound before running fleet-footed towards Michael's room, clutching their shoes. They were inside his bedroom with the door firmly shut before the maid reached the penny.

"Good plan," said Lawrence, re-tying his shoes. He turned towards the sleeping form in the bed.

"Oh dear. This doesn't look good," he murmured.

Violet sat on the counterpane and shook Michael's shoulder. "Wake up," she whispered.

A gentle snore escaped from Michael's recumbent form.

Violet shook him again and moved her mouth to his ear. "Wake up," she hissed urgently.

His eyes fluttered open and closed just as quickly.

"This is hopeless," said Lawrence, reaching for a tumbler of water, which he splashed onto Michael's face. "Wakey, wakey," he said, slapping him firmly on the cheek.

Michael opened his eyes with a start and stared woozily, trying to focus. "Lawrence, is that you?" he asked.

"Shh. Keep your voice down."

"Where is everyone?"

"Downstairs. You need to get out of here."

"Why? It's my home."

"You're in danger."

Michael's eyes fluttered again.

"Smelling salts," hissed Lawrence, holding his hand out.

"Good idea." Violet fished around in her purse and produced a small brown bottle.

"Here. Take a whiff of that," said Lawrence, holding it to Michael's nose. Michael's head jerked back as he screwed up his eyes.

"Alright. I'm awake. Put it away."

"Gladly," said Lawrence, handing the open bottle to Violet. "Now, pay attention. Felix Crossley is on his way. He wants Luna, and if not, he'll take Aurora."

"I don't believe it," said Michael. "Francis has finished with Crossley."

"No, he jolly well hasn't. Francis and Major Savage are competing to gain Crossley's favour. Fortunately, your clever wife has the better of them. But she has asked us to get you away from Netherwood immediately."

"Why should I trust you when you have hidden Luna from me?"

"Nobody knows Luna's whereabouts for good reason. She is in grave danger, and Francis has betrayed you. You're vulnerable to his control. Do you understand? And if you stay here, he will use you to get to Aurora."

"Where is she? I must find her."

"Downstairs, and no, you must not. Aurora has carefully planned her dealings with Crossley."

"How?" Michael sat up and uncertainly swung his feet over the bed.

"You look terrible," said Violet, staring at Michael's emaciated legs poking out from a pair of ill-fitting pyjamas.

"I haven't been well," said Michael.

"Nonsense. They've been drugging you. Here. Put this

on." Lawrence grabbed a dressing gown from a hook on the back of the door and thrust it towards Michael.

"Not until you tell me what Aurora is doing."

"We don't know," said Violet, resting a gentle hand on his shoulder. "But she made us promise to take you away from Netherwood, and we agreed."

"I'm not running away and leaving my wife in danger."

"Yes, you are," said Lawrence. "You are a hindrance here. Aurora stands a fighting chance of success if she doesn't have to worry about your safety."

"It shouldn't be this way. I've let her down. Why did I make such poor choices?" groaned Michael, putting his head in his hands. "Are you sure about Francis?"

"I'm afraid so," said Violet.

"Then I've brought evil into my home and left my wife and daughter unprotected. I don't deserve to escape the consequences."

"That's not your choice," said Lawrence.

"I can't go."

"You must. We'll get you out of the house and settled somewhere safe in Bury. Then we'll return for Aurora."

"Promise."

"I do."

"Very well." Michael tied his dressing gown cord and stood, swaying as he fought the effects of the drugs in his system.

Lawrence walked towards the window and peered outside, sighing as he spotted the wrought iron railing beneath.

"We'll have to use the stairs," he said.

"They'll see us," said Violet.

"What else can we do?"

"I don't know." Lawrence and Violet cast anxious glances as they considered their options.

"How about the window on the dogleg?" asked Michael.

Lawrence clicked his fingers. "Brilliant. It's safer and a shorter drop than this window. But let's not take any chances." He tossed the counterpane to one side and stripped a pair of sheets from the bed. "Now, just the maid to take care of. Any ideas?"

"I'll ask her to fetch me a drink," said Michael.

"Will she do it?" asked Lawrence.

"More to the point, how quickly will she do it?" said Violet. "Because if she sets foot on the staircase before we're all out, the game's up."

"Rats." Lawrence twirled the sheet absent-mindedly as he thought.

"I know. I'll tell her the scratching is keeping me awake again," said Michael.

Lawrence grimaced. "The what?"

"Someone locked the cat in one of the bedrooms last week. It made the devil of a row enough to wake me anyway, and I haven't been aware of much lately. Which housemaid is on duty? One's young and the other not so much."

"This one is definitely north of forty," said Lawrence.

"Good. That's Marion. She likes animals."

"Wait," said Violet. "Won't she worry that you're awake?"

Michael shook his head. "They still feed me. I am conscious some of the time. It's hard to believe they've been drugging me. I genuinely thought I had flu."

He cocked his head and looked suspiciously at Lawrence.

Lawrence knelt and pulled Michaels's pyjama leg up to

the knee. "Look at your limbs, Michael. This isn't normal. You've been off your feet for some time."

"Like I said, I've been ill," said Michael falteringly.

"You've lost all your muscle tone, which comes from a prolonged spell of lying in bed."

"God help me for being a trusting fool."

"Speak to the maid. Let's get this done."

Michael closed his eyes, and his lips moved as he said a little prayer. Then Lawrence and Violet ducked behind the door as he opened it and walked outside. They heard the murmur of voices, and moments later, the door opened again.

"Quickly," said Michael. "Marion has offered to check all the rooms, but she's started next door and could be out at any time.

Lawrence placed a steadying hand around Michael's shoulders and ushered him down the landing, with Violet following behind. Then, leaving Michael leaning against the banister, he opened the window. Lawrence tried the latch and frowned. "Not strong enough," he murmured. Then he knotted the two sheets together and secured them to the newel post before dropping the makeshift rope from the window. It swung about eight feet from the ground. "Oh, Violet. I wish there was another way. This is a long, risky drop."

"Don't worry about me," said Violet, removing her footwear. She reached outside and dropped the shoes, which landed safely and quietly on the lawn. "Shall I go first?"

"Yes. That works best."

Violet clambered onto the narrow window ledge, turned, and grasped the sheet rope. Lawrence nervously eyed the newel post and placed a steady hand on the banister as the rope tightened. Violet half climbed, half slithered down the rope, landing with a gentle bump. Lawrence ran to the window, his heart in his mouth, but Violet was already on her feet and replacing her shoes.

Lawrence turned to Michael. "Think you can manage?" he asked.

"Probably. Though whether I should is a different matter."

"You must," said Lawrence, firmly.

Michael tried to climb down, but his weak arms and wasted musculature took their toll. Lawrence glanced at his watch, realising in horror that it was five minutes to nine. Crossley would be there at any moment. As if on cue, the sound of baying guard dogs cut through the night and a car's bright headlights swept the lawn. Violet darted towards a bush, then emerged moments later, jabbing her finger against her watch face.

Slowly and painfully, Michael eased himself down the rope, dropping off abruptly when he lost his handhold. He lay for a few moments, sprawled on the floor, his legs splayed but Violet ran towards him and helped him to his feet. He took a step and fell,

"Get up," she said. "I'll help you."

The guard dogs barked again, this time closer. Violet dragged a limping Michael towards the bush, and three large German shepherds powered past, baying at the car in the driveway.

"Call them off," growled a voice from the car. Lawrence, now on the rope, swayed precariously as the knot between the sheets began to fail.

He shimmied lower, but not in time to escape the notice of the dog handler, running towards the driveway.

"What do you think you're doing?" yelled the guard.

Lawrence released the rope and dropped to the floor, his

scarred left hand on fire. He rolled onto his shoulder as he fell, absorbing the blow, then ran in the opposite direction, attempting to lure the dog handler away from Violet. The handler whistled for the dogs, and they came thundering towards him, their slavering jaws eager for fresh meat. Hot on his heels, the guard grabbed Lawrence's jacket and missed by a whisker, but the dogs were quicker, and he felt their rancid breath as he headed for a low-boughed tree. Grabbing the branch, he swung his legs up and hung sloth-like for a moment before easing himself into a sitting position against the trunk.

The guard arrived, panting, by the side of the old oak. "You can stay there all night for all I care," he said as the dogs sat beneath, baying for blood. Lawrence tried desperately to catch his breath, despairing at his position, and hoping that Violet and Michael had escaped the grounds. He cast an eye towards the drawing room window, dread in his heart as three shadowy shapes rose, roused by the sounds from outside. Then suddenly, without warning, glass shattered explosively from the windows as a blast ripped through Netherwood, leaving it a blazing inferno.

Chapter Forty-Four

A PARTING OF THE WAYS

THE BLAST BLEW Lawrence from the tree, and he landed painfully on his rear, yelping as his coccyx hit the earth. The guard dogs had vanished, running in an undisciplined pack from the blast while the guard sat in stunned silence some distance away. Lawrence did not wait for the man to come to his senses but turned tail and sprinted towards the bushes where he had last seen Violet and Michael. They were not there. He ran towards the rear door, but it was dislodged and impassable. Throwing caution to the wind, he risked the driveway and fled towards the main entrance. He hurled the door open, but an evil cloud of smoke billowed outside. Lawrence covered his mouth and steeled himself, ready to take on the flames. But just as he prepared to move, a firm hand clamped on his shoulder, and a shiver of dread crawled up his spine.

"You," snarled Crossley.

Lawrence turned to face him. "I wondered when you'd turn up."

"She's gone," said Crossley, a momentary sadness flickering over his bleeding face, shredded by flying glass.

"Who?"

"My scarlet woman."

"Oh God. Is Aurora still inside?"

"They all are," spat Crossley. "Look." He marched Lawrence towards the drawing room window, the outside now peppered with shards of glass and pieces of the once luxurious drapes. A fire still raged inside around a large crater in the middle of the room. Farrow's wheelchair lay on its side with his blackened corpse nearby. What remained of Major Savage's head hung perilously over the hole. Stephens was nowhere to be seen.

"I can't see Aurora," said Lawrence. "She may still be inside."

"She isn't," snarled Crossley. "Nobody left this house."

"I must find her."

"You won't live long enough. You've ruined everything again." Crossley whipped out an ornate knife and pointed it towards Lawrence, who backed away. Crossley lunged forward and jabbed the knife again, surprisingly agile for a large man. Lawrence sidestepped and prepared to run, but Crossley placed a meaty arm around his neck and drew the knife to his throat before muttering a series of strange incantations. Lawrence tried to pull away, but Crossley's anger strengthened him. He spun Lawrence around with lightning dexterity, tripping him up with a well-placed knee. As Lawrence fell to the floor, Crossley leapt on him, wielding the knife, and prepared to strike Lawrence between the shoulder blades. The sound of a nearby fire claxon distracted Crossley mid-strike.

"I'd better make this quick," he sneered.

But as he readied himself for the kill, a pair of head-lights blazed in front of him. He stared, puzzled.

"That's my vehicle."

The engine rumbled, and the car moved towards them. Still holding the knife, Crossley covered his eyes from the dazzling headlamps and watched, transfixed. Lawrence seized the moment and thrust him off before rolling to one side. The car weaved slowly towards Crossley, who paced menacingly towards it while Lawrence ran alongside as the rear door flew open.

"Get in," yelled Michael.

Lawrence needed no further invitation, hurled himself inside and slammed the door.

The car crept towards Crossley, who leapt on the bonnet and stared into Violet's eyes as if about to mesmerise her. Violet hesitantly drove the large automobile, momentarily panicking as it failed to gain traction.

"Faster," yelled Lawrence.

"I can't."

"Stop the car," growled Crossley. "Or I'll rain the fires of hell on you."

"Do your worst," said Lawrence. "Violet, put your foot down."

Violet pressed and pulled, but the car ground to a halt.

Crossley slithered down and dropped to the side, battering the driver's window with his knife, which cracked beneath the onslaught. Another blow and the glass shattered. Violet stared at Crossley's bloodied face and shrank back at the madness on full display.

He lunged towards her with the knife. Lawrence flung himself over Violet, taking a cut to his arm as he shielded her from the blow. The knife flew into the air and dropped to the ground.

"I'll kill you all, I swear it," screamed Crossley, searching for the blade. His hand closed over it as he fell across the grass, and he returned to the car, slashing towards the window. Violet accelerated, more by luck than judgement, knocking Crossley off his feet and momentarily winding him.

"Quick, get out," commanded Lawrence as Crossley lay gasping for air on the ground. Violet opened the door and jumped into the back seat while Lawrence sprang behind the wheel. Crossley grasped the knife and struggled to his feet. But Lawrence, sensing an opportunity to humiliate his enemy, grinned, tipped his forelock and rammed his foot onto the pedal. The car lurched forward, knocking Felix Crossley to the ground again.

"You're a dead man walking," screamed Crossley, howling with pain. "I will track you down and kill every one of your miserable family. I have acolytes in every corner of the globe waiting to serve me. They will find the damned child, and I will make you pay for my loss. Watch out. There will be a large and attractive bounty on your heads."

Lawrence tooted the horn and thundered down the driveway, almost colliding with the fire truck as he sped from Netherwood.

"Where are we going?" whispered Violet.

"Home for one last time."

Chapter Forty-Five

THE ORTEGA

LAWRENCE LEANED over the rails on the deck of the *Ortega* as she pulled away from the dock, tears pricking his eyes as he lingered over his last sighting of England. To leave his country was a desperate wrench but knowing he would never see his wife and child again was more than he could bear. He had tortured himself over the decision he knew he must make while driving in silence from Bury St Edmunds to Cheltenham, pausing only long enough to pack, pick up Daisy and lay his hands on his cash and valuables. Once consolidated, he divided his savings between Michael and Violet, leaving a small amount for himself.

They had said their goodbyes in the drawing room of the rented house in Cheltenham in a scene eerily similar to the day Vera left. When Lawrence first mooted the idea of separating forever, Violet refused, insisting that they should stay together despite Crossley's threat. But Lawrence was adamant. Aurora had exemplified bravery, sacrificing her life to end Crossley's. She had failed, but only just, and destroyed Francis Farrow, Stephens, and Major Savage in the process. If Crossley had been a split second earlier and had stepped through the front door, she would have fulfilled her desire to rid the world of a monster. As fortunate as his name, Felix had escaped the conflagration. But revenge, never far from Crossley's heart, had nested there, and Lawrence knew he would hunt them to the ends of the earth.

Aurora had been streets ahead. She had always appreciated the danger, and her final word of advice was to travel alone. Lawrence had understood what Violet ignored. That they would never be safe if they were readily identifiable. Three adults travelling with a young teenage girl would be easier to find than three separate groups. And the same logic would apply to living arrangements. Crossley would be seeking a family of three, not a single woman and her daughter. Violet and Daisy were safer alone.

Aurora had shown the way, taking the brave and lonely step of saving her husband and child by destroying Netherwood, knowing she would die. If she could make the ultimate sacrifice, Lawrence could keep his family safe, however much it hurt.

They had cried together during their last moments in Cheltenham, Daisy sobbing into his shoulder and telling him she loved him. It had taken everything Lawrence possessed to escort them to the taxi to take them away forever. He would not let Violet tell him where she would live, but they had already agreed it could not be in England. So now, as he pulled away from Liverpool docks, he had no way of knowing where in the world his family might be.

Lawrence was travelling steerage. His funds allowed a more comfortable passage, but he could not bear to dine well and make small talk with strangers. He could get lost in third class and avoid company. It would be safe, and he had already limited his life's expectations to making the best of a melancholy situation where his only comfort was the certainty that Violet and Daisy were better off without him.

Lawrence wiped his eyes and walked towards a tarpaulin-covered lifeboat. He leaned against it and watched the twinkling lights growing ever distant as he remembered his last conversation with a bowed and broken Michael. Lawrence had tried to help his friend, but nothing could assuage Michael's guilt, knowing he should have been stronger and kept his brother distant. He had allowed a serpent into their home who had struck at those he most cared for.

Michael had chosen a life of penance. He did not tell Lawrence where he would go, only that he would live the life of a monk in solitary retreat. Lawrence refrained from dissuading him. He had known Michael for many years and understood his need for self-punishment and introspection.

Lawrence shivered in the chill evening wind. He should go below deck and eat his evening meal, but he was so miserable that he couldn't face the thought of food. Besides, he must make the most of the English weather now that he was bound for Barbados to settle somewhere on the island. Not that he cared where he lived or that a Caribbean island could ever compensate for losing his family. Lawrence had no particular draw to Barbados. He had arrived at the ticket office without caring where he went and had opted for the next available passage to the west. The teller had handed him a ticket for the *Ortega*, destined for Bridgetown, where his new life awaited. But God, it hurt. Lawrence put his head in his hands and blinked away tears, his heart aching at the enormity of his loss.

An hour passed before he felt ready to move, and he rose, legs aching, and took the stairs to the steerage eating hall. He managed a slice of bread and butter and a weak tea before going back on deck to contemplate the stars before bedtime.

The ship was far from shore, and all he could see in the inky blackness was a new moon half hidden by billowing clouds and a smattering of stars. He felt alone and adrift, his life anchor gone, and his world in disarray. A passing woman's young son, dressed in an ill-fitting suit, momentarily cheered him with a shy smile. Lawrence nodded and forced a grin, but the loneliness still weighed heavily upon him, and he carried on walking. Then Lawrence felt a gentle tug as he made his way along the deck. He turned to see the teenage boy.

"Can I help you?" he asked.

The woman, now standing in the shadow of a towering funnel, glanced forward and aft before nodding. The boy removed his hat, revealing a tumble of curls, and Lawrence's mouth fell open. "Daisy," he whispered. She nodded.

"Violet?"

The woman stepped aside, removed her hat and wig, and ran towards Lawrence. As he stood, trembling with shock and happiness, a surge of hope filled his heart, and he hugged them as if he would never let them go.

"How did you find me?" he whispered.

"I followed you," said Violet. "The years of detective work paid off."

"But you promised to stay apart. We're in danger."

"I've walked past you twice since leaving Liverpool. You didn't recognise me, and Crossley won't either. Besides, our lives aren't worth living if you're not part of them. So, we're here, and you're stuck with us."

"I love you," said Lawrence, pulling them towards him

again. They stood in silence, watching the ship hove through the choppy sea, contemplating their new lives together. Wherever they went, whatever danger lay ahead, Lawrence knew he could face anything now. Life had never been sweeter.

Also by Jacqueline Beard

vinci-books.com/cornishwidow

Innocence, secrets, and a gift she can't control.

Connie Maxwell has a secret. Though broken in body, her spirit
runs free. Dreamwalking might be useful if only she could control
it. But it's one thing roaming the Cornish Coast and quite another
witnessing a murder - especially when she can't influence the
outcome.

Turn the page for a free preview…

The Cornish Widow: Prologue

I WAKE WITH A START. The window has unlatched in the night and is slamming against the stone walls of our cottage. It is dark outside, and I reach for my stick, feeling its comforting weight in my hands before I limp towards the window. A bolt of lightning flashes through the sky as I fumble for the latch, and I place my hand on the windowsill, not noticing the pool of rainwater until it is too late. Then I stand on my tiptoes and catch the buffeting frame, almost losing my balance as I close it. I wipe my wet hands on my nightdress and shiver. How long was the window open? I can't tell because I don't know how long I have been sleeping. I've been dreaming again. Another dream so vivid that I cannot separate it from reality.

I sit on the end of my bed, wondering whether to light a candle. I don't know the time, and I haven't got a clock in my bedroom. It would serve no purpose. I rarely have appointments, and my condition leaves me unable to travel alone. A timepiece is no use to someone like me.

My thoughts return to the dream. It was lucid, real, but then they usually are. And I always remember them. I started keeping a journal of my dreams, but as I so rarely forget, the journaling seemed redundant in the end, and I abandoned it. Tonight's dream was unusually unnerving. I found myself in a house somewhere up north. Well, anywhere is north of here, but this was a good distance away. Two middle-aged ladies occupied the property, and the younger of the two was fast asleep when I arrived. I stood beside the bed, watching for a moment as her chest rose and fell. Then a muffled noise came from outside, and I passed through the wall and onto the landing just in time to see the older woman creep downstairs. I followed behind, confident that she wouldn't see me. They never do. She opened a door, and I waited for her to light a candle, but she reached for a wall switch instead, and the room lit up in seconds. They must have been wealthy as the house had electricity, which is unusual in a terraced property. Where I live, there is a limited electricity supply at the nearby hotel, but our little cottage runs on gas lamps, and I can't see Mrs Ponsonby changing things. She would disapprove.

I watched the woman as she fussed around the kitchen. She approached a cupboard, opened it, and started pushing things around as if she were looking for something. She didn't find what she was searching for and quietly closed the doors, muttering under her breath. Then she opened another door to a nearby room and removed two clothing items from a coat hanger before laying them over the table. I couldn't see much of the second outfit, but the first was a knee-length skirt with a fitted jacket. They must have different styles up north as the clothing was a world apart from the simple, feminine fashions I know. All my skirts are long, of course, to hide my leg. My friend Mary wears a calf-length dress, and she looks every inch the fashionable lady. But this tailored outfit was very modern in appearance.

Once the older woman had moved the clothes, she opened a second cupboard behind the door and rummaged inside, feeling for an object. A relieved half-smile spread across her face as she located it. She walked towards the sink and placed a brown bottle on the surface before easing the stopper free with her thumbs. Then she washed the dust off her hands and sniffed the contents, recoiling at the smell. There was a drawing on the label that I couldn't quite see, and I drifted towards it for a closer look. The bottle was the old-fashioned kind, and I remember seeing a similar one in Mr Pennigan's shop when I was much younger. The object on the dog-eared label was all that remained of a skull and crossbones – poison.

The woman put her hand into her dressing gown pocket and removed a second bottle. This one was slim and made of blue glass, and someone had fastened a dropper to it with an elastic band. She took the dropper, placed it in the neck of the brown bottle, squeezed the bulb, and transferred a few drops of liquid. Then she rinsed the dropper under the tap and wiped it dry. Finally, she replaced the top and vigorously shook it.

I knew what she was doing. It was obvious. There was no need to follow her up the stairs and watch her put the doctored medicine bottle by the younger woman. But I did it anyway. I tried everything to warn the sleeping woman. I touched her, prodded her, and I even tugged her bedclothes. Then I tried to scream, but it was noiseless. There was nothing I could do. I would have waited, but the storm woke me up, and she had gone. And although it's happened before, I cannot will myself back into a dream state. I am powerless to help her. But of course, it is just a dream – life-like and lucid, but existing only in my imagination. I press my cheek into my pillow and listen to the sound of waves crashing against the shore, then thank God that I haven't just witnessed a murder.

The Cornish Widow: Chapter One

CONSTANCE

Thursday, November 13, 1930

I WAKE bleary-eyed to a new day. I couldn't get back to sleep last night and lay awake until dawn, fighting the urge to go downstairs and make better use of my time. I have nearly finished my book, *Women in Love* by D.H. Lawrence, which I hid in the bottom drawer of the bureau as my guardian, Mrs Ponsonby, would have kittens if she saw it. She hasn't forgotten Lawrence's last scandalous book, and though this one doesn't come close in content, it is not worth the aggravation of her seeing it.

I am twenty-five years old – an adult – yet still living under the guardianship of a woman I know little about. Mrs Ponsonby doesn't like me. She never has. I am nothing more than a responsibility, a duty. She might be a groomsman taking care of a horse for all the affection she shows me.

Our cottage is small and basic, but we do not lack creature comforts. I eat well and can always call upon Elys for help. She is our housemaid and lives in, attending to Mrs Ponsonby's every whim. If I want something, I ask for it, and it usually arrives. I can go outside within reason, although Mrs Ponsonby frowns on any travel beyond Newquay, at least without her permission. We don't have a telephone, but the hotel staff let me make or take calls. I only need to ask Dolly, the receptionist, if I want to speak to someone, which because of my situation, is infrequent. The local people are friendly, and the omnibus is reliable, although I may not travel alone. All in all, I cannot complain about the physical aspects of my life.

Someone unknown pays for my upkeep. Mrs Ponsonby dresses smartly and enjoys all the trappings that a woman her age could want. But I don't know who funds our home, and she won't tell me. I've often asked her and sometimes begged her, but she says that no good would come of it. Mrs Ponsonby occupies the largest bedroom, inside which is a walk-in cupboard. She always keeps the door locked, and I know because I've often tried to open it over the years. She wears the key on a chain around her neck and is never without it. Mrs Ponsonby fell down the stairs one night and severely sprained her ankle. They took her straight to the hospital, and I thought my luck was in. But despite her pain, she remembered the key and passed it to Elys for safekeeping. I tried to persuade Elys to lend it to me, but she refused and wouldn't budge on the matter. "It's more than my job's worth," she said. So, my benefactor remains a mystery, as do my origins.

My life started when I was about five or six years old. No. I should re-phrase that. My memories begin from then. I know I wasn't born in Cornwall, but I cannot remember anything before arriving here. As hard as I try, anything further back is dark and hazy. No other words can adequately describe the terrible void. I used to think there was something wrong with my head. But that was before Doctor Maltravers arrived. He replaced stuffy old Doctor Kimbrell, who was older than his years and set in Victorian ways. It wouldn't have surprised me if he'd produced a jar of leeches from his bag instead of medicine, although he never did. Doctor Maltravers is quite the opposite. He trained in London and took a particular interest in psychiatry. He says that most people suffer from childhood amnesia, but my case is extreme. He thinks it's my brain's response to childhood trauma. He might be right, for all I know, but with no relatives to hand, I can neither confirm nor deny his theory. It makes sense, though. My scarred left leg with its wasted muscles is shorter than my right, and Doctor Maltravers thinks this might have happened from lack of use. He asked if I had a bath chair when I was younger, and of course, I couldn't tell him because I don't know. It is embarrassing, and I feel naïve and stupid to know so little about my early life.

I rise, get dressed and hook my stick over my arm, leaning heavily on the bannister as I go downstairs. It's Tuesday, and book changing day at the hotel. I want to return three of my four books, though not the hidden one, of course. Elys is setting the breakfast table and calls me over.

"Do you want some porridge, Connie?"

Mrs Ponsonby flashes a glare from the chair in the opposite room. She thinks Elys is too familiar for a domestic servant. It's 1930, for heaven's sake and about time she came off her high horse.

"No thanks," I say, walking towards the coat stand. "I'm going for a walk."

"Where?" asks Mrs Ponsonby curtly.

"To the beach and then the hotel," I answer, waiting for her response with a prepared one of my own. It's a conversation we have almost every day, and the content rarely varies.

"Well, don't go too far," she continues as if I could go any distance without a chair or transport.

"Only to the Lizard and back," I say facetiously. She scowls, and I leave, pausing only to share a knowing smile with Elys. Poor Elys. I don't know how she does it. I get out whenever I can, which isn't often, but it's more than Elys does.

I fasten the top button of my coat as I leave the cottage and head towards the beach. Our home is immediately behind the hotel, and both buildings are elevated, which makes for a steep walk. If it were up to Mrs Ponsonby, I would never go outside. She doesn't like me walking anywhere, much less to the beach. She says it will do untold damage if I fall over, but I won't get any stronger if I sit around all day indoors. I know the limits of my endurance. If the weather is mild and the tide is out, I can manage a walk to each end of the bay, which works out to about half a mile. We live in a hamlet with a scattering of houses, and the hotel, of course. The nearest village is Trevarrian, but I can't get there under my own steam because it's too hilly. As for Newquay, there is a walk across the cliffs for those lucky souls with functioning limbs. But it is beyond my capability without help.

The wind whips my scarf from the top of my coat as I approach the ramp towards the beach. The path is steep, but one of the odd-job men at the hotel erected a wooden fence a few years ago, and it helps to have something to hold on to, especially if it's wet. Today is dry, the tide is out, and the expansive beach is a joy to behold. I walk towards the water where the sand is firmer, and before long, I turn around to see stick marks peppering the once-pristine sand. I inhale the salty sea air and watch the seagulls shrieking overhead. There is not a soul on the shore – unusual for this time of day. Mostly, the holidaymakers can't keep away. But it's cold, and I expect they have sensibly huddled around the fire back at the hotel.

I will join them soon enough, but first, I head towards my favourite cave. I know it's an extravagance to have a choice, and I don't take my residence by the seaside for granted. There are about half a dozen small caves within a few hundred yards, and one is more spacious than the others. Last year I dragged a wooden chair to the cave and left it there, half expecting someone to take it away over the summer. But instead, the holidaymakers treated it as their own, adding a wooden packing crate and a small but hardy pot plant. A month or two later I discovered a small suit-case. Someone had put half a dozen books inside, to which others were subsequently added.

I can see the cave ahead of me now, every detail of its entrance as familiar as my home. I walk inside and head towards the chair. It is damp but not enough to seep through my coat. I turn it around to face the sea and sit with my stick across my legs, watching the waves ebb and flow. It is peaceful and soporific, and despite the cold, my eyes grow heavy. But I must not fall asleep here. It's hard enough to keep control of my dreams from the relative safety of my bed. So, I take a quick inventory of the cave's contents; everything is still there, with nothing new added. Satisfied, I prepare to walk back.

My route back to the hotel takes longer, of course. I tire quickly, and my limp gets worse the longer I stay on my feet. I start my daily walk with a straight back, but a lack of concentration leaves me hunching again. I stop, look forward and straighten my shoulders. It is easy to fall into bad habits, and I have enough medical problems without adding to them. I trudge back, doing my best to ignore the pain in my hip and brace myself for the climb up the ramp. Some days, it brings me close to tears. Moving on the flat or a slight downward incline is not onerous, but a slope is usually painful no matter how shallow. It's because my legs are different lengths. The cobbler has always made my boots and builds the left heel taller than the right, but it is never enough, and I often feel unbalanced. I grit my teeth and begin the climb, with the lyrics to 'It Had To Be You', looping in my head as a distraction. It works, and I find myself at the top of the ramp and head towards the hotel's entrance with little exertion. I open the door and go inside.

The Cornish Widow: Chapter Two

PORTH TREGORYAN

THE PORTH TREGORYAN hotel perches high on the cliffs just feet from the shore and facing towards Newquay. It is a handsome stone building with a gothic feel, yet far from being ancient, it is only a little older than I am. But there is something about the hotel that evokes caution, as though if not currently occupied by ghosts, they could arrive at any moment. Despite this, it is a welcoming place, and for several years the owners have extended their hospitality to the locals. This generosity includes access to the hotel library, although I am the only one who takes advantage. Their loss is my gain and provides me with a haven in which neither Mrs Ponsonby nor any of her informants can bother me.

I visit the library most days, but always on a Thursday when the reading room truck arrives from Newquay. Quite how a private hotel has arrived at this arrangement with a subscription library, I don't know. But I expect it involves the exchange of money or the acquisition of new books. I must ask Peter when I see him. And no sooner does the thought pop into my head than Peter is walking down the corridor. I am about to follow him when a head pops up from behind the counter.

"Morning, Miss Connie," says Dolly, the receptionist. She is sporting the hotel's grey and white uniform and is looking immaculate. I don't know how old Dolly is. She could be in her late twenties or perhaps early forties, but it's impossible to tell. Dolly is slender, almost skinny, which amplifies the problem in assessing her age. I could ask her, but it might seem bad-mannered, so I have held my tongue up to now. Dolly lives in the upper rooms of the hotel and stays in Porth Tregoryan all year long. Hotel work is seasonal, and most of her friends go home when the summer is over, but after three years of loyal service, Dolly is part of the scenery. I count her as one of my close friends and can barely remember the hotel without her.

Dolly smiles at me, revealing crooked teeth and a slight overbite. It is a shame as she has a pretty face and melting brown eyes with the longest eyelashes I have ever seen.

I return the smile. "Good morning to you too. And how are you today?"

"Very well," she says, beaming. Dolly is always smiling and would still perform her duties with good humour if the hotel fell off the cliff. She is a perfect employee, spreading happiness and calm around her. If I had to stand at the reception desk all day, I would bite people. Not that I could stay on my feet for half an hour, much less eight.

"It's busy today," says Dolly, stifling a cough.

I frown. "Oh dear," I say. Some people like people, but I like books, and I prefer to read them quietly. Occasionally it is nice to see a friendly face in the library and exchange a few pleasantries, but only if I'm left alone to read once I have done my bit.

"You've just missed Peter," she continues, and for one moment, I think I see her wink. But it must be my imagination. Peter Tremayne is five years my junior, and if I had a brother, then my feelings towards him would be the same. There is not a flicker of romantic interest between us, and I'm not sure Peter even likes girls. But he is an interesting young man, and we get on very well, all things considered.

"I'll look for him," I say, lifting my stick as I carefully step up. I have missed that step too often, ending up on the floor on my hands and knees. It's a stupid place to put one, but despite the indignity of frequent falls, I still forget. I limp up the hallway towards the rear of the hotel, where the large reading room overlooks the sea. Dolly was right. The room is full of people, and I ignore them and search for Peter. I see him swapping books at the end of the room. He spies me and waves.

"What have you bought?" I ask eagerly, forgoing the usual small talk. I have read most of the books in the hotel library and am dreading the awful prospect of having nothing to read.

"You like Agatha Christie, don't you?"

"You know I do," I say eagerly.

"Here. Take this before someone else does," says Peter, placing a book on the table. "You'll be the first to read it."

I pick up the book and reverently open the cover. "But where's Poirot?" I ask disappointedly.

"Not here," he says. "This book features a new character called Miss Marple. One of a series, I believe. It's hot off the press and only arrived last week. You will love it."

I look at the title page – *Murder at the Vicarage* – and I know he is right. I want everyone to leave the room so that I can read it in peace. Failing that, I'll take it home and devour it in front of the fire, and a thrill of excitement courses through me as I anticipate the twists and turns of a new story.

"What else?" I ask excitedly.

Peter waves a hand towards the shelf, and I rifle through his treasures while he finishes his chores. There are about two dozen new books, which should be enough to keep me going for a while. E.M. Forster, F. Scott Fitzgerald, and a non-fiction book by someone called Sigmund Freud. I recognise one or two of the covers, but most are new to me. I pore over the books and finally select two with the most exciting descriptions. Then I find Peter, who is now sitting in the corner nursing a cup of tea. He stands up as I arrive, waiting until I am sitting comfortably with my stick safely tucked to one side before resuming his seat. For a young man, he has excellent manners.

"How are you?" he asks.

"Tolerably well," I say.

"I see you've been beachcombing." He points to my stick and the grains of sand liberally scattered across the hotel carpet.

"Oh, dear. I usually remember to clean it," I say, annoyed that Peter has mentioned the mess in public. I look around, but nobody is listening – they are all preoccupied with their books. One man is writing in the corner with his head bowed in concentration.

"What have you been up to then?" Peter asks.

"The usual," I say. "Reading, avoiding Mrs P, my daily constitutional and yet more reading. How about you?"

"Much of the same," he says. "I say, have you seen today's paper?"

"No. You know Mrs Ponsonby doesn't like them and won't have them in the house."

"She's a funny old stick," says Peter.

"There's nothing amusing about my captor," I say darkly.

"Still lacking the maternal spark?"

"Not a suitable subject for levity," I say, crossing my arms. "I have come to terms with my parents abandoning me, but why they thought it was a good idea to leave me with her, I will never know. It's unforgivable."

"You're still alive," says Peter, and for the first time in my life, I want to hit him.

"That's enough," I say.

"No, seriously. I know you don't like Mrs Ponsonby but think about it and then tell me three good things about her."

"It will take all day."

"You're not trying. I promise it will make you feel better."

I sigh. It is all I can do to stop myself from leaving, but I suppose I ought to humour Peter. He is generally good to me and must see some value in this seemingly pointless exercise. "She keeps me fed and clothed," I say.

"Good. We'll count that as one. Next?"

"She doesn't beat me."

"I'm not accepting that. Try harder."

"She's brave. Billy Baxter's dog tried to bite me when I was younger, and she chased it down the road with a stick. Everyone else was terrified, but not Mrs Ponsonby. Actually, there's an odd-looking sword in the outhouse. I bet it's hers."

"Excellent. Last one."

"She's got a sense of humour when she's not being mean and checking up on me. She listens to the radio sometimes and laughs. But if I walk in, she stops and re-sets her miserable face."

"So, she's nurturing, brave and funny," says Peter.

"No," I snap. "You're putting words in my mouth."

"You said them. My mother likes her."

"She would," I say, not embellishing on the subject. I like Peter's mother, but if he's going to bring her into it, then I'm not playing.

Peter raises an eyebrow. "You don't like Mrs Ponsonby because she's strict," he says. "But it's because she cares, not because she doesn't."

"You don't have to live with her." I glower. "Change the subject, or I'm going."

"You haven't asked me about the newspaper."

"I forgot," I say when what I really mean is that I don't care.

"There's an interesting death notice inside. A woman called Alice Thomas died in Plymouth hospital."

"I should think it happens a lot," I say, wondering whether it would be rude to start reading my books now.

"Yes. But there's going to be an inquest next week," says Peter, "and Malcolm's asked if I'd like to go."

I shrug. "Why would you? And anyway, I thought you didn't like him?" Malcolm is Peter's much older cousin. He is a reporter with the Cornish Advertiser, not an especially well-regarded paper, but well suited to Malcolm, who enjoys digging up dirt.

"I don't," says Peter, honestly. "But I've never been to an inquest before, and I expect it will be interesting."

"I'm sure you're right," I agree.

"Still, nothing may come of it, but I'll let you know what he says."

"Good. Please do."

"Anyway, I've got to go now. It's drama club tonight."

I shake my head and smile, watching Peter's eyes sparkle. He is in thrall to Oliver and Felicity Grenville, a pair of actors trying to fund a Newquay drama group. The unofficial throng meets at their house every second Thursday, and it is the highlight of Peter's week.

"Off you go," I say. "Will I see you this time next week?"

"Before then, I expect," says Peter. "I'll be back in the next few days, and I'll come and find you."

"Enjoy yourself, won't you?" I watch as Peter walks from the room, sandy hair flopping over his glasses. He strolls casually with his hands in his pockets, nodding as he passes the hotel guests. They smile back, and I can almost hear them thinking, 'what a nice young man.'. They are right. He is.

I sit back and look around the room. It is quieter now. Some residents have left, and one is stirring a cup of coffee while she reads. The bald man by the window is still scribbling in his journal. He hasn't stopped and is writing with a sense of urgency. I cannot help but stare. A few moments pass, and he looks up. Our eyes meet, and I blush and turn away, pretending to pick a hair from my jacket. I enjoy watching people, but I hate getting caught. It always seems so intrusive.

Grab your copy...
vinci-books.com/cornishwidow

Author's Note

I loosely based this book on the Great Wyrley Outrages, a series of anonymous letters and animal mutilations occurring in South Staffordshire at the turn of the century. I thought long and hard before writing about this case. The subject matter is distasteful, and the abhorrent racism towards the Edalji family is hard to take. I deliberately glossed over the details of the animal mutilations and focussed on the anonymous letters, which were more interesting from a psychological perspective. Although Lawrence disliked Arthur Conan Doyle in my book, Sir Arthur was a genuine hero in real life, using his influence to free George Edalji from undeserved imprisonment.

After consulting numerous books and online resources, I found myself questioning George's innocence. I wish I could feel differently, given the unfair treatment and blatant prejudice he endured. However, acknowledging the presence of racism does not mean we should overlook signs of guilt.

I believe George, in his naivety, wrote the earlier letters as a childish prank, inadvertently casting suspicion on Elizabeth Foster. This misstep led to the terrible and unjust retaliation he later faced. I do not believe George had any involvement in the animal mutilations.

Conan Doyle secured George Edalji's release in 1907. He never returned to Great Wyrley and settled in Welwyn Garden City, where he died in 1953. Though pardoned, George Edalji did not receive compensation for his imprisonment, though his sister Maud relentlessly campaigned on his behalf for years. Horace Edalji remained estranged from his family, changing his name, and moving to Ireland with his wife. The perpetrator of the Great Wyrley Outrages is still unknown, but many theories and fascinating accounts are available on the internet.

Jacqueline Beard, Cheltenham, 2025